Mystery at Blackbeard's Cove

By Audrey Penn

Illustrations by Joshua Miller and Philip Howard

SCHOLASTIC INC.

New York Toronto London Auckland Sydney
Mexico City New Delhi Hong Kong Buenos Aires

ISBN 0-439-80589-9

12 11 10 9 8 7 6 5 4 3 2 1   5 6 7 8 9 10/0

Printed in the U.S.A.   23

First Scholastic printing, October 2005

In memory of Clinton Gaskill

To Lena Austin Donlon, Todd Mugford, and Jennifer Esham, I dedicate this story. And to the families of Ocracoke Island, North Carolina, most especially the children. Thank you for sharing your culture and devotion to history and heritage. You are a wondrous source of pride, and I will carry you in my heart forever.

The Price on a
Pirate's Head is
a Buck-an-Ear.

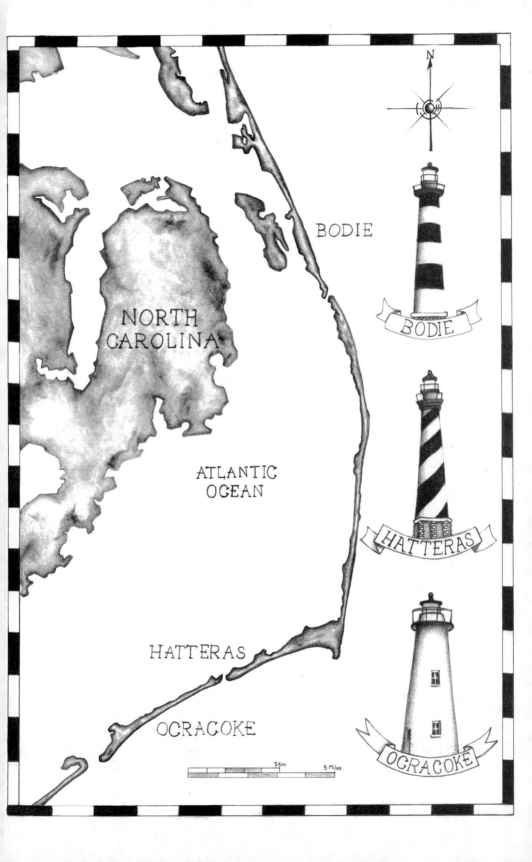

We hung a lantern 'round its neck,

The nag we brought to race.

'Twas fortune we were after

On Jockey's Ridge we paced.

The boats they came a sailin'

With pickin's sweet and ripe.

The beacon 'round the old nag's head

Lured ships aground at night.

PROLOGUE

It was a fair race. On the morning of June 25, 1718, high atop Jockey's Ridge on the Outer Banks of North Carolina, six horses raced across the perilous mountain of sand until a single surviving horse was declared victor.

Basil Hawthorne led his prize Appaloosa back down the sandy slope to receive the owner's prize: a horse-shaped ale stein frothing over with local ale. That same night, as a dense fog rolled onto the sandy shores, the winning Appaloosa was led back up Jockey's Ridge to once again prove his worthiness. Upon reaching the top of the mountainous dune, Basil Hawthorne slipped a candle-lit lantern around his prize nag's head, then braced his steed's front legs with sticks and rope. The lamplight bobbed and swayed as the horse limped back and forth across the dangerous peak, sending a false beacon of hope to ships steeped in fog, inviting them to safer waters. Falling for the ruse, the floundering ships ran aground.

While Hawthorne and his cohorts lured the ships inland, promising a false refuge to all souls on board, other members of the land-pirate brigade spread out among the villages of Nags Head and Kill Devil Hills and sold tickets to the impending event. Colonists who purchased the tickets were promised a looting and plundering to satisfy any desire for entertainment. Following the pirate's plundering, the lucky ticket holders would board the grounded ship and take possession of those items not already claimed. Years of such land pirating gave Nags Head its name and reputation while proving to be both entertaining and profitable.

Hidden by darkness, Governor Spotswood secretly witnessed the pirate raid on the night of June 25th. When the last of the ticketholders claimed his plundered prize, the governor and his agents stormed forth and arrested the entire lot of thieving pirates and colonists. The goods were confiscated, brought to Williamsburg, Virginia, and put away for the rightful owners to come and claim. Unfortunately, while on route to North America, the rightful owners had been relieved of their worldly goods by a band of sea pirates sailing off the coast of Cuba. They, in turn, were unburdened of the same items by a thieving group of pirates near the Bermuda Islands. The land pirates of Nags Head were the third set of piratical hands to claim ownership. Thus, the return of the loot to its rightful owners seemed unlikely.

Meanwhile, just prior to the governor's raid, young Melanie Smyth had gingerly fingered the vast array of items set out on the ship's galley table. In particular, she drank in the beauty of a pair of crystal and sterling candlesticks. When inquiring whether the pair of candlesticks counted as one ticket or two, she was assured her first ticket would include both candlesticks. The gentleman in charge took quill and ink to her ticket, thus providing Miss Smyth with a receipt. The front of the ticket read: "June 25, 1718, one pair crystal and sterling candlesticks." When the ink was set with powder, the receipt was turned over and the artist's stamp and initials were copied.

Miss Smyth's second receipt read, "June 25, 1718, one sterling silver trowel."

When the ink on both tickets was dusted and dried, Melanie Smyth pocketed the two receipts and left the ship in possession of her two candlesticks wrapped in thick brown paper and the polished silver trowel. She was soon relieved of her newly acquired valuables by Governor Spotswood himself, who had a policy of never arresting young women. Melanie and several other young ladies were sent home with a scolding and a gloved handshake. Their male counterparts were sentenced to a night in jail and enough ale to loosen their lips on the whereabouts of other pirate ships, most particularly Blackbeard's.

Years later, Melanie Smyth presented the pair of tickets and the accompanying story to her favorite grandson on the occasion of his marriage. In time, her grandson passed both tickets and story onto his granddaughter, who, in time, passed them onto her grandson, and so on and so on for ten generations. Theodora Teach McNemmish received both the tickets and the accompanying story from her grandfather on the occasion of her sixteenth birthday.

Walk with caution,

Walk with care,

Island treasures everywhere.

Misty skies,

Sands of old,

Hidden cache of jewels and gold.

Skip the tides,

Dance the sea,

A pirate's life for me, for me,

A pirate's life for me.

C H A P T E R   I

On a quiet stretch of beach out among the sand dunes of Ocracoke Island, North Carolina, an old, bent woman turned from the sea and grinned.

"So!" she exclaimed in her high-pitched whistle of a voice. "You're back!"

Her gray eyes sparkled as a large, bearded man walked toward her through the dim, hazy mist of an early October morning.

"Did you get them?" she asked excitedly. "Did you get all sixteen?" Quizzing the man, she prodded him with her walking stick, trying to pry the large, nylon duffel bag from his shoulder.

"Not so fast, Theodora." The gruff-looking seaman put up a restraining hand. "You'll get your precious seashells when I get my precious money."

"Of course, of course," agreed Mrs. McNemmish. "But how do I know there's really whelk shells in that bag? How do I know you haven't filled it with sand and sea wash?" Captain Ezekiel Beacon had better things to do than argue with this ancient O'cocker. "You're crazy, you know that, old woman? You could have bought twice as many whelks in a shell shop for what you're paying me."

Mrs. McNemmish shook her head defiantly. "Snow Ducks are made from Carolina shells. That's the way it is. That's the way it's always been. Now, show me my shells before I swat you with my stick."

Zeek Beacon opened his duffel and displayed the sixteen, cone-shaped shells on the cold, damp sand. A jury of laughing gulls inspected the cache from above while the widow bent down for a closer look. "Satisfied?" rushed the agitated captain.

Mrs. McNemmish clasped her hands and gasped audibly. Grabbing hold of the captain's arm, she lowered herself to the ground. Her tiny fingers swept across the treasure trove of perfectly sculpted pink and tan shells while her twinkling eyes soaked in the beauty of their crowned heads and cascading funnels. "They're perfect!" she told the diver who had acquired them. "They're absolutely perfect!"

Zeek Beacon was nervous. His eyes shifted from one sand dune to the next, then as far up and down the 13-mile shoreline as his vision would allow, constantly fearful of onlookers. "I'm thrilled you're happy, old woman. Now pay me so I can get out of here."

Mrs. McNemmish leaned heavily on her walking stick and pulled herself back up. She dusted the damp sand off her skirt apron. "The truth is," she explained demurely and somewhat hesitantly. "I haven't got your money. At least, not the kind you're used to getting. But!" she added quickly. She knew not to provoke Zeek's temper. "I want you to have these." She pulled a handful of large, white flower seeds the size and shape of pistachio nuts from her pocket and proudly presented them to the captain. "These seeds are very precious and very valuable," she assured him. "One hundred times the value of those whelk shells."

"Seeds! You want to pay me with seeds?" Zeek Beacon fumed. Grabbing the widow's arm, he hurled her frail body to the ground. The handful of seeds scattered. "Do you see those shells, Theodora? They took me a month to collect. A month! That's including riptides and shark attacks! I am not in the habit of trading them for beans, chickens, or hog meat! So unless you have something more valuable than magic seeds, our business is over." Beacon knelt down and slipped the whelks safely back into his duffel. Standing to leave, he grabbed the widow's shawl, yanked her back to her feet, and pulled her pale, frightened face flush against his own. The smell of alcohol on his breath made her cringe.

"There are shell shops all along the Outer Banks that will pay me top dollar for these whelks, Theodora. That's the only reason I don't strangle you where you stand." He pushed the widow aside and turned to leave, but in so doing, noticed the drawstring handbag loosely hanging from the old lady's wrist. He eyed it suspiciously. "I remember that bag. That's the pirate's ditty bag you found with the Jamaican coins and snuff inside." He regarded the widow with renewed interest. "What's in the bag now, eh, McNemmish?" He reached forward and yanked the ditty off her wrist. Its meager contents of white seeds and small seashells scattered onto the sand.

"Well, well, well, what have we got here?" whistled the captain. He bent down and plucked a sparkling, round object off the matted sand. Brushing it clean, he placed the trinket in the center of his palm. "Very nice, McNemmish. This may be your lucky day."

He twirled the large, ruby-cluster ring in front of his right eye, then glared at the widow curiously. "Where'd you get this?"

Mrs. McNemmish gently caressed the ditty bag, running its broken strings through her fingers. "I found that ring years ago," she told him as she knelt down and recovered each and every precious seed and shell from the sand. "It was a gift of old booty."

"A gift, huh? Is it real?"

"Of course it's real!" Mrs. McNemmish stood up and stared at the captain's harsh features. She smiled impishly. "It's a beauty, ain't it?"

Beacon spit-cleaned the cluster of blood-red rubies, then polished it on his coat sleeve. "Not bad. Not bad. I might consider trading this for the sack of whelks." He tugged on his beard and glared down at the living, breathing artifact standing beside him. "How do I know these rubies are real?"

"Because I'm telling you they are!" Mrs. McNemmish grinned to herself as she played to the captain's greedy ear. "That ring is from Blackbeard's booty. Found it myself locked in one of his sea trunks. It's a real prize. Might have come from the same ship your great-granddaddy Israel

Hands sailed on alongside of the devilish Blackbeard himself."

"Well then. That would make it more mine than yours, wouldn't it?" Zeek Beacon narrowed his icy, blue eyes and pocketed the ring. "Okay, old woman. Keep your shells. But if this ring's a fake, I'll be back. You hear me, Theodora? I'll be back."

There is a place on Ocracoke

Where inlets form a cove,

Where Blackbeard came with

plundered goods

Three hundred years ago.

He said the only living soul

To ever see his wealth,

Would be the devil in disguise,

Which was his devilish self.

But I have Blackbeard's blood in me,

A pirate's heart have I,

And I have searched that very cove

And found the

brigand's prize.

N

CHAPTER II

Mrs. McNemmish stoked the fire in her fireplace, lit her favorite clay pipe, then sat down and rocked in her favorite rocking chair. The chill of October seeped through her ancient bones as well as through the cracks in her tiny fishing shack. The warm fire and a good smoke were all the company she needed.

"He didn't want the seeds," she told Squash, reviewing the morning's events with her favorite tabby cat. "Of course he took the ring. I knew he would." She stared into her fireplace as if it were some mystic window sparking her imagination. She had always gotten great joy out of that ruby ring. She would miss it terribly. A simple glance at the bobble reminded her of secret places and unearthed treasures. When she held it, vibrant images of swashbuckling pirates, fancy-dressed ladies, and overflowing trunks painted her imagination. Beacon had no vision. For him, the ring meant money in his pocket. A shallow value for a priceless heirloom.

Tired by the morning's events and lulled by Squash's gentle vibration, Mrs. McNemmish nodded off into a peaceful, late-morning nap. She was awakened by Beacon violently smashing his way into her shack with the bottom of his boot.

"You startled me!" gasped the widow. Her swift movement frightened Squash, who leapt off her lap with a loud, angry meow. "Next time, you might try knocking," she told the captain.

She came to her senses and placed her precious pipe on the fireplace mantle. She turned toward Beacon cautiously. "I thought you left the island."

"I did." Beacon roamed about the cottage, lifting knickknacks off shelves and tables, then returning them to their places. He toyed with the sixteen whelk shells soaking in the kitchen sink. "I took the ring to a friend of mine up in Kinnakeet. He's a jeweler—of sorts."

Mrs. McNemmish snickered. She could only imagine what "of sorts" meant. "Well?"

"He says the rubies are extremely rare and valuable. So is the setting."

"I see. Well then. I have my shells, and you have your ring. Business is complete."

"Not quite." Beacon's tone was sharp and threatening. He lifted a whelk shell out of the sink and juggled it from one hand to the other. He stopped abruptly and cast a menacing look at the widow. "I want the rest, Theodora."

"The rest of what?"

"The rest of the jewelry." A wave of anger and desperation stirred in his voice. "If you've had that ring all these years, then there's a whole lot more where it came from. Do you know what I think, Theodora? I think you're a liar. I think those stories you tell kids about Blackbeard's treasure really are true. I think those buried and hidden treasure chests you talk about aren't really buried or hidden at all, but are here, somewhere on this island, and you know where they are." His acid stare bore down into her eyes and he spoke with whispered malice, "I want the rest of the treasure, Theodora. I want it all and I want it now."

Mrs. McNemmish took a step back. She couldn't breathe with him staring down at her like that. "Or what?" she asked him cautiously. "You'll kill me? Go ahead. I already have one foot in the grave. Even if there was a treasure, which there isn't, what makes you think I'd share anything with you?" Disgusted, she reached for her walking stick to shoo him away, but Zeek Beacon was faster. He snatched up her cane and swung it like a hammer, smashing the priceless clay pipe on the mantle with a single, shattering blow.

Mrs. McNemmish jumped back with a startled outcry. "Stop it, Zeek! What's the matter with you? You have your ring. That's all there is. That's all there ever was. There was never any treasure and you know it. That ring and my Arthur's pipe were the only booty ever found."

Zeek's expression was frightening. He stormed across the open room and pointed to a hanging shelf. "Then

where did this lantern come from? Or this ale stein?"
Beacon swung the cane like a baseball bat, first shattering
the horse-shaped ale stein, then driving the lantern into the
wall. "Should I start on the whelks, Theodora, or do I get
the rest of the treasure?"

"Knock it off, Zeek!" Thirteen-year-old Daniel
Garrish, a slightly built redhead, and fourteen-year-old
Billy O'Neal, who was tall for his age and husky from a
large appetite, stood in the doorway holding Mrs.
McNemmish's groceries. Daniel's heart pounded as he
pushed farther into the tiny, green house. "Are you all
right, Miss Theo?"

Beacon flashed an angry glance at the boy and poked
him in the stomach with the stick. "Keep out of this,
Daniel."

Billy stormed into the kitchen and placed the grocery
bags on the kitchen table. Besides the obvious mess on the
floor, he saw the broken pipe on the mantle and Mrs.
McNemmish's anguished expression. "I'm getting Teddy,"
he announced to Daniel. He turned to fetch the sheriff, but
Beacon stopped him with a smack to the head. Billy toppled backward onto the kitchen table, knocking over the
contents of both bags. "You're not going anywhere," Zeek
growled. "No one is!"

Eleven-year-old Mark Tillet and thirteen-year-old
Stefanie Austin heard the commotion from the sound side
of the house. Stefanie, her auburn ponytail gleaming in the
sun, grabbed Mark by the hand and dragged him through
the widow's back door.

"What a mess!" squawked the girl. Oblivious to the
situation, she frowned at Beacon, who was still thrashing

about the room like a maniac. "You're not supposed to be on the island," she told him with arms folded indignantly. She turned toward the widow with a smirk of tattletale satisfaction. "He's not supposed to be on the island. He got busted."

Daniel rolled his eyes and waved a hand toward the back door. "Get lost, Stefanie. You'll only make him madder."

"I can stay if I want to."

"You're all staying!" ordered Beacon.

"Oh, yeah? Well, I don't have to stay if I don't want to," Stefanie sassed him right back.

Beacon was rapidly losing patience. "Listen to me, rat pack. I want you all to keep your mouths shut about me being here, or I'll shut them for you. Especially you, mighty mouth," he told the young girl. He bent over and pinned his face up against the widow's ear. "You had better get me what I want, old timer, or I'm taking you and your favorite sea urchins over there for a nice, long swim! And don't think for a second I won't do it." Breaking the widow's cane in half, he thundered across the room and out the door.

"Whew!" Mrs. McNemmish took a nice deep breath, then sat back down in her rocking chair. "Thank you, children. I must say, he took the wind out of my sails."

"What a creep," moaned Billy. He picked up the spilled groceries, then grabbed some glue out of a kitchen drawer and began piecing together the widow's walking stick. "I thought he was going to break one of us."

Daniel found the broom and swept up the broken pieces of antique ale stein and lantern. "Are you sure you're all right, Miss Theo?"

"I am now, thanks to you four." She surveyed her tiny home, feeling more sad than angry. "Stefanie, dear, check to see if Squash and the kitties are all right." She rose up slowly and gathered the remains of her precious clay pipe into her hand. "It was a fine pipe," she told her visitors.

She looked up and saw the youngest of the children trembling against the farthest wall. "Come sit beside me, Mark. We'll have a talk."

Mark sat down at the foot of the rocking chair and smiled up at the widow through eyeglasses the thickness of soda bottle bottoms. Mrs. McNemmish smiled back, enjoying the play of the firelight reflecting off his lenses. After a moment or two, Mark shrugged, and Mrs. McNemmish assured him she was fine, using a simple, calm nod.

The widow and young Mark often shared conversations in this silence. They could say nothing to one another all afternoon and have a grand time. Mark didn't talk because of some terrible thing that happened to him that no one knew about because he wouldn't say. Most people were used to his expressions and what Mrs. McNemmish called his "pirate sense," something she said both she and Mark had.

"This was my Arthur's favorite pipe," she told the children with a deep sigh. "It was a gift of old booty." Mark pursed his lips and shook his head.

"Thank you, Mark. That's very kind." Mrs. McNemmish looked over at Stefanie, who was sprawled out on the bed with all four cats. "This pipe once belonged to your great-grandfather times three. He received it from Blackbeard himself, who passed it on down through my sweet Arthur's kin. Arthur loved to smoke it. Said it had a wonderful draw. All that history gone in the blink of an eye."

"You shouldn't have let Zeek come inside your house, if you ask me. He's not supposed to be on the island. He got busted."

Mrs. McNemmish hid her grin. "So you said. Actually, it was my own fault he busted in here the way he did." She invited the children to come closer. "You see, I didn't have enough money to pay him for the whelk shells he dug up, so I bartered for them with a ring. Now he thinks I know where Blackbeard's treasure is hidden, and he wants me to give it *all* to him."

"Blackbeard's treasure?" laughed Billy.

"Zeek never was too bright," admitted Daniel. "What makes him think there's a hidden treasure?"

"Because, child...there is."

Billy whirled around so quickly, a stream of white glue soared across the kitchen, landing on the wooden floor. "What do you mean, there *is* a treasure?"

"I mean, there is a treasure. And I know where it is."

"Wait a minute." Daniel asked the next question slowly and deliberately to make certain he had understood what the widow was saying. "You're telling us that Blackbeard really *did* have a hidden treasure, and *you really know where it is?*"

New life blossomed in Mrs. McNemmish's expression as she awakened to the children's reactions. "That treasure is as real as the sand and the sea and as close to you and me as a whisper. And," she added, "I not only know where it is...I know what's inside."

Stefanie rolled her dubious, brown eyes to the ceiling. "Yeah, right," she uttered loud enough to be heard by all.

Billy crawled along the floor and wiped up the remainder of the spilled glue. "If you knew where Blackbeard's treasure was hidden, why didn't you tell anybody?"

"Because she's making it up, that's why," scoffed Stefanie. She leaned back against the wall and scooped the kittens onto her lap. "She's always making things up. My mom says it's because her arteries got too hard."

"Gawd, Stefanie! Could you be a little ruder?" blushed Daniel.

Mrs. McNemmish laughed heartily. "Your mother is probably right," she admitted.

"Come on, Miss Theo. Did you *really* find Blackbeard's treasure?" asked Billy.

"I not only found it, I managed to keep it a secret for nearly seventy years." She pointed to Stefanie with a shaky, bent finger. "See that trunk over yonder? Read me the initials on the brass plate, child."

Stefanie let out a long, put-upon sigh, then got up and did what she was asked. "It says 'E.D.T.'"

"E.D.T.," repeated the widow. "Edward Drummand Teach."

"You said that trunk belonged to Edwina Dillan Timberlake," said Daniel.

"That's so no one would bug me. But the truth is, it belonged to the greatest buccaneer who ever lived: Blackbeard, King of the Pirates. Of course, no one knows for sure if Edward Drummand Teach was his real name. Not even the pirates who sailed with him knew for sure. But that," she proudly pointed out, "was his trunk."

Billy rubbed his chunky hands together and enticed Mrs. McNemmish with bouncing eyebrows. "I don't suppose you'd let us take a peek inside, would you? We wouldn't tell anybody about it. Honest."

Stefanie shook her head and went back to petting the kittens. "Hey, Billy. Did you know the word 'gullible' isn't in the dictionary? If she really found Blackbeard's treasure, do you think she'd still be living in this crummy, little shack? Of course not. She'd be living in some fancy condo up at Jones Point."

Daniel blushed so horribly, the tips of his ears glowed. Racing over to the bed, he slapped a hand over Stefanie's mouth. "Do you know how an oyster makes a pearl?" he screamed into her ear. "By keeping its mouth shut!"

"Now, now," stated the widow. "It was a fair question." She looked at Stefanie and winked. "First of all, except for a ditty bag filled with snuff and a little black bag filled with white seeds, most of the stuff I found in that trunk was useless. Just a bunch of old clothes, a few empty gun holsters, and a whole lot of pewter dinnerware. But you have to remember, my Arthur built this shack when houses like it were quite fashionable. Just about every house on the island looked like this one. Someday you'll understand the power and sweetness of holding onto a memory. But keep in mind, this house is on hallowed ground, so moving to a new one was out of the question." She motioned for the children to follow her out back. "The rounding of those trees at the high point yonder is Teach's Hole, where he moored his boat and lost his head, right? Well, it was here, on this spot of ground, that he had his house and lookout. While he was in Blackbeard's Cove doing his trading, one of his men

would be on the lookout from here. That way, they had
the advantage of seeing ships come in from both the sea
and the sound. Blackbeard could go from his trading post
to his moored boat and make a quick getaway without the
fear of being caught."

"Then how come he got killed?" argued Stefanie.

"Well!" exploded the widow. "If Maynard and his men
hadn't snuck up on him when he was sleeping off his grog
and asleep on his boat, he never would have lost that battle. Blackbeard would have won hands down!"

When the children and Mrs. McNemmish returned
inside, Billy seemed confused. "If all you found was the
ditty bag and some snuff, where'd the ring come from?"

A glint of a smile crossed the widow's face as she recollected. "There's more to the treasure than the single chest,"
she admitted. "But that we'll keep for another day."

"You didn't actually tell Zeek about that treasure,
did you?"

"I did and I didn't," explained the widow. "When he
found the ring in my ditty bag, I told him it was gift of old
booty. He assumed there was more where it came from
and demanded I hand it over. He says he wants it all."

"All of what? I thought you said there was just a bunch
of old clothes and stuff," said Stefanie.

"Like I said. There's more than just that chest," teased
the widow.

"She's making this up," insisted Stefanie.

"'Tis as true as you and me," Theodora assured her.
She looked at the children and grinned mischievously.
"Do you know what else I found?" Her face flushed with
excitement. "I found the skeleton of a real Spanish maiden!

She was all laid out in Spanish lace and golden trinkets. On her hand, she bore the most glorious ruby-cluster ring I'd ever seen. That's the ring Zeek has now. Lying next to her was another gentleman's bag. This one was filled with Jamaican coins, English snuff, and more of those large, pearl-white seeds. I spent the gold years ago. And I must admit, the snuff went quickly. I've kept only the seeds."

"What did you buy with the money?" asked Stefanie.

"Sand," giggled the widow. "Lots and lots of sand."

"Say what?" Stefanie stared at the widow, then switched her glare over to Daniel. "Hard arteries."

"I don't mean to be gruesome," interjected Billy. "But...what did you do with the body?"

Mrs. McNemmish looked surprised. "I buried her at sea."

"You dumped her in the ocean?" Stefanie's eyes practically flew out of their sockets. "You dumped a lady's corpse into our ocean? That is so gross!"

"Not at all, child. That was a proper burial in pirate times. Besides," she teased the girl. "There wasn't much left of her. Poor thing was all jewels and bones."

Mark glanced at the widow and giggled. He knew what was coming next.

"What did you do with the jewelry?" Stefanie asked her quickly.

"I buried it with her. All but the ring."

"You what?!"

"Hey, Stefanie. Don't get your tail in a knot," said Daniel.

Mrs. McNemmish laughed joyfully. Leaning forward in her chair, she gathered the youngsters closer to her. "I am the oldest islander and last surviving descendant of Blackbeard's sister from Bath. Someday, I'm going to claim my birthright as Edward Teach's great-great-grandniece times two-and-a-half and be a pirate by his side on the ghost ship *Queen Anne's Revenge*."

"Don't you have to be dead first?" scoffed Stefanie, still sullen over the lost jewelry.

"Absolutely!" applauded the widow. "And after I'm dead, and after I'm buried at sea, I, Mrs. Theodora Teach McNemmish, will reveal the secret of Blackbeard's Cove and the whereabouts of his hidden treasure. The very secrets I have kept to myself all these many years. Whoever buries me at sea will be as rich as Midas and hold in their hands the wealth of the world. And Mrs. McNemmish keeps her word."

"She's nuts *and* squirrels!" said Stefanie, rounding the corner to her house. "Her veins didn't get hard. They petrified."

"Granted, she's a few teeth short of a comb," chimed in Billy, "but I don't think she's completely whacked out. I think she really does know where Blackbeard's treasure is hidden. She didn't tell anyone about it because they would have hauled it off to a museum or someplace where she couldn't take care of it."

"She didn't take care of it!" griped the girl. "She dumped it in the ocean. What kind of a idiot dumps perfectly good jewelry into the ocean?"

"I agree with Billy," said Daniel. "She must be telling the truth about the ruby ring, or why else would Zeek be on her case?"

Stefanie waved an indifferent hand. "What difference does it make? You heard her. She's not going to tell anybody where the rest of the treasure is hidden unless she's buried at sea, and that's not going to happen."

Mark stopped walking, looked at the two older boys, then at Stefanie, and shrugged.

"What do you mean, why not? Because no one in the world is stupid enough to bury her there, that's why," Stefanie informed him.

"We could do it," said Daniel. "We could bury her at sea."

"WHAT?"

"Miss Theo would love that!" agreed Billy. "We could even tell her we're going to do it so she can enjoy knowing about it before it happens!"

"First of all!" screeched Stefanie. "She's almost a hundred years old! She'll probably never die. And second of all, I don't like dead people. They're dead."

"What's that got to do with anything? Look," said Daniel. "Miss Theo's always doing nice things for other people. This is something we could do for her. I say, when Miss Theo dies, we bury her at sea!"

"And if we end up the richer for it, hey, what's wrong with that?" added Billy.

Mark clapped his hands and nodded approvingly.

"You're as nuts and squirrels as she is! You're ALL nuts and squirrels!" Stefanie was still grumbling half a block away as she trotted up her porch steps and stormed into her house. "Ghouls!" she shouted out the window.

"To Mrs. McNemmish!" cheered Billy.

"And to Stefanie, who's nuts and squirrels!"

"I heard that!"

I have seen the brigand's ghost
Aboard his mighty ship.
I have heard the cannon roar,
I've seen his cutlass rip.
I have stood upon the deck
With Blackbeard by my side.
I shall dream a pirate's life
Until the day I die.

CHAPTER III

Mrs. McNemmish stood facing her fireplace mantle. Her work was done. Eight, spanking-new, whelk-shell Snow Ducks sat drying above the warmth of a crackling fire. "You know," she admitted while cradling Squash in her arms. "These are the nicest Snow Ducks I've ever made."

Smudge, a kitten named for her soot-colored coat, Oink, the pinkest kitten, and Minute, the tiniest of the three, mewed in agreement. They had learned from past experiences that not agreeing meant sleeping outdoors.

"Okay, Squash, down you go." Now that her weeks of work were complete and the hour was late, Mrs. McNemmish slipped into her rocking chair and visited her old friend, memory. She loved thinking back to the days when she and her young, dashing husband brewed coquina tea and steamed oysters over the open fire. It was a good memory. She was glad she had kept it.

Just before dawn, the widow was startled awake by a ship's whistle sounding off the coast of Ocracoke Inlet. It was the heart-wrenching call of a ship in danger.

Grabbing her shawl and walking stick, she rushed outside and down toward Springer's Point. The dark night and rolling fog were blinding, but the ninety-six-year-old native knew every inch of the island and almost floated over the tall grasses, bits of ancient and decayed shipwrecks, and hidden boat-slip walls. The biting wind and dulled lighthouse beam brought to mind a similar day, years ago, when her loving husband and two strapping sons were lost at sea. She prayed no souls would be lost today.

Again, the ship's bells cried out, and Mrs. McNemmish quickened her step. Breathless and weary, she stopped along Point of Beach and looked out over the black water and breaking dawn. Her lungs ached from the chilling mist as she waited fervently for the ship to ring out its perilous cry, or perhaps to get a glimpse of the troubled craft. She waited for nearly an hour. The absence of a Coast Guard cutter was troubling. She waited anxiously and alone until golden shards of sunlight crept above the watery horizon, piercing the darkness with the hope of daylight. Still, no rescue boats arrived. In time, the ship's bells faded. The vast "Graveyard of the Atlantic"—the watery grave of pirates and sailors past—fell quiet. Slowly, the salty southern sky filled with the morning cries of laughing gulls, great black-backed gulls, egrets, and brown pelicans, while the rumblings of breaking waves and the soft, rushing wind of passing ghosts tumbled onto the silky shore.

Mrs. McNemmish took a handful of sand and let it rain down from her palm. The wind was from the north. A storm was brewing. She slapped her hands clean and was about to leave the point, when she spotted a sprinkling of ship's lights off the eastern shore. Curious, she held her hand to her forehead and squinted into the sun. Suddenly, a loud, thunderous explosion bit through the morning silence as cannon fire shook the beach beneath her. Mrs. McNemmish shrieked, then crumbled to the ground. Sea oats and sand from the Try Yard Dune rained down onto her legs.

A moment later there was a second explosion, then a third. The widow was blanketed in sand up to her waist. Her head vibrated to the shrill of a deafening ring. Then...the gunfire ceased as startlingly as it had begun. The ship's bell fell silent. The ground beneath the quaking dunes settled. Mrs. McNemmish lay quietly trembling, her breathing shallow and faint. Slowly, yet courageously, she lifted her head off the ground and looked around. Fire and smoke filled the yellow sky. She raised herself onto an unsure elbow. A shiver rose up her spine and her skin tingled. Somebody laughed! It was a loud, chilling laugh that echoed like thunder and clutched the widow's ancient heart.

"Who's there?" she called out timidly. She sat up and searched the long stretches of sand dunes and shoreline, but saw no one. She squinted out to sea and watched the ship's flickering lights growing closer and closer, brighter and brighter. Slowly, the swirling cloud and mustard smoke that bridged sea and sky feathered apart, making room for the misty fresh glow of morning. Still, she saw no one.

Mrs. McNemmish sat mesmerized, gaping into the distance, when a tall ship's yardarm appeared out of the luminescent cloud that hovered above the water. She witnessed in amazement the massive bow and hull that loomed behind, floating into view. Three towering ship's masts nearly scraped the awakening sky as their billowing, unfurled sails swelled with a mixture of Gulf Stream and ocean breezes. Breaking waves and flapping canvas melted into one thunderous sound. Atop the mid-mast, a large black flag snapped and curled. Mrs. McNemmish once again squinted into the distance. As the ship grew closer, she could make out the outline of a giant figure of a man standing against the portside rail. He was waving his arms and shouting madly:

"Arise, ye spindly sponge! Are ye going to sit there all morning soaking me in, or are ye coming aboard?"

"Aboard?" asked the widow, pointing to herself. She glanced around the beach, but saw no one else he might have been addressing. "Sir, if that be an invitation, I accept."

"Aye. Then let's get on with the matter."

Mrs. McNemmish grabbed her walking stick, rose to her feet, and brushed herself clean. She stood graciously and ladylike, awaiting the arrival of her transport. A bronzed, half-naked seaman approached the beach in a wooden dingy, left it rocking in the shallows, and walked ashore. He greeted the old woman with a crude bow, then scooped her up into his muscular arms and carried her aboard.

As the lady and her escort approached the seafaring vessel, the sun grew larger in the sky. A family of curious dolphins swam along the side of the dingy as blue crabs and sand dollars walked beneath the oars. Pelicans diving for breakfast sent a school of fish flaring in all directions, their silver scales twinkling like diamonds beneath the paling water. Mrs. McNemmish looked up as the gentleman with the haunting laugh came into view. He was a towering man, more than 6'5" tall, and boasted a huge, black beard that covered his chest. His face had a devilish glow to it as he held a fiery mug of grog to his lips. The black, white, and red flag above him pictured the skeleton of the devil toasting death with an hourglass and spearing a heart dripping with blood.

"Lay alongside and climb aboard!" roared the pirate Blackbeard. He helped the old woman over the rail, then removed his glove and presented his hand. "Welcome aboard the *Queen Anne's Revenge*." The pirate Teach brushed back his coat and bowed gracefully.

Theodora Teach McNemmish lifted the skirt of her nightgown and curtsied. "I thank you for the invitation." She twittered and grinned sheepishly as she inspected the grand master of piracy from stem to stern. "My, my, my. You are certainly well put together. Thoroughly ripped, as the kids would say."

Blackbeard found himself momentarily speechless as Mrs. McNemmish further perused her infamous ancestor. She particularly liked the long, black frock that flared at the calves. Today he was wearing high, black boots with huge cuffs, although his normal boots, according to record, were low cut for quick escapes. His wide-brimmed hat and burgundy plume shaded his massive features, while he boasted three guns and as many holsters across his chest.

"So!" boomed the brigand. "Ye want to be a pirate."

"Aye, sir. Piracy runs in my veins."

"We'll see about that," chuckled Blackbeard. "Would ye kill?"

"I would in self-defense," admitted the widow.

"Would ye rob?"

"Only what was mine to begin with," confessed McNemmish.

"Would ye set a ship ablaze?" asked the buccaneer.

"Nay, mate. I'd save it for myself."

Blackbeard roared with laughter. "Ah, y'ar a spineless jellyfish, ye are, McNemmish!"

"I'm a Teach same as you!" insisted the widow.

"Aye, that ye are, that ye are," agreed her relative. The pirate turned and pointed to one of his men. "Do ya see me mate yonder by the boom?"

"The man, Israel Hands?" asked McNemmish. "He's Zeek Beacon's great-grandfather times three."

"Aye, that be the one. He's as much of a lily-livered scoundrel as yer Beacon is," Blackbeard assured her. He waved an arm and beckoned the man to his side. "Lay down yer sword and come here, ya withering piece of hemp."

Blackbeard greeted Israel Hands with a pleasant slap on the back, then withdrew a gun from his holster and blasted off the man's kneecap. The injured Mr. Hands fell screaming to the floor.

"Give the man a pint and two weeks pay!" Blackbeard ordered his helmsman. He turned and faced his pale, horrified guest and offered an explanation. "I do that now and again so they don't forget who I am."

"Captain!" Blackbeard's quartermaster, William Howard, poised a spyglass out to sea. "There's a man o'war off our starboard bow. It's Beacon and his men!"

"Beacon?" gasped McNemmish, barely recovered from Blackbeard's demonstration.

Edward Teach grabbed the glass eye and growled. Folding back the front of his coat, he revealed three more guns and as many knives. "McNemmish, sound the bell! All hands on deck! Howard, hard-a-starboard and take the wind out of that blackguard's sails."

The widow's heart pounded as she swung the clapper of the polished, brass bell. She could see her own golden reflection flushing back with excitement as a hundred men jumped into action at their captain's orders.

Blackbeard stroked the thick, matted beard that covered his massive chest. His eyes crinkled in thought as he lopped off a long swatch of hemp cord from the main spool and cut it into a dozen smaller pieces. He dipped each piece into a prepared mixture of saltpeter and limewater, then wove them through his beard like the knotted ribbons in a fishing net. A longer piece of hemp was wrapped around his head just below the rim of his hat. Teach kept a close watch over his men as he ignited the hemp, but loosened his grip on them as the rope began to smolder. A dull smoke rose upward from his beard and around his forehead, filling his nostrils with an aromatic hallucinative. Blackbeard grew giddy and loud, hungry for action. He ordered Howard to forge on ahead toward Beacon's ship.

"Ship's company, prepare to fight!" cried the mighty Teach. "Ye, too, McNemmish." He slapped a cutlass into her hand. "This is war, Madam! Are ye a pirate or a fish-monger's wife?"

"I, sir, am a Teach, same as you." The widow accepted the cutlass, nearly staggering to the floor from its awesome weight. Duty called, and she was prepared to fight. She braced herself as Beacon's men swarmed over the gunwale and onto the well-swabbed decks of the *Revenge*. Guns fired. Swords clashed. Men screamed in terror as they fell into their black, watery graves.

"Well, if it ain't the old woman of the sea," laughed a sailor.

Mrs. McNemmish froze. Her heart pounded, half from excitement and half from fear. Turning slowly, she faced the dreaded scoundrel, Captain Ezekiel Beacon. Beacon aimed his pistol at the widow's eyes and grinned coldly. "Trick or treat, Theodora?"

Mrs. McNemmish glanced over the sailor's shoulder and smiled inwardly. "Aye, mate, trick or treat indeed." She bravely inched forward and shoved the point of her cutlass into Beacon's broad chest.

Beacon jumped back, then chuckled sarcastically. "You can't win, McNemmish. Your cutlass is no match for my bullet."

The widow sighed deeply. "Aye, mate. My cutlass is slow compared to the flight of a bullet." She raised the tip of the cutlass and aimed it at Beacon's throat. "But my wits, sir, are not."

Beacon's smug grin disappeared as the widow pushed him back toward the deck rail. "Say good-bye, McNemmish," seethed the pirate.

"Good-bye, Zeek," sang the widow. She glared up into

Beacon's stormy, blue eyes and pushed him farther back—this time into the ready blade of Blackbeard's sword.

Beacon cried out in anguish as he fell forward onto the widow's shoulder.

"Good work, McNemmish!" Blackbeard hailed his relative as he withdrew his sword and joined another bloody clash with a cluster of Beacon's crew. "I'm pleased to call ye 'pirate,' McNemmish! And proud to call ye a Teach."

Mrs. McNemmish drank in Blackbeard's words, but Beacon's hands were growing heavy, and she was tiring rapidly.

"I'm not finished with you yet," wheezed Beacon. He tightened his grip on the widow's shoulder.

"Blow it out your pipes, Zeek," crowed the feisty McNemmish. An icy chill ran down her spine as she looked across the ship's bow. Blackbeard was fully engaged in another battle, so she would have to finish her battle with Beacon alone.

"I said," hollered Zeek, "I'm not finished with you yet."

"And I said, 'Blow it out your pipes!'" said Mrs. McNemmish. She slowly opened her eyes. The dream was over. The warmth of her tiny shack and the sound of her crackling fire were comforting, but the pressure of Zeek's large hand on her shoulder began to hurt. Reaching up, she pried off his fingers one by one, then turned and faced the raving captain. "What is it you want, Zeek?"

"I told you what I want. And I told you what would happen to you and those kids if I didn't get it."

Mrs. McNemmish chuckled to herself, remembering the moment Blackbeard shot off Israel Hand's kneecap.

"I'm not going to show you anything," she told Beacon. "I've hidden the cache where it can't be found. Not by the likes of you. Blackbeard's treasure is like an old woman's dream—filled with riches and brimming with mystery. The real prize will go to those who deserve it. And Mrs. McNemmish keeps her word."

Beacon was furious. Grabbing the edge of the rocking chair, he spun it around violently.

"Look here, you old witch. I've had enough of your stupid riddles. Now, either you show me the stuff, or I'll show you to your grave." He grabbed the widow's arm and yanked her forward, but the frail woman slumped back into her chair.

Beacon froze. An icy fist clutched his throat. His hand trembled as he released the widow's arm and backed away. "Theodora? Miss Theo? Hey...come on, old woman." Again and again, he called her name, but it was no use. Mrs. Theodora Teach McNemmish was dead.

Those of open heart and mind,

Who seek the truth within,

Must follow paths, alas unknown,

The journey thus begins.

Unleash the strength that you possess,

Give heart to what you know,

There lies a secret in your tears,

When God cries, flowers grow.

CHAPTER IV

Halloween came to Ocracoke Island on a gray, joyless day. Usually tales of ghost-ship lights and headless horsemen are born on such mornings. But today, the soft Spanish moss that hung like matted spider webs wept from the live oak branches that canopied historic Howard Street. It wept for all who lived on the island.

By early afternoon, the Ocracoke School gymnasium was overflowing with native islanders, off-island residents, and longtime visitors. In the background, a symphony of church bells and boat whistles echoed across the Pamlico Sound, throughout the Silver Lake inlet, and up into the heavens in honor of the passing of old Mrs. McNemmish. The tiny village that sat at the southern tip of the 13-mile-long sand bar felt the loss of the widow as one, united in heart and soul by the loss of one of its own.

"We are witnessing the end of an era," pronounced the Reverend Lyle Woods. "How fitting it is that Miss Theo passed away on the morning of her favorite holiday. I can only imagine the infinite number of ghost and pirate stories she is taking with her to the next world." The reverend paused dramatically. "Mrs. Theodora Teach McNemmish, relative to many and friend to all, was as wise as she was gracious and loving. She will be sadly missed by all of us. We shall celebrate her life when we lay her to rest in the McNemmish family cemetery on Saturday morning."

When the town meeting ended, Sheriff Teddy Jackson gathered together Daniel, Billy, Stefanie, and Mark and walked them outside. "Grab your bikes and follow me over to the widow's house. There's something I want to show you."

Stefanie shook her head. "I don't want to go over there. Dead people give me the creeps, even if it is Mrs. McNemmish."

"I'm with Stefanie," said Billy.

"Miss Theo's not in her house. She's been moved to the clinic before being taken to the church. You'll be fine. I promise."

But when the children arrived at the widow's shack, they weren't fine. They didn't know how to feel or how to behave. The usual warmth and unspoken invitation that had always been present had been replaced with a cool stillness and haunting quiet.

"It's creepy," said Daniel, speaking for all of them. "It's like she's here, but she isn't here."

"She is still here in a way. But that's okay," Teddy assured them. "Theodora wouldn't mind you being here. As a matter of fact, I think she'd be upset if she knew y'all were uncomfortable. You know, when I stopped by this morning to take her up to Hatteras, I thought she was asleep in her rocking chair. I couldn't believe she was gone. Anyway, while I was waiting for the reverend and the doctor to show up, I noticed those eight Snow Ducks up on the mantle."

"Those are her Halloween ducks," said Daniel. "She makes them every year and gives them to the kids who don't already have one."

"I know. But this note was with them. It's addressed to you guys." He took the letter off the mantle and handed it to Daniel. "It's probably the last thing she wrote before she died."

Daniel stared at the letter, then timidly took it out of Teddy's hand. "What's it say?"

"I don't know. It was addressed to y'all, so I didn't read it. The four Snow Ducks on the right belong to the four of you. Your names are taped to their feet."

"We already have our Snow Ducks," said Billy. "We got them ages ago."

"Well, maybe she forgot you had them. Or maybe she just wanted you to have new ones. When you're ninety-six years old, and your name is Theodora Teach McNemmish, you do pretty much whatever you want to do."

Daniel retrieved his Snow Duck off the mantle and examined it tenderly. The body and head of the duck were constructed out of two of the whelk shells Zeek Beacon had found. In addition to the whelks, the duck had two oyster-shell feet, two clamshell wings, and two coquina shell eyes. A single, white, belly-button seed plucked from the widow's ditty bag was glued right in the middle of the bottom whelk.

Billy inspected his duck as well. "Maybe this is one of those seeds Mrs. McNemmish found with the body!"

"Body? What body?" asked Teddy.

Daniel scowled at Billy, then answered nonchalantly. "Oh, it's just some silly story she told us. She was always making stuff up. Stefanie said it's because of her hard arteries. Who are the other ducks for?" he asked, quickly changing the subject.

Teddy wrinkled his brow at the "hard arteries" comment, but let it slide. "That's just it," he told them. "I don't know who the other ducks are for." He took one of the remaining Snow Ducks off the mantle and pointed to the foot. "This one is for N.E."

"Who's N.E.?" asked Billy.

"I don't know. Take a look at the other three." He handed one each to Billy, Daniel, and Stefanie.

"Mine says S.E.," said Stefanie.

"This one is for S.W.," said Daniel.

"Mine's for N.W.," said Billy. "These are compass points."

"I think so, too. But compass points to where, or what?" Teddy put the ducks back on the mantle, then checked his watch. "I have an errand to run. Why don't you guys stay here and read your letter in private. I'll be back in a few minutes." Mark waited for Teddy to leave, then took his Snow Duck and sat down in front of Mrs. McNemmish's rocking chair. He looked up into the empty chair and stared at nothing through his magnified lenses.

"We're all going to miss her," Daniel told him quietly. He stood with his hand on Mark's shoulder for a moment, then turned to Stefanie and Billy. "Can you believe how weird this is? First she tells us about Blackbeard's hidden treasure and how she wants to be buried at sea so she can be a ghost on his ghost ship, and then she ups and dies."

"Maybe those are burial instructions," suggested Billy, pointing to the envelope.

"Burial instructions?" asked Stefanie. "For what? The Snow Ducks?"

"No, silly. For her!"

Mark looked up and motioned for Daniel to open the letter.

Daniel stared at the pale blue envelope, then slowly tore it open. He unfolded the note paper and read out loud:

In the chest a secret lies,
Hidden from a thousand eyes.
Fortune comes to those who seek,
In the shell, a precious key.
Follow me and you will find
A treasure like no other kind.
Keep alive the stories told,
A pirate's cache is not all gold.

Stefanie gave a huge sigh of relief. "Well, at least they're not burial instructions."

"It's better!" Daniel read the note a second time to make sure he had understood the contents correctly. "She left us the stuff in that trunk!"

Stefanie turned and snatched the letter out of Daniel's hand. "Where does it say that?"

"Right there. 'In the chest...'"

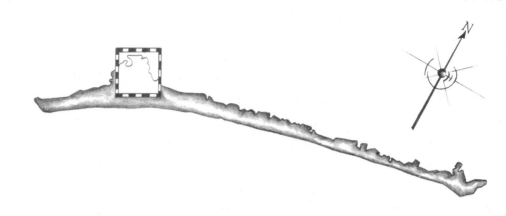

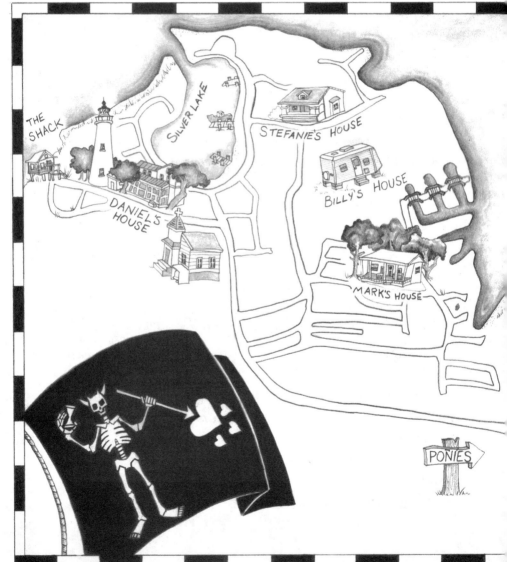

"Let me see." Billy reread the poem and agreed with Daniel. "It definitely says 'in the chest,' and there's the chest. Quick, let's open it."

Mark put up a restraining hand, then gently took the letter away from Billy and read it to himself. When he was finished, he looked at his friends and shook his head firmly.

"Have you lost your mind?" Stefanie asked him.

"No! He's right," Billy admitted, embarrassed that he hadn't thought of it himself. "We don't get to open the treasure chest until Mrs. McNemmish is buried at sea."

"WHAT!"

Daniel bit his lip pensively. "We can do this. Just grab her coffin, sail it out to the ocean, and dump it. We said we'd bury her at sea when she died—and she died. We'll have to hurry, though. The funeral's Saturday."

Stefanie was livid and looked it, having turned bright red and puffy around the cheeks. "We are not burying Mrs. McNemmish at sea! People don't bury people at sea. Especially when those people are us! Mrs. McNemmish is being buried in the cemetery in two days. That's where people get buried when they're dead. They're buried by burial people who bury people who are dead! This is the dumbest plan y'all have ever come up with. I'm going home."

"You can't go home. Not until we figure out how to bury the widow at sea. We have to do it, Stefanie. Besides..." Daniel pointed to the trunk with the initials E.D.T. carved on the front brass plate and smiled at the girl enticingly. "I bet the key in that poem is inside a seashell in there. Don't you want to know what she left us? If we bury her, we can see what's inside the trunk. There could be gold and diamonds in there."

"You are so stupid." Stefanie grabbed the note out of Mark's hand and reread it. "She's talking about a key in a shell that a thousand eyes will never find. It can't be in that trunk because that's the first place she knew we'd look. No offense, but you're listening to a woman who had barnacles on the brain. I mean, what good is telling us about a key if she didn't tell us where to find it? You know what I think? I think that trunk is full of those shells she collected for ninety years, and that key is the key to her underwear drawer, and that ring Zeek got really came out of a cereal box!"

"The poem says the secret is in that chest and the key is in the shell, which means the key that's in the shell is in that chest!"

"So what! We are still not burying her at sea!"

"Maybe it's a test," suggested Billy. "Maybe she wanted to see how smart we are. I mean, what if the key really isn't a *key* key. It might be a *key* key, but it might be a *hint* key."

"Ha!" Stefanie pointed at Billy, giving him a nod of approval. "That proves she's crackers because you can't hide a hint key in a treasure chest!"

"Ha yourself," grumbled Daniel.

Once again, Mark shook his head firmly.

"No, Mark! We are not burying her at sea, so y'all can just forget about it!"

"We gave her our word."

"You did not."

"Well, we sort of gave her our word." Daniel glanced out the window, worried that Teddy would return to the shack before the argument was settled. "We made a pact with each other that we'd do this."

"I didn't!" Stefanie reminded him.

"Well, the rest of us did and we need your help." Daniel put his hand out and waited for the other three to put theirs on top. Billy and Mark added their hands at once. "Come on, Stefanie."

"It'll be okay," Billy assured her. "If we bury the widow in the Graveyard of the Atlantic tonight, she can be a ghost on Blackbeard's ghost ship by tomorrow and then we'll be as rich as Midas, just like she said."

"What about it, Stefanie?"

Mark reached out with his other hand, asking for hers.

"Well?" prodded Daniel.

Stefanie hesitated. "No. I can't. I'm not going to bury Miss Theo at sea tonight, or any other night."

"That's okay," Billy told her gently. He turned to Daniel and Mark, who still had their hands clasped together. "We can do it by ourselves. It's what she wanted. We have to do this for her."

Stefanie moved toward the door. She was trembling, and her throat was closing. She couldn't breathe. "You shouldn't be doing this," she said in a broken voice. "It's wrong! It's not Christian. You can't bury *anybody!* You're just kids! Mark, what's the matter with you?"

"Gawd, Stefanie, calm down," said Daniel. "You'll give yourself apoplexy."

Billy spoke calmly and honestly. "We can do this, Stefanie. I know we can. All we need is a plan."

Daniel walked to the back window and pointed. "If we can get the coffin out of the church, back up Lighthouse Road, and around the back of Mrs. McNemmish's house without being seen, we can load it into a boat, easy."

"We'll have to carry her over to the ocean side," Billy said, agreeing with Daniel's assessment of the situation. "If we dump her in the sound, she'll float back to the village."

"Stop it!" cried Stefanie. She pushed Daniel away from the window, and turned to leave. "You are not doing this! I swear I'll turn y'all in."

"No you won't, and yes we are! And we're going to need two boats: one for us and one to carry Miss Theo's coffin. I can bring one of my dad's outboards to the cove at midnight," figured Daniel. "But I need you to meet me there with one of your dad's boats."

"We'll have to work fast," Billy advised them. "The fishing crews gather at the creek around four a.m."

"Teddy's back." Daniel looked at Stefanie and spoke urgently. "We are going to do this. We are going to bury Mrs. McNemmish in the ocean at midnight. It's what she wanted and it's up to us to do it. Now, are you with us or not?"

"Come on, Stefanie. We really want you with us." Billy looked at her with puppy dog eyes. "Pleeeeeease."

Mark looked at Stefanie pleadingly. He more than anyone would want to do this for the widow.

Stefanie heard Teddy's footsteps and jumped. "All right!" she agreed. "But I swear: If we get caught, I'll kill all three of you."

"If we get caught," said Billy, "we're dead where we stand."

In the blackness of the night,

There sails a yellow moon.

Witches sing of Halloween,

And ghosts cry out in tune.

Bury me beneath the sea,

So I may sail on high.

I shall live a pirate's life

The very day I die.

CHAPTER V

Daniel blinked away raindrops as he steered his father's boat into Blackbeard's Cove near Teach's Hole, just south of the widow's shack. The starless sky and black water blended into the bleak backdrop of bewitching trees that swayed and hovered above the stone-filled landing. Unsteady nerves turned Daniel's spine to ice. Not only had he swiped the ranger's boat, but he had picked a particularly creepy, dark, and eerie night to do it. His eyes darted back and forth across the sandy footpath that led to Blackbeard's hideout. In the darkness, his feet became entangled in the spread of English Ivy that covered the woods, and he tripped over the old English bricks that were the foundation for Blackbeard's trading post three hundred years earlier. He arrived at the rain-filled well beside Sam Jones's gravesite and sat down for a rest. He wondered how many ghosts were hiding out there, peering down at him from trees that looked more like mangled animals than trees.

Stefanie, too, was cold, wet, and scared. She had turned her father's boat back twice before reaching the cove just after midnight. If Captain Austin ever found out she took the boat, he'd filet her. She really wanted to be home. She wanted to be in bed. She wanted to be anywhere but where she was. Her heart pulsed in her throat. Her hands shook so hard she could barely moor the boat. Man, she hated the boys.

Daniel whistled softly when he saw Stefanie walking the footpath so as not to frighten or surprise her. Once together, Stefanie grabbed hold of Daniel's coat sleeve, and the two stumbled and fought their way to the far side of Blackbeard's lair.

"My ankle's caught in the ivy," whispered Stefanie.

Daniel reached into the pocket of his dripping wet parka and pulled out a pocketknife. He quickly cut her loose and led her to where their bikes had been hidden earlier. Mounting their bikes, they rode to the Assembly of God church on Lighthouse Road, their only light coming from the small lamp on the front of Stefanie's handlebars. When they arrived at the church, Billy and Mark met them behind the small, white, clapboard building.

"All of the doors and windows on the first floor are locked," Billy filled them in. "The only way inside is through the steeple window. Follow me." He hugged the rain-soaked clapboards along the side of the church making his way to the front of the building. Stefanie and Mark followed without incident, but Daniel let out a yelp when he backed into a prickly yucca plant. "Be quiet," whispered Billy. "The reverend's bedroom window is right next door." He gathered everyone together, and pointed to the top of the church. "Daniel, you'll have to climb onto the porch overhang, then crawl to the bottom ledge of the steeple window and pull yourself up. Then all you have to do is climb through the window, jump to the floor, and let the rest of us in."

Mark nodded in agreement, but Daniel looked at Billy as if the boy had three heads. "What do you mean, I'll have to climb through the window? I'm not doing that! I'll kill myself!"

"Good," yawned Stefanie. "Then we can all go back to bed."

"You have to do it," said Billy. "I'm too big, and Stefanie and Mark are out."

"Why am I out?" objected Stefanie, suddenly outraged at being passed over for the job. "Because I'm a girl?"

"No, no. I didn't mean you're out because you can't do it. I just think it's better if Daniel gets hurt instead of you."

"Oh. That's okay then." Stefanie tightened her coat collar and pulled down her hat. "Well, hurry up and do it already. It's freezing out here and I'm soaked."

"Why can't we just break a window and climb in that way?" asked Daniel.

"That's sacrilegious," explained Billy. "The steeple window's already unlocked. Once you let us in, all we have to do is steal the coffin, dump Miss Theo into the ocean, and get home before anyone notices we're gone."

"It's a good thing that's not sacrilegious," mocked Stefanie.

"I thought about that," said Billy. "But since we're giving the widow a real burial, the robbery part is okay." He reached up and unscrewed the front porch light. The church and grounds went black.

"What did you do that for?" cried Daniel.

"So no one can see us."

"Now I can't see us! I don't think this is going to work."

Stefanie folded her arms and squawked, "That's what I said, but no one ever listens to me."

"Shut up, Stefanie." Daniel made two attempts at jumping onto the overhang from the side railing, but couldn't hold on. "Mark, get down on your hands and knees." He waited for the youngster to get on all fours, then using Billy for balance, he tried jumping off of Mark's back.

"Stop squirming," Daniel told the boy. But Mark started giggling and wiggling as soon as Daniel pressed his shoes into his back. Screaming with laughter, he collapsed onto his stomach and rolled over. Daniel's arms flapped helplessly as he tumbled backward onto Billy's chest, sending his friend careening over the side rail and into the reverend's pumpkin garden. A moment later, there was a loud pop. Everyone looked up as a portion of the gutter broke loose, hovered in midair for one brief, death-defying second, then dropped onto the cement porch with a loud clank.

Stefanie jumped back and applauded. "Way to go, y'all! If you don't wake up the reverend, maybe you'll wake up Mrs. McNemmish."

"Do you think you could shut your trap for five minutes?" grumbled Daniel. He got to his feet and crouched over Mark. "Way to go, Sherlock. I could have broken my neck. The reverend's going to kill us when he finds that piece of gutter. Are you okay?" he asked Billy, who was returning from the pumpkin patch.

"I'm fine, but there's mashed pumpkin all over my pants. Hmmm, I smell like a pie." He got back onto the porch and told Mark to get back onto his hands and knees. "This time, I'll stand on your back and Daniel will get on my shoulders. If you laugh, I'll beat you up. Stefanie, you catch us if we fall."

Stefanie pulled out a tissue and blew her nose. "I have a better idea," she said with a crackling voice. "Don't fall."

Mark giggled, but remained still. Daniel pressed the tips of his sneakers deep into Billy's neck, then pushed himself onto the overhang. Billy reached up and shoved him the rest of the way. "Hurry up. It's getting late."

Daniel scrambled farther onto the overhang, skidding and slipping from one wet roof tile to the next. On his way to the steeple window, several of the large, green tiles slid out from underneath his sneaker and sailed to the ground. "If I fall off and get killed, I'll be grounded for life," he thought to himself. Finally at the top, he pressed his face against the windowpane and gazed down into the chapel. Soft candlelight flickered throughout the church, giving the room a warm, inviting glow. Mrs. McNemmish's coffin rested in the center aisle between four ten-foot-tall brass candlesticks. The casket had been carved by Jeffrey Tillet and was made from her favorite—cedar wood. A hand-quilted blanket made especially for her by the women at the Schoolhouse Road Methodist Church lay across the top of the casket, celebrating her life in story squares. Both the casket and the blanket had been made years earlier in honor of this occasion.

Daniel was terrified. "I don't think I can jump from here. I might break something," he called down.

"What did you think you were going to do once you got up there? Fly to the floor?"

"I thought Billy had a plan."

"This was my plan."

"Some plan."

"Just do it!" shouted Stefanie. "I'm getting pneumonia!"

"Okay, okay." Daniel wedged his fingers underneath the base of the wooden frame and slowly pressed the steeple window open. Shaking off the excess water, he lifted one leg over the ledge and into the chapel. "Man, that treasure better be worth all this. Hey! There's a stack of folding chairs behind the front door. Maybe I can land on the chairs." He was about to lift his other leg over the windowsill, when Mark shot his hands up in the air and motioned for Daniel to stop moving.

"What's the matter?"

"Mark says Teddy's coming," said Stefanie.

"Rats! Daniel, just stay there. And be quiet!" In a panic, Billy grabbed Mark and Stefanie by their coat sleeves and dragged them around the back of the building just as the sheriff's car pulled up front.

Daniel sat paralyzed, half in and half out of the window. It was raining harder now, and the wind had shifted. It was getting colder by the minute, but sweat poured down Daniel's neck when Teddy Jackson and his dog Mustard got out of the car.

"Come on, boy. Let's go check on Theodora." Teddy clicked on his flashlight when he spotted two green shingles lying in the middle of the front yard. "The wind must be stronger than I thought," he told Mustard. He glanced up at the roof, but didn't see anything suspicious. "Uh, oh!" He walked over to the front stoop and kicked the piece of gutter with his foot. "Either Santa got to the church a month early, or someone decided to pull a Halloween prank."

Meanwhile, Mustard was leading his own investigation. Staring straight up at Daniel, he wagged his tail and whined.

Daniel bit his lip and shrieked under his breath. "Go away, you stupid mutt!" He waved away the frisky pup, but Mustard thought Daniel was playing and barked.

"What's the matter, boy? Halloween got you spooked?" Teddy swung his flashlight up and down the front of the church, passing lightly over Daniel's right shoe. "Remind me to replace the front light," he told his K-9 partner.

Daniel's mouth went dry when Mustard made a second attempt at getting his attention. "Go away," pleaded the boy. "My butt's falling asleep."

Teddy pulled a ring of keys out of his pocket and unlocked the church door. Stepping inside, he gave a quick glance around the chapel. Daniel watched as the sheriff approached the widow's coffin. "Sleep well, Miss Theo. We're sure going to miss you around here." He straightened the quilt with a gentle hand, then turned to leave.

"I'll tell you what, Mustard. Why don't you and I set up a couple of rows of seats? It'll give the reverend a head start in the morning."

"No!" freaked Daniel. "I need those folding chairs!" He watched in silent horror as his stepladder shrank in size, one folding chair at a time, until it was half the height.

Outside, Billy checked his watch. It was a quarter past one in the morning and they hadn't even gotten inside the church yet. It was another fifteen minutes before Teddy called it a night and came outside. The children heard him lock the front door, then head for the backyard.

"Oh no! He's coming back here," panicked Billy. He grabbed Mark and Stefanie and yanked them around to the other side of the church and back to the front yard, where they hid behind the brick-enclosed church bell.

"I have to sneeze," Stefanie muttered from behind her glove.

"Oh no, you don't." Billy slapped his large hand over her mouth just in time to muffle the sneeze. Teddy didn't hear the smothered explosion, but Mustard did. He broke loose and ran straight for the children. With one leap, he knocked Stefanie to the ground and licked her chin.

"Get off of me," groaned the girl. "You smell like a wet rug."

"Shh! Mustard, get out of here," said Billy.

"Mustard!" called Teddy. "Where are you, boy?"

Billy picked up the young yellow lab and tossed him onto the other side of the bell. Mustard thought Billy wanted to play and barked excitedly.

"There you are!" Teddy jogged toward Mustard as the dog continued to bark in front of the bell. "Something behind there, boy?" Teddy was about to peek behind the brick enclosure, when another one of the green roof tiles sailed to the ground. The young sheriff jumped. "Must be the Halloween ghosties. Come on, Mustard, let's go home."

The children held their breath as Teddy and Mustard got back into the car and drove away. Billy waited a few extra moments to make sure Teddy wasn't coming back, then bolted out from behind the bell. "Daniel, are you okay? Man, I thought we were toast!"

"My butt fell asleep."

"Well, wake it up. This is taking too long."

"Ya think?" Daniel wiggled around until some feeling was restored to his backside, then continued climbing through the window. Grabbing the sill with gloved hands, he dangled for an instant, then dropped onto the shortened stack of folding chairs.

The crash was noteworthy.

The metal chairs collapsed into a heap onto the parquet floor with Daniel sprawled out on top. When he tried to stand up, his foot got wedged between the seat and the back of the top chair, and he lost his balance. His arms flailed about aimlessly as he toppled forward onto the back of the last row of hardwood pews. His right hand reached for the armrest and missed, knocking over one of the ten-foot-tall candlesticks. The long, tapered, rose-colored candle continued to flicker brightly as it flew out of the holder and rolled down the full length of the carpeted center aisle and underneath the drape-covered staircase. Tiny flames flared like the tips of birthday candles, leaving a bright, golden trail down the center of the aisle, across the staircase curtain, and up the steps leading to the pulpit. Like golden streamers that burst from a Fourth of July sparkler and hover in the clear night air, dancing flames played across Daniel's closed eyelids. Billy's frantic pounding arrested him from his nightmare.

"What's going on in there?" shouted Billy. "Daniel! Open the door!"

Daniel yanked the chair off the stack and dragged it with him to the front door. He opened it just as the quilt on Mrs. McNemmish's casket went up in flames.

"Oh, man!" shrieked Stefanie. "Let me guess. This is or isn't sacrilegious."

"Mark, help Daniel," yelled Billy. "Stefanie, get Mrs. McNemmish out of the aisle."

Billy leaped over the chairs and raced toward the reverend's office. Meanwhile, Stefanie, who admittedly didn't do well with dead people, grabbed Mark by the hand and aimed him toward the front of the church. "I'll take care of Daniel. You take care of the coffin. Just keep walking until you bump into the gurney! Be careful when you pull the blanket off the casket! It's on fire." She reached down and helped Daniel shake off the offending chair. "Nice job," she told him.

Billy grabbed the fire extinguisher off the wall of the reverend's office, then he ran back into the chapel and blasted foam over the rug, curtains, pulpit, and coffin, quickly dowsing the flames. When he was finished, the church podium and first ten pews were covered in black soot and foamy-yellow fuzz.

"Well," choked Stefanie. "That was fun."

"We're in, aren't we?"

"Yeah, we're in. Now, let's get out," coughed Billy. He stowed the extinguisher under the front pew, grabbed Mark, and pushed the coffin and gurney toward the front door.

Stefanie stuck her head outside to see if the commotion had raised any islanders. "I don't see anyone. Let's go."

Daniel limped to the head of the gurney while Stefanie took charge of the foot. Mark and Billy placed themselves on either side. Together, they carefully guided the table through the door and onto the front stoop.

"Stefanie, watch out!" shouted Daniel.

Stefanie looked up and asked, "What's wrong?" as she stepped backward, missing the first stair. She let out a startled squeak as the gurney fell forward, pushed her down the next two steps and onto the sidewalk, landing with a thunk on her backside. The coffin jerked out of the boys' hands while bumping and rocking sideways on the top of the table. The gurney then rolled over the tiny, white picket fence that lined the sidewalk, and lurched to a stop on the reverend's side lawn.

Mark, who was completely blinded by the darkness, tripped over Stefanie and stumbled into the brick-encased bell on the side lawn. It rang out—gong, gong, gong, gong—while Stefanie's scream pierced the night like a steamboat whistle. Daniel hobbled over to the bell to stop it from ringing a fifth time while Billy steadied the gurney and kept the coffin from falling off the table top.

"Oh, gross!" Billy looked at his friends, his entire body convulsing.

"What's the matter?"

"I heard Mrs. McNemmish roll around in the coffin."

"Ooh, yuck. That is so nasty," winced Daniel. "Shoot! We woke up the reverend! Come on, y'all. Move it!"

Billy, Mark, and Stefanie grabbed the gurney and high-tailed it off the reverend's yard while Daniel shut and locked the front door. He caught up with the others just as they were rounding the sound side of Lighthouse Road.

"We moored the boats behind the widow's shack about a hundred yards before you get to the hole," Daniel panted. "When I say turn, turn!"

But Billy was overanxious to get the coffin into the boat and set sail for the ocean. As soon as he saw the moored boats in the faint light of a Coast Guard buoy, he gave the gurney an extra heave. The gurney shot forward onto the widow's sandy front lawn. The moment the two front wheels hit the sand, the front of the gurney sank. The metal table, as well as the four children, came to a sudden, grinding halt. Mrs. McNemmish's coffin, however, did not. It took off like a 747, flew through the air, sailed onto the beach, and slid into an outgoing wave. It finally sloshed to a stop some fifteen feet away. No one moved. No one even breathed. They all just stood there with their mouths open, gaping into the dark, stormy distance.

Stefanie covered her mouth. "Oops."

"This is a nightmare," uttered Daniel. He pulled a small penlight out of his pocket and shuffled toward the beached coffin. He stopped when he reached the casket and turned. "She fell out."

"She WHAT?"

"She fell out. The lid broke, and Theodora fell out of her coffin!"

"I'm going to puke," said Stefanie.

"Well, put her back in," ordered Billy.

"You're the biggest one here. You put her back in!"

"I'm not touching her. She's dead."

"Of course she's dead. That's why we're here!"

"Well, somebody put her back in before the rest of us freeze to death."

"You do it!" shouted the boys.

Stefanie hid her hands behind her back. "I don't touch dead bodies."

"Well, neither do we!"

Mark walked forward and squinted down at the frail body that lay silently in the shallow water and sand. Bending over, he gently and respectfully touched the end of her shawl, but the lifeless body repelled him and he quickly withdrew his hand. He looked up tearfully.

"Come on, y'all," Daniel said urgently. "Mark and I can't do this by ourselves, and if we don't put her in the coffin and get out of here soon, somebody's going to see us." Neither Stefanie nor Billy moved. "We can't bury her if we're caught!" hollered Daniel. "We rang the stupid bell!"

"Okay, okay." Billy closed his eyes, swallowed the giant lump in his throat, then joined Daniel and Mark beside the widow and her coffin. "You get her arms, and I'll get her legs." Together, the three boys gently lifted Miss Theo and, once again, laid her to rest in her satin-lined coffin. With trembling hands, Stefanie straightened the widow's dress and favorite shawl. A photograph of Mrs. McNemmish's late husband, Arthur, and their two strapping sons peeked out of her pink skirt pocket.

Daniel wandered away from the others, returning with two halves of the coffin lid. "We've got a problem."

"Now what's wrong?" asked Stefanie.

"We were supposed to poke holes in the lid once we got to the ocean so the casket could fill with water. If it doesn't fill with water, it won't sink. Don't you get it? Without water in the coffin, it could float back to town with the tide, and without a lid, we can't fill it with water because Mrs. McNemmish will float out of the coffin."

"So what are you saying?" asked Billy. "You want us to poke holes in Mrs. McNemmish?"

"Don't be gross," croaked Stefanie. Her voice was raspy, and she was coughing constantly. "Can't you tie her in?"

"With what? My pants belt?" Daniel's ankle hurt and he was losing his patience. "Wait a minute. I have an idea."

He limped over to his father's boat and back again carrying a large, green fishing net and a roll of duct tape.

"What's that for?"

"You'll see." He pointed to Billy. "Help me cover the coffin with the net. I can secure it underneath with nautical ties and duct tape so she won't float out."

Together, the boys worked quickly, tying and securing the net. For the first time since the evening began, the four friends stood together and stared down at the wonderful, gentle woman who had been part of their lives and heritage since they were born.

Stefanie watched the icy rain trickle across the netting. The drops reminded her of glistening pearls, and she suddenly remembered Daniel's joke about the oyster keeping its mouth shut. "Maybe we should have a funeral," she suggested.

"We will out at sea," said Daniel. "We really have to go."

It was a quarter to three in the morning before Mrs. McNemmish's coffin was finally placed in the back of Captain Austin's boat. Billy and Daniel donned their life jackets and climbed aboard Ranger Garrish's boat. Mark tied the two crafts together.

"Hide the gurney and the top of the casket where they won't be found," Daniel reminded Stefanie. "And don't forget to put our bikes back."

"We won't." Stefanie turned to walk away, then turned back. "Don't get dead," she told the boys.

"We won't."

Mark looked at Daniel and pointed to the coffin.

"We'll give Miss Theo a really nice funeral," he assured the youngster.

Billy turned on the motor and put the boat in gear. "We'll see y'all tomorrow." Glancing out at the black waves and ripples of undertow, he added, "I hope."

'Round and 'round the winter wind,

Rolling waves and tides that spin,

Chasing years around the globe,

With sailing ships and tales of gold.

Blackbeard sang his toast to life

With blackening sky and firelight,

The laughing gulls, so full of zest,

Are Ocracoke, my soul at rest.

CHAPTER VI

Billy took the helm of the ranger's boat and skill-fully steered the tandem crafts out of the sound, through the tiny inlet, and out toward the open sea. Daniel sat beside him, deep in thought.

"We could go to jail for this."

"No way! We'll probably get some kind of reward. Especially when we tell everyone it's what she really wanted." Billy spoke as he carefully navigated the two boats around shallow sand bars that dotted the coast-line. At the young age of fourteen, he had already acquired the skill of captains three times his age and experience. "Besides," he told Daniel confidently. "They'll never catch us. Miss Theo wouldn't let that happen. Would you, Miss Theo?" He shot a quick, off-the-shoulder glance back toward the widow's casket and let out a blood-curdling scream.

"What?" Daniel whipped around in his seat so fast he nearly toppled over the side of the boat. "Oh, God! Oh, God!" He stumbled to the rear of the craft and stretched out over the back rail. "Where is she?"

"I don't know! I don't see the boat anywhere!" Billy shut off the motor and drifted to a stop just shy of the mile marker. Daniel reached into the water and grabbed the end of the towrope Mark had used to secure the two crafts. It had come undone! "We're dead! We're dead where we stand."

"Not yet, we're not." Billy held his bare hand in the air. "The wind changed. It's coming from the east. She must be drifting back toward the island!"

Daniel freaked. "What if somebody sees the boat? They'll know it's Captain Austin's boat. What if it floats up next to one of the shrimp boats and they look down and see the coffin? They start loading in less than an hour!" Billy turned the boat around and gunned it back toward the Ocracoke inlet. "She's got to be around here somewhere," he assured Daniel.

"What if she isn't? What if the boat turned east and headed out to sea? What if it picks up the current and goes up toward Hatteras? Or what if it goes south to Portsmouth Island? It could have gone anywhere! Man, we are so dead, we are beyond dead."

Billy raced back toward the island, carefully dodging inlet shallows while keeping his headlights aimed and his eyes peeled on the black water. "There she is!" He slowed the boat as he passed through the inlet and followed the low water markers in the direction of Howard's Reef, a small, sandy island in the sound. "Uh, oh."

"What?"

"She's headed for the Coast Guard station. This could be a problem."

"Wait! She's turning!" Daniel pointed toward the entrance to Silver Lake where the night crews would be hauling supplies onto their spider-legged shrimp boats. "She just went through the ditch!" He and Billy watched as Captain Austin's boat slowly drifted into the harbor, passing the moored boats and restaurant docks.

"We have to follow her," said Billy.

"Are you nuts?"

"We can't just leave her there." Billy thought for a moment while he assessed the situation. "I'll turn off the motor and we'll float in behind her. It's dark. Maybe no one will see us. Shh!" He cut the engine and allowed the boat to ride the small turbulence caused by the rainstorm. Within minutes, the ranger's boat drifted into Silver Lake harbor following the exact same path the Austin boat had taken.

"Shoot!" Daniel slapped a hand to his forehead. "She's headed straight for the dock at the Jolly Roger Restaurant. Poor Jake's going to think he drank some bad brew."

"Forget that," said Billy. He handed Daniel a rowing paddle and took one for himself. "We need to circle around to the front of the boat and then back up to it so we can tie them together."

The two boys rowed as slowly and silently as they dared, ducking down every time they heard a voice or noise coming from one of the docks. They aimed for the

Jolly's loading dock and caught up with Captain Austin's boat just as a small Coast Guard skiff sailed into the harbor almost directly behind them. Billy quickly rowed his boat between two others that were docked and tied to the wharf. They lucked out when the Austin boat rocked its way underneath the dock, which cast a large shadow over it.

"Get down!" whispered Billy. He and Daniel quickly pulled in their oars, then dove to the floor and waited breathlessly as the skiff wove in and out of the docks. For one scary moment, they could see the side of the Coast Guard boat just inches away from their own.

Daniel thought his heart would fall out of his chest, it was pounding so hard. "It sounded so easy. Steal the coffin, bury the body in the ocean, and get rich."

"Yeah, well," sighed his accomplice. When the skiff moved away, Billy peeked up over the side and gave Daniel a nudge. "They're gone. Sit up." Checking that the coast was clear, the boys slipped their oars back into the water and gently eased the back of their boat into the front of the Austin craft. When they were close enough, Daniel tied them together for the second time that night.

"Okay. Let's go," he said anxiously.

"Are you sure?"

"Yes! Go!"

Billy didn't need encouragement. He waited for several of the fishing boats to start their engines, then he started his and glided out of Silver Lake Harbor. Once out of the ditch opening, he hit the gas and flew back toward the inlet. The sea was growing increasingly choppy due to the freshening wind and rain. Billy fought the incoming tide, skillfully guiding both crafts past the deep-water buoys.

About a mile out, he reached for the gear to shut down the motor when the craft lurched forward, dragging the Austin boat with it. Both crafts rocked so violently, pitching forward and backward and slamming into each other, that Daniel was knocked off the bench and onto the floor. Billy, too, was thrown back and forth from one side of the wheel to the other as rain and seawater sprayed across the bow. "We're caught in a whirlpool!" shouted Billy. "You'd better hang on to something!"

Billy grasped the wheel tightly as the cyclonic ocean spun beneath him. Daniel reached out and grabbed hold of an oarlock.

Billy worked the wheel as hard as he could, trying to keep his boat from capsizing. Suddenly, his feet slipped out from under him and he was shaken loose from the wheel when the Austin boat slammed him from behind. Daniel was propelled up and off the floor. He crashed into the back of the captain's chair, smashing his left shoulder. Pulling himself up, he climbed over the chair and reached for the unattended wheel. He seized it just in time to keep the boat from toppling over. High-breaking waves slapped against the hull of the boat, followed by a loud scraping noise. The backside of the hull had been breached by the Austin boat. "It's leaking! Billy, take the wheel!"

Billy struggled to lift his head. He was horribly dizzy and his eyes were blurred from both the rain and the bump on his head. Staggering to his feet, he reclaimed the helm.

"I can't see the lighthouse!" Billy shouted frantically. Without a fixed point of reference, he would continue to spin out of control until he, or the boat, or all of them were pulled under.

Daniel reached into the hold, pulled out several life jackets, and shoved them against the side of the boat. He, too, was dizzy, but managed to temporarily stop the leak.

A flash of pitchfork lightning followed by a deafening crack of thunder added to their fear and ill fate. The storm was turning harsh. Looming, black clouds fluttered on and off like distant fireworks, teasing them with welcomed light and then going dark. The boats continued to heave and swirl, locked into the increasingly turbulent water.

"I see the lighthouse!" shouted Daniel. He stumbled forward and pointed in the direction of the rounding beam. "There it is!" He waited a moment then pointed toward the beam again. "Can you see it?"

Billy caught sight of the lighthouse lamp every few seconds. With each sweep of light, he struggled to hold fast, keeping his craft facing the shore for longer and longer periods of time. Suddenly, there was a loud popping noise from underneath the floor of the craft. Daniel's boat lunged forward, carrying with it the Austin boat as the ocean spit the two crafts clear of the whirlpool.

Billy turned off the motor and plopped down into the captain's chair. The boat rocked with the waves, but steadied slightly when he lowered the anchor. He turned to see if Daniel was okay.

"Oh, my God! Daniel! Daniel, where are you?" He grabbed the large flashlight and skimmed it across the water. It was impossible to see anything between the curling waves and streaming rain. Another flash of lightning filled the sky, and Billy saw Daniel fighting a wave. He grabbed an oar and leaned out over the side. "Daniel! Grab the oar!" Daniel looked up and saw Billy. He swam toward the paddle and grabbed it around the middle, wrapping both arms around the lengthy handle as a wave curled over him. When he surfaced, Billy planted his feet on the inside wall and pulled the oar with every ounce of strength he had left. He finally leaned over the side of the boat, seized Daniel's arm, and dragged him over the rail. Both boys dropped to the floor gasping.

"Did you drown?" Billy asked him, finally able to speak.

Daniel was still gasping. "I don't think so. How 'bout you?"

"No. I'm okay. Man! That was a four-ticket ride!" Billy climbed to his feet and made sure the coffin hadn't flown off the Austin boat. "The casket's full of water, but it's still on the boat, thank goodness. You look like a drowned rat."

"I feel like a drowned rat." Daniel sat up straight and felt a small knot on the back of his head. He reached into the hold to get a blanket and winced from the pain in his left shoulder. "How am I supposed to explain a banged-up ankle, a knot on my head, and a bruised shoulder when I get up for breakfast?"

"Easy," said Billy. "Don't complain."

Daniel sat still for a few moments and gathered his thoughts. "Thanks for saving me."

"No problem." The truth was, Billy was hurting from the night's battles as much as Daniel was. "My stomach can't make up its mind whether or not it's going to puke up the gallon of water I swallowed."

"Just don't puke on me," Daniel told him. "Man, I just want to get out of this boat, get into bed, and sleep for a week." He walked to the back of the boat and stared down at the coffin wearily. "Let's just do this and go home."

"Maybe you should say something before we, you know, dump her overboard," suggested Billy.

"Bury, not dump." Daniel gazed down at the shrouded casket and thought about the vivacious, loving woman who lay inside. "Maybe Stefanie's right. Maybe we shouldn't be doing this. I mean, don't you think it's kind of weird that all those things went wrong? It's like someone's telling us not to bury her here."

"You're just quamish from the ride," Billy told him. "Besides, this isn't about Stefanie, and it isn't about us. It's about Mrs. McNemmish. She really believed that if someone buried her at sea, she would become a ghost pirate on Blackbeard's ship. My dad says if you can't prove something one way, you can't prove it another. We don't know but that she wasn't right. If we don't bury her at sea, it'll be our fault if she doesn't become a pirate on Blackbeard's ship."

"I know all that. It's just weird, that's all." Daniel removed his hat and straightened his rain-drenched collar and coat. "Take off your hat," he told Billy.

"But it's pouring!"

"What difference does that make? You're soaked anyway."

Billy removed his hat and pushed back his hair. "Go ahead."

Daniel cleared his throat, and addressed his words to the late Mrs. Theodora Teach McNemmish. "We have come to bury our friend Mrs. McNemmish in the Graveyard of the Atlantic so she can become a ghost pirate on the *Queen Anne's Revenge*. Mrs. McNemmish was the oldest living relative of Blackbeard's sister from Bath and everyone on the island loved her, including us. We hope she has a wonderful life on the ghost ship."

"How can she have a wonderful life if she's dead?" asked Billy.

"She understands! Man, you've been hanging around Stefanie too much. Anyway, we hope you have a great *after-life* on Blackbeard's ghost ship. What else should I say?"

"Say something about how much everyone will miss her."

"We will miss her," Daniel said sincerely. "But we'll sure never forget you. Anyway, we're really sorry about your coffin lid, and the mess we made in the church, and losing you, and getting all that water in your casket. We just had a really hard time getting you here. But I guess you already know that. Anyway, everybody's going to miss you. Especially Mark. Oh! Clinton brought an old rocking chair over to the Community Store porch and put your name on it. Come and sit there anytime you'd like. And listen. You know all those pirate stories you told us about Blackbeard and his treasure? Well, they were really great stories. So if they turn out to be fake on account of your hard veins and everything, don't worry about it. It's okay. We would have done this for you, anyway. But if they turn out to be real, we really want to thank you in advance."

"That goes for me, too," said Billy.

"We hope you have a great life as a pirate," said Daniel. "You're a terrific lady."

"You'll make a great first mate," added Billy.

"I guess that's it," said Daniel. "Oh! We postponed Halloween in your honor. We're going to have our carnival and auction and stuff next week. I'll egg some cars for you. And we'll visit the McNemmish gravesite at midnight. If we see Blackbeard walking around Try Yard Creek without his head, we'll tell him hey for you."

"Amen," chattered Billy. "Can we go now? I'm soaked to the bone and freezing."

"I guess."

With the service concluded, the boys jumped onto the Austin boat and took hold of Mrs. McNemmish's coffin. Together they managed to lift it barely over the wall, where it toppled into the water upside-down.

"This isn't happening," wailed Daniel.

"Grab the oars before she floats away!" shouted Billy.

Daniel jumped back onto his father's boat, grabbed both paddles, then hopped back onto the Austin boat just as the coffin began to bob farther out to sea. Reaching over the side, Billy and Daniel brought the coffin back toward their boat, then flipped it over using the flat end of the paddles and a timely wave. Now, Mrs. McNemmish could face her precious Ocracoke sky one last time. It wasn't long, however, before curling waves swelled and broke atop the casket, showering a mixture of ocean and Gulf Stream water over Mrs. McNemmish's body. The coffin soon filled with a blanket of saltwater and heaven's tears. Daniel and Billy watched silently as their beloved widow slipped quietly away from her gentle life on the island, to the ghostly world of the hereafter where the prospect of piracy peppered her imagination. They watched with pride and in awe as the daring, brave woman they called friend disappeared into her black, watery grave.

"God be with you, Miss Theo. You're a pirate now."

"Aye! That ye are," cheered Blackbeard. He held up a frothing mug and toasted her spirit:

> *A pirate's days are never done,*
> *As long as there's a rising sun.*
> *His knife held high, his courage fast,*
> *It's piracy for us at last.*
> *Y'ar Blackbeard's mate at last.*

If "reason" be food for thought,
Let "imagination" be dessert.

CHAPTER VII

"The sheriff's office in Ocracoke Island, North Carolina, today reports the mysterious disappearance of a body from the Assembly of God church on Lighthouse Road. According to Deputy Sheriff Teddy Jackson, the church was broken into sometime after 1:00 A.M. this morning. Reverend Lyle Wood heard a commotion and, upon entering the church, discovered that the gurney and coffin containing the body of the late Mrs. Theodora Teach McNemmish were both missing. In addition to the robbery, the church suffered a small but damaging fire and some damage to the outside of the building."

"The gurney, along with the two broken pieces of the casket cover, were found later this morning in

Reverend Wood's backyard. There will be further information pending an investigation. In other news..."

Daniel's elbow slipped on the kitchen tablecloth, nearly plunging him headlong into his cereal bowl. He told Stefanie to hide the stuff where it wouldn't be found—not in the reverend's backyard, for crying out loud!

Daniel's dad, Ranger Todd Garrish, turned off the television and slammed down the remote. "What kind of crazy maniac would break into a church and steal that sweet old lady's coffin? Especially with her still in it? A dingbatter, that's who. Some deranged tourist with nothing better to do than walk right down the middle of our roads blocking traffic, sink their tiny little cars in our sand dunes, and swipe corpses out of our churches because there's not enough *entertainment* on the island. Well, they'll get plenty of entertainment where they're going."

"Calm down," said Elizabeth. She reached across the table and removed her husband's coffee cup. He was edgy enough already. "You don't suppose Zeek had anything to do with this, do you? He was always so mean to her, and Candy saw him on the island a few weeks ago."

The mention of Zeek Beacon sent Daniel jumping so violently, he tipped over in his chair.

"My, you're jumpy this morning," said Mrs. Garrish, helping her son back up. "I guess the news has all of us upset."

"You have no idea," moaned Daniel. He picked up his chair and returned to his cereal. What if they questioned Zeek about the widow, and he blabbed about seeing the four of them at her house? They'd have to tell everyone that they knew about the ring Zeek stole from her. Then everyone would find out about the treasure. Then Zeek might tell everyone that the four of them had gone to the widow's shack to get the rest of the treasure, and that they stole the widow's body for ransom just to prove that the ring was his, and that he didn't know about the treasure, *and* they'd have to prove he was lying before he could prove that they were lying, even though they weren't. Worse! They might interrogate the four of them, and that would mean Stefanie would have to talk, and that would be the end of that, because she couldn't keep her mouth shut if it meant keeping the whole island afloat.

"It couldn't possibly be Zeek!" Daniel blurted out suddenly. "Zeek doesn't even go to church. Dad's right. It was definitely a dingbatter. Some tourist probably wanted a souvenir, so when they saw the really nice handmade coffin that Mr. Tillet made, they must have thought it was for sale but couldn't find a clerk, so they took it home and will probably send the money later. And I bet they didn't even know someone was in it, and then they probably caught the first ferry off the island so they could show everyone back home how good we make stuff down here."

Todd Garrish truly wanted to say something in response, but when he opened his mouth, absolutely nothing came out.

"That was a very interesting, uh, thought," stammered his mother. "Very creative."

"Thanks."

Todd cleared his throat. "I believe your mother only mentioned Zeek because of the way he treated Theodora. No one said they suspect him of taking the coffin. And I just mentioned the dingbatters because I was angry. I'm sure there's a logical explanation. All I know is, it's a pretty sad state of affairs when you can't leave the body of a loved one in a church overnight." The ranger reached for his rain gear, kissed his family, and headed for the back door. "I'll run over to the church and give Teddy a hand with the fingerprints. He's already brought the Coast Guard in from Hatteras." Stepping outside, the ranger lifted his hood and shied away from the wind and biting rain. He thought about Daniel's raving and chuckled. "They wanted a souvenir? Give me a break."

Daniel gagged on his orange juice as the words "fingerprints" played over and over in his head. "Coast Guard!" he groaned to himself. "We are so dead."

Seven-year-old Lena Garrish waited for her parents to leave the kitchen and then gave Daniel a toothless grin, proudly revealing four, new, empty spaces.

"I know what happened to Mith Theo'th coffin," lisped the freckle-faced redhead.

"You do not," said Daniel.

"I do, too. Giant alien carpenter anth landed on the church roof and gnawed through the theiling. I think they needed Mith Theo'th wooden coffin tho they wouldn't thtarve to death and could take over the world. Uncle Wade thaid tha'th why tho many people thtopped going to church."

Daniel looked at his sister with envy. "Your story's better than mine."

Clinton Gaskill sat rocking on the front porch of the Community Store. His cat Ollie slept on the wooden floorboards beside him, her tail swishing back and forth, missing the curved rockers by a hair. The Community Store was the hub of Ocracoke Village and nothing much got past Clinton. He spent most days spinning fish tales and whittling pelicans out of driftwood. No one knew

Theodora Teach McNemmish better than he did. Today, he thought only about her.

Billy O'Neal trudged up the store steps and plopped down on the bench rail opposite the aged gentleman. "Do you think she's finally a pirate?" he asked Clinton.

Clinton chuckled. "Theodora? That old woman's been a pirate since the day she was born. Half the stuff in her house she either traded or bartered. My God, you would have thought she was Blackbeard himself returned from the grave, to hear her talk about it. Lost her head often enough." He stared out onto the rain-soaked parking lot and remembered the days the ferryboats brought the groceries and mail. "Did she ever tell you that on Tuesdays, we'd sneak out and nab old Josiah's mare so we could be the first ones to the dock? Theodora liked to know who was getting what before they got it. She liked postcards best. Said she could travel all around the world without ever leaving paradise." He drew on his pipe and waved a shaky hand. "Ah, who knows if she is or if she ain't a real ghost pirate. She's happy now, I'll tell ya that much. But where in the world is she?"

"Maybe she's not really dead," Mark's younger sister Jennifer suggested. "Maybe she just walked out of the church and took the coffin with her so she could use it when she was really dead."

Mark rolled his tired eyes to the ceiling, then slapped his hand to his forehead.

Jennifer got up and walked away. "Says you!"

Marylee Austin kissed Stefanie on the forehead, then studied the thermometer in her hand. "Your temperature's over a hundred! You were perfectly fine yesterday. You'd think you were out in the storm all night. Well, you'd better stay in bed. I'll check on you later."

Stefanie waited for her mother to leave the room, then wriggled farther down under her soft, fluffy cover. Her ten-year-old brother Matt flew into her room and flopped down on the bed beside her. "Maybe Theodora turned herself into a piece of paper and slipped out between the cracks in the coffin. Then the wind came and blew her away. She's a bird, she's a plane, she's Paper Woman!"

Stefanie picked up her pillow and threw it at Matt, hitting her target square in the face. "Out!" she demanded. When he was gone, she closed her eyes and scooted further down under her cover. "They're going to catch us. The fishnets will slip, Mrs. McNemmish will float up onto the dock of the Silver Lake Lunch Bucket, some tourist will croak from a heart attack, and we'll be arrested." She sat up and grabbed a tissue just in time to catch a stream of sneezes. "That treasure better be full of diamonds and gold, or I'm going to bury Daniel, Billy, and Mark myself. Achoo!"

A pirate's word was what she gave,

Its value worth its weight.

A story by a crackling fire

Was worth a piece of eight.

When silently the sun does rise,

What secrets will impart?

A lady's word upon her death

Is gifted from her heart.

CHAPTER VIII

Reverend Wood initiated the Baptist church phone tree at noon and, by three o'clock, had a packed house. Daniel, Billy, and Mark chose to sit together in the last row.

"We have come here today to lament over the missing remains of our beloved Miss Theo. We can only pray that she is being cared for with respect and with love. We hope that those responsible for her disappearance will have a change of heart and return her to the church for a proper, Christian burial. In either case, we will have her funeral on Saturday as scheduled."

"That's stupid," whispered Billy. "We already gave her a funeral."

"Shh!" Daniel squirmed in his seat. "Did you see the way he just looked at us?"

"Who?"

"The reverend."

"He didn't look at us."

"Yes, he did. Look, he's staring at us now!"

"No, he isn't."

"Yes, he is!"

May Belle Gaskin turned around in her seat. "Quiet down, boys."

Daniel wiggled. He hated wool pants, but his mother thought they were more respectful than blue jeans. He hated memorial services. Especially this one. "I'm telling you, Reverend Wood saw us last night. He probably saw Stefanie hide the gurney and cover in his backyard! How stupid can you get? She put the stuff in his backyard! And what if my dad and Teddy and the Coast Guard match up our fingerprints to the ones on the lid?"

"Will you children be quiet!"

"There's nothing to match," whispered Billy. "We wore gloves."

Mark jabbed Billy in the side with his elbow and signaled for both boys to zip it up.

Billy leaned in closer to Daniel. "Stop worrying. If anyone saw us last night or matched up our fingerprints, we'd have been arrested by now."

"Arrested!" Daniel was so startled by the suggestion, he inhaled his chewing gum. Billy slapped him on his back to keep him from choking, and the gum flew out of his mouth and landed on the back of May Belle's hat.

"What are you doing?" shrieked Daniel, recovering enough to gasp in horror.

"I'm getting the gum."

"Just leave it there."

"I told you boys to be quiet!"

Billy sat back and giggled silently while the reverend continued to drone on in the background. "Theodora Teach McNemmish had an extraordinary love of life and people, and had a high regard for personal property. I sincerely hope the people who took her also have a high regard for personal property and see the error of their ways."

"I sincerely hope she doesn't float back to the island," whispered Billy.

"That's not funny. There! Did you see the way he just looked at us?"

"He didn't look at us!"

"Yes, he did."

"Shh!"

Following the service, Teddy grabbed the youngsters before they could make their escape. "I don't suppose you guys know anything about poor Miss Theo's disappearance, do you? I mean, maybe you guys heard someone talk about it and didn't put two and two together. Or maybe that letter she wrote you had some kind of clue in it. We could really use your help if y'all know something."

Daniel turned so pale, his freckles stood out like domino dots. "I...uh..." He shook his head then turned and looked at Billy. "Actually, I never really saw the letter. Billy read it."

"Huh?" Billy turned his baffled expression toward Daniel, then turned and frowned at the sheriff. "Gosh! In all the excitement, I forgot..."

Mark clasped his hands and nodded.

"What did he say?" asked Teddy.

Billy interpreted. "He said the widow's note said 'Thank you.'"

"Thank you for what?"

"Thank you for delivering her groceries, I guess," said Daniel.

"You always delivered her groceries."

"That's probably why she thanked us."

"Actually, it was a one-time thank you letter for all the times she didn't thank us for delivering her groceries."

"Oh." Teddy scratched his head. "Well, if you think of anything that might help our investigation, let me know."

"We will. As a matter of fact, we're going to go look for the widow right now," said Daniel. "Just in case someone put her someplace." He climbed onto his bike and sped away from the school gymnasium before Teddy could quiz him further. Billy and Mark hopped onto their bikes and followed.

Teddy stared after them. "See ya later," he called out quietly. To himself, he thought, "You can count on it."

The boys rode off in three different directions and wandered around the island aimlessly for about half an hour. They met up again at the widow's shack, careful not to have been followed.

"That was close," said Billy. He climbed off his bike, then he, Daniel, and Mark hid their bikes on the side of the widow's shack behind a row of tall yucca plants. "I don't think he suspects anything."

"I do," said Daniel. "I think he knows we did it and is waiting to pounce on us."

Billy shook his head. "If he knew, he would have hauled us off to his office. I'm telling you, he's really stumped."

"Even if he doesn't know we did it, he *thinks* he knows we did it, and that's just as bad."

"Thinking and knowing are an ocean apart," said Billy. He turned the corner and was surprised to see Stefanie waiting on the back steps of the shack.

"What are you doing here?" asked Daniel. "Why weren't you at the meeting?"

"I'm here to get my treasure, and I didn't go to the meeting because I'm sick." Her voice was scratchy and nasal, and her eyes were puffy and bloodshot. "I'm probably dying."

"No such luck," Daniel teased her.

"Did you hear what they said on the television? Now everyone knows she's missing."

"Of course I heard what they said. They blasted it loud enough. My dad thinks some dingbatter did it. Even the reverend talked about it." Daniel quickly opened the widow's back door with the key he had slipped off his father's key chain. "We have to hurry. I have to put this back before my dad knows it's gone. That is, if we're not arrested first."

"Arrested! Why, what happened? Did you get caught?" Stefanie turned so abruptly, she smacked Billy in the forehead with her umbrella. "Y'all got caught, didn't you? I knew you'd get caught. Didn't I tell you you'd get caught? You didn't tell them about me, did you?"

"We didn't get caught," laughed Billy. He took the umbrella away from her and closed it. "Man, you're lethal with this thing."

Stefanie wasn't listening. As soon as Daniel had the door open, she made a beeline for the widow's treasure trunk. Her fingers itched to get hold of whatever riches the widow had bequeathed to them. She could practically feel the gold and diamond necklaces around her neck. "Come on, come on."

Daniel locked the door behind him. "I still say we could get arrested."

Billy dismissed the idea with a wave of his hand. "Who's going to believe a bunch of kids could break into a church and steal a coffin?"

"Anybody who saw the inside of the church, that's who."

"Hey! The trunk's locked!" Billy tried yanking off the offending piece of metal, but the padlock wouldn't budge.

"That wasn't there yesterday," said Daniel. "Teddy must have put it on. I'll go get some bolt cutters."

"Forget that." Stefanie reached up and removed a small barrette from her hair. She slipped the tip of the barrette into the lock and gave it a sharp twist. The bottom of the lock fell open. "Way to go, Fingers!" Billy knelt down and quickly removed the lock from the trunk. With sweaty palms and heart racing, he pushed open the huge, mahogany lid that kept him and his three best friends separated from their life's fortune. "Whoa! What is this stuff?"

Mark lowered his head into the trunk in order to see better and lifted out a gold, filigreed sword and scabbard.

"Wow! That's from the Civil War!" said Daniel with awe. He carefully removed it from Mark's hands and laid it ceremoniously across the top of Mrs. McNemmish's bedspread. "What a beauty! This could have been at Gettysburg or Vicksburg!"

"Or Fort Hatteras or Fort Clark," added Billy, who absolutely loved history. "Wow, look at this. A whole uniform." He held it up to the front of his chest and looked at himself in the widow's mirror. "I bet this belonged to the widow's great-granddaddy. There's tons more stuff in here. Buckles, buttons, epaulets..."

"Any gold?" asked Stefanie.

"I think the buttons are gold," said Billy.

"Whoa! Look at this!" shouted Daniel. He lifted out a ship's bell that had been wrapped in a bath towel. "This is amazing!" The tarnished brass bell and clapper were carefully unwrapped and placed on the floor next to the trunk. "It's dated 1709! This should be in a museum or something. I wonder what they'd pay for something like this."

"Museums don't pay for stuff," Stefanie enlightened him. "You have to donate it. Museums are like huge, enormous garage sales, only instead of selling the stuff they get, they charge admission for people to come and see it. But first, they change the label from 'old' to 'antique.' That way they can charge you more for looking."

"We could do something like that," said Daniel. "We could open up our own museum and charge people to come and see this stuff."

Mark agreed.

Billy reached into the trunk and pulled out several handfuls of old photographs. "There must be a hundred pictures in here. Oh man, look at this. It's a captain's log dated 1718." He gingerly handled the leather-bound log that had been wrapped in a linen pillowcase. "The last entry was November 21, 1718! That's the day before Blackbeard was killed."

Mark raised his eyebrows.

A chill ran up Daniel's spine and out to his fingertips as he reached over and touched the bound manuscript. "What if this log really *is* Blackbeard's log? Do you know what this would be worth? People have been looking for this for three hundred years!"

"How freaky would that be?" agreed Billy.

"What do you think we should do with it?"

"Sell it," said Stefanie.

"You can't sell it. It's priceless," said Daniel.

"Priceless means you can't wear it and you can't spend it," sniffed Stefanie. "It's just another word for 'nobody's buying.' Y'all haven't found one thing in there that's worth anything." She stood behind the boys and peered over their shoulders as they delved further into the chest. "Haven't you found even one diamond yet?"

"Not yet," said Billy.

"Emeralds?"

"Not yet," said Billy.

"What about gold coins or doubloons?"

"Nope."

"What about rings, or necklaces, or…"

Mark giggled.

"Give it a break, Stefanie! If we found anything, we'd tell you," barked Daniel.

"We'll find something for you," said Billy. "The good stuff's probably on the bottom."

"What about the duck with the key?" asked Stefanie. "Did you find the duck with the key?"

"Does it look like we found the duck with the key?"

Mark gasped as a car rounded the corner and pulled up in front of the widow's shack.

"Shoot! It's Teddy!" Following Daniel's lead, the children scooted toward the front window and hovered below the sill.

"Maybe we should hide," whispered Billy.

"Where? In the kitchen drawer?"

"What if we just tell Teddy the widow wanted us to have what was in the trunk?"

"Are you crazy?! Then he'll think we took her for sure."

"Will y'all shut up before he hears us!" Stefanie peeked up over the window just in time to see the sheriff and Mustard walk toward the front door.

"Quick, he's coming!"

Billy, Daniel, and Stefanie made a mad dash toward the back door, when Mark clapped his hands, signaling them to stop.

"He'll see us!" worried Daniel.

Stefanie got down on the floor and crawled back over to the window. "Look at this, y'all. Miss Lilli's roosters got out again. Mustard's chasing them back to her house and Teddy's chasing Mustard!"

"Way to go, roosters," cheered Billy.

Daniel kept a watch out to see if Teddy would return to the widow's shack. He was rewarded when the sheriff and Mustard returned to the sheriff's car and drove away. "Man, was that lucky."

"Well?" asked Stefanie.

"Well, what?" asked Daniel.

Stefanie let out an exasperated sigh and glared at all three boys. "Why are y'all just standing there? Mrs. McNemmish said we would find a duck with a key in a chest, and that's the only chest around here, and we still haven't found the duck. So start looking."

"Yes, your bossiness."

She watched over their shoulders while the boys pulled out more Civil War and seafaring artifacts. The more fragile items were placed on the widow's bedspread while the sturdier things were set down on the floor beside the trunk. Mark noticed a small, white, leather pouch that Billy had placed on the floor next to him and opened it. He spilled its contents into his hand. Squinting through his lenses, he counted more than thirty white seeds the size of pistachio nuts. Several of the seeds trickled between his small fingers and onto the floor.

"You know what? I'll bet those seeds are worth something," Billy told him.

"They're just seeds," said Stefanie.

"I know. But if they weren't valuable, why would the widow have kept them all these years?"

"Because she was a psycho."

"Don't be disrespectful," Daniel told Stefanie. "Billy's right. Those seeds were really special to her. If she found them with the other pirate stuff, maybe they were really important. Maybe they were Blackbeard's bargaining chips or poker money. This is really cool stuff."

"That does it! I have had it with Civil War junk and old bells," shouted Stefanie. "I have a fever, I'm thirsty and tired, and I expected a whole lot more than white seeds and soldier's pants! I mean, what's the matter with y'all? This stuff is not cool! Seeds are not cool!" She picked up several of the seeds and flaunted them in front of Daniel's startled face. "Seeds are not a treasure!" Suddenly, her voice cracked and she stopped long enough to pop in a cough drop. "A treasure has diamonds, and rubies, and emeralds, and gold coins," she croaked. "Where are the diamonds? Where are the gold coins? And where are the doubloons? There have to be doubloons. Whoever heard of a pirate treasure that didn't have doubloons?" She finished her proclamation with a muffled, "Ugh," turned ashen white, and slid to the floor. Her eyes rolled back in her head, and she looked like she was about to faint. "The room's spinning."

"Great." Daniel rushed to her side and offered her a hand up. "Go home, Stefanie. You look terrible."

"I don't want to go home."

"You look really sick," Billy told her. "If you do have pneumonia, you'll just get sicker staying here. If we find any gold or diamonds, we'll bring them over to your house, I promise." Billy helped Mark scoop the seeds up off the floor and return them to their pouch. "Why don't you keep them," he told Mark. "I think they were really important to the widow. Do you want me to walk you home?" he asked Stefanie.

"I'm not going home!" Stefanie stood up and held her ground. "I'm not leaving until we find the real treasure. Well, don't just stand there. Look for the duck!"

"We did look for the duck. This is the only stuff we found. Look, I don't mean to be rude," Daniel told Stefanie. "But could you stop breathing on me? I'm already sore from our little outing last night. I don't need to catch whatever you have." He went back to the trunk and lifted out a twelve-inch metal bar with engraved printing on one side. It took Daniel a moment to figure out the lettering because of the old world filigree. "Look at this." He gathered the others around him as he read. "Qu...e..ns...R..v...ng." He read and reread the letters out loud, unable to make heads or tails out of the meaning, when Mark's eyebrows suddenly flew above his glass rims, and he clasped his hands excitedly. He pointed to the carved ship on the widow's bedroom mantle.

"No way!" crowed Billy, who understood immediately. "Daniel, this plaque used to say *Queen Anne's Revenge!* This must have been in a cabinet or something inside his ship! How cool is that?"

"Yeah, cool," sniffed Stefanie.

Daniel was ecstatic. "You know those divers who just found the *Revenge?* Well, I bet they'd give anything to have this plaque. This is really historic! We're going to be famous!" While he and Billy continued to admire the plaque, Mark rooted around inside the trunk and uncovered a large piece of sheepskin that was rolled into a tube. Stefanie helped him remove two pieces of ancient parchment paper that were rolled inside.

The first parchment was a hand-sketched map dated 1760. Black ink detailed the area of the Atlantic Ocean known as the Diamond Shoals east of the Outer Banks. The other piece of parchment was a page of *The Boston News-Letter* dated Monday, February 16, to Monday, February 23, 1719.

Billy moved over to see what the two were studying. "Wow! Do you think this is a treasure map?"

"Of course it's a treasure map," declared Stefanie.

"Maybe that's our reward," suggested Billy.

"How do you know it's real?" asked Daniel.

"Daniel Garrish, you wouldn't know a real treasure map if you fell over it." Stefanie pointed to the parchment and nodded her head emphatically. "This definitely looks like a real treasure map. Besides, you don't know that it isn't." She narrowed her eyes and stared at the map intensely, then shook her head. "Yep. It's real."

"You're full of bologna. You don't know it's real any more than the rest of us do."

"Oh yeah? Well I can prove it's real. People back then were more honest about maps and stuff than they are now. They didn't draw fake maps. How else could they steal the stuff?"

"Well, if it is a treasure map, it's all ours," grinned Billy. "I bet that's where Blackbeard's stuff is hidden."

"Excuse me," interjected Stefanie. "But that had better not be the only place Blackbeard hid our treasure, because I don't think Miss Theo meant for the four of us to take a rig over to the Diamond Shoals where you can't take a boat anyway, dive to the bottom of the ocean where the sunken treasure ships are kept, and scoop the treasure out of the treasure chests with our bare hands, do you?" She considered the idea for a moment and bristled. "If that map is the map to the only treasure she left us, I'm going to be really annoyed."

"You know," Billy told Daniel, "I bet your dad would take us out to the shoals if we asked him to. We could show him the map."

"Before or after we go to jail?"

"My gawd. What did she think we were, scuba divers?" Stefanie continued to babble on about Mrs. McNemmish and the fact that Blackbeard's treasure had better not be out at the shoals. She left the map for a moment and picked up the ancient newspaper. She read out loud: "'Boston, by letters of the 17th of December last, from North Carolina, we are informed that Lieutenant Robert

Maynard of His Majesty's Ship *Pearl* (commanded by Captain Gordon) being fitted out at Virginia with two sloops, manned with fifty men and small arms but no great guns in quest of Captain Teach the Pirate called Blackbeard who made his escape from thence, was overtaken at North Carolina, and had ten great guns and twenty men on board his sloop." She read on silently for a bit. "It says that Blackbeard swore he wouldn't give quarters and then Maynard swore he wouldn't give or take quarters either, 'whereupon he boarded the Pirate and fought it out, hand to hand, with pistol and sword.' What's giving quarters?" she asked the boys.

"It meant that neither side would take prisoners," explained Daniel. "Even if a pirate surrendered, the pirates from the other ship would still kill him."

"Huh. Too bad." Stefanie read on: "'The engagement was very desperate and bloody on both sides, wherein Lieutenant Maynard had thirty-five of his men killed and wounded in the action, himself slightly wounded, Teach and most of his men were killed, the rest carried prisoner to Virginia, by Lieutenant Maynard, to be tried there who also carries with him Teach's head which he cut off, in order to get the reward granted by the said colony.' Then it goes on to talk about the weather."

"Hey, Stefanie. Do you know what they did with Blackbeard's head after they chopped it off and hung it on the bowsprit?"

"No. And I don't want to know."

"First, they showed it to the judge in Williamsburg to prove he was dead, then they stuck his head on a pole outside of the courtyard so everyone could laugh at it. Then...they auctioned it off!"

"Somebody bought his head?"

Billy laughed. "Yeah. Some man from England bought it for two dollars and nineteen cents."

"You're making that up."

Mark shook his head.

"That's disgusting," said Stefanie.

"That's not all," added Daniel. "The guy who bought it took it to a taxidermist, who ripped off all the skin and stuff. Then he took it to a silver smith to have the skull made into silverware and had a drinking glass put inside of it."

"Blackbeard's head is a drinking mug!" whooped Billy.

Mark giggled.

"I don't think that's very funny. That was somebody's head, even if he was a pirate."

Daniel was enjoying Stefanie's reaction. "They say if you drink from the mug, you actually get to share Blackbeard's devilish dreams."

"All y'all are disgusting," she told the boys.

"That's not even my favorite part of the story," Billy teased her. "I like the part where they chopped off Blackbeard's head and threw his body overboard. While they were hanging his head off the bowsprit, twenty-one pirates said they saw his body swim around the ship at least a dozen times. Of course, I don't believe that. But I bet he swam around it at least once."

"He did not."

"Actually, nobody knows how many times he swam around the ship," said Daniel. "But you know how a frog can still wriggle after it's dead? Well, Blackbeard was still fighting when his head was lopped off, so his arms kept flapping like Aunt Ida's jaw. When his body hit the water, he just took off like a jet ski. It's true. Lots of pirates saw him swim without his head. It's even in the diary Elizabeth Wahab's great-granddaddy times three kept. It's on her dresser!"

Stefanie went from ashen white to pale green. "Thanks for sharing."

"You're welcome."

Stefanie plunked herself down in the widow's rocking chair. "If you ask me, this whole treasure hunt's been a waste of time. We were promised treasure, but a captain's log, a bunch of swords, and a bag of white seeds are not treasure. I want diamonds, and rubies, and emeralds, and gold, and not some outdated map that may or may not be totally bogus and says 'Diamond Shoals' instead of 'Diamonds!'"

"Well, I hate to tell you, but there's nothing else left in the trunk."

"What?" Stefanie shoved Billy to one side and looked in it for herself. "Well, that's great. That's just great," snarled the girl. "I'll probably die of pneumonia in some horrible, rat-infested prison cell somewhere where people think grits and hush puppies are dirt and shoes, and for what? Because a crazy, old woman wanted to be dumped in the ocean and become a ghost pirate with her relative Blackbeard, who probably won't know her from Adam."

"Buried," said Daniel. "Not dumped."

"Whatever! The point is, Miss Theo said that whoever buried her at sea would be as rich as Midas and would know the secret of Blackbeard's treasure and find the key in the shell. Well, Midas had gold, and treasures have diamonds, and maps are too hard, and take too long, and are definitely too much work, and we haven't found a key or a shell. So, where's the good stuff, huh, Mrs. McNemmish?"

Stefanie got up, stomped around in circles, then stormed off toward the back door. On her way out, she turned back around, bristled over to the trunk, and gave it a good, hard, angry kick. There was a sudden, loud bang as the floor of the trunk dropped open.

Stefanie stumbled backward, yelling something about it must have been broken before she kicked it. The boys scrambled to their feet, tripping over each other, and raced back to the edge of the trunk. All three stood gaping into the black void with eyes bulging and hearts pounding.

"Whoa!" exclaimed Billy. "Steps!"

Those of greed and devilish ways,

Have justly gone to watery graves.

Their future lies beneath the earth,

Lost for good, and lacking mirth.

It's those with wind to fill their sails,

Who seek an old maid's pirate tales,

That soar like gulls above the sea

And carry always Blackbeard's key.

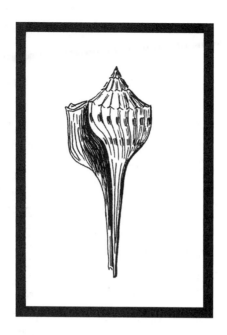

CHAPTER IX

Daniel knelt down beside the trunk and stuck his head as far down into the hole as his neck would allow. "Where do you think they go?"

"They go down, where do you think they go?" said Stefanie.

Mark giggled.

"I know they go down, mullet brain. I meant, where do you think they go after they go down?"

Billy, too, stuck his head into the trunk and gaped into the pitch-black surprise. "Maybe it's an old well like the one at the cove." He removed a dime from his pocket and dropped it down the opening. It landed silently. "Maybe it's a dried-up well."

"You can't have a well that deep on an island," said Stefanie.

"You can't have a trunk with a hole in the bottom and a ladder going down it either, but you're staring at one."

"That's besides the point."

"Do you have a better idea?" Daniel quizzed her.

"Yes." Stefanie ran into the kitchen, grabbed a flashlight off of Mrs. McNemmish's countertop, and handed it to Daniel. "Go down and look."

"I'm not going down there!"

"Chicken." She offered the flashlight to Billy.

"No, thanks. I've had enough excitement this week."

"Why don't you go down?" suggested Daniel.

"I can't. I'm too sick. See? Cough, cough."

"Well, I'm not climbing down any ladder that may or may not hold me and might plunk me into a hole that may or may not be full of water. Besides," Daniel added. "My ankle and shoulder still hurt from last night."

"All y'all are such wimps. I bet the treasure's down there," she enticed the boys. "First one down there gets dibs on the really good stuff." She grabbed Mark by his coat sleeve. "Come on, Mark. We'll go down."

"Ooh! I knew you'd do that!" Daniel snatched the flashlight out of her hand and aimed it down the ladder. "I still can't see anything."

"That's because it's so deep. You have to go down and look."

Billy took a deep breath and let out a long, loud sigh. "I know I'm going to regret this. Come on. I'll go with you." He stepped over the side of the trunk and gingerly tested the steps. "It feels okay."

"I'm coming with you," said Stefanie.

"No way," said Daniel. "You and Mark stay up here."

"I agree." The deep, harsh voice came from the doorway. Zeek Beacon entered the shack and slammed the door behind him. "I'm proud of you, Daniel. It's nice to know there's still chivalry in the world." He walked over to the trunk, casting a glance at the items strewn across the widow's bedspread and those laid out on the floor. He whistled approval at the assortment of antiques and other artifacts. "Well, well, well! Looks like somebody found the birthday prize." He pushed Daniel to one side and glanced down the gaping hole. "I've gotta hand it to the old lady. She was full of surprises. Get out of the trunk, Billy."

"What do you want, Zeek?"

"A little respect from you, for one thing," he told Daniel. Before he perused the trunk, he snatched the leather bag out of Mark's hand. A quick peek revealed a handful of white seeds. "She tried to pawn those things off on me, too," he said, tossing the bag back to the kid. He noticed Mark's eyes drift toward the kitchen floor and followed the path. "Whoa! Nice map."

"Hey! That's ours!" Stefanie told him.

"Shut up, mouth." Beacon lifted the flaking piece of parchment off the floor and laid it open on the kitchen table. He examined the unique map closely while keeping one eye peeled on the children. He caught Billy inching toward the back door.

"Freeze, termite!" He pulled a gun out of his belt and aimed it at all four children. "No one moves."

"Or what?" Daniel challenged him. "You going to shoot us?"

Beacon lowered the aim of the gun to Daniel's leg. "It don't have to kill to hurt," he warned the boy. "Ever hear about my great-granddaddy's kneecap?"

"Yeah. Blackbeard shot a hole through it."

"If you don't shut your trap, I'll teach you how it feels." He waved his gun and motioned for the kids to sit on the kitchen countertop while he took a closer look at the map. He traced its faded lines and crude measurements with the tip of his switchblade while his eyes sparkled with possibilities.

"Miss Theo left that map to us," Stefanie informed the man.

"Well, Miss Theo's dead, or haven't you heard? She's dead and gone, and no one knows about this map except for me, you, and that slug bait you're sitting next to. So at the moment, that makes it mine."

"You're a bully, you know that?" wheezed the girl. "I hope my germs make you really sick and you die from germ rot." She coughed and sneezed in his direction and grinned. "Oh excuse me."

Beacon grumbled. "I don't believe I've ever heard of germ rot. So why don't you just shut your mouth before you die from brain squeeze." He returned to the map with a curious, almost childlike smile. Suddenly, he smacked the table so violently, all four children jumped. "This is it! This is the missing Howard Map! Do you know what this means? No! Of course you don't. You're too stupid to know." He gloated like a child who had just discovered chocolate. He rewrapped the map and tucked it into his inner coat pocket along with the valuable newspaper clipping. He looked around thoughtfully for a moment then, waving his gun in the air, instructed the children to climb into the trunk and down the ladder.

"I'm not going down there," squawked Stefanie, followed by a chorus of sneezing and nose blowing. "I'm too sick."

"You were all fired up about going down before I interrupted. I'm just giving you permission."

"You can't make us go down there," said Daniel.

"You know, I'm getting really tired of arguing with you twits. So, why don't you just shut up and get on the ladder before my gun accidentally goes off in your direction. Move it!"

"I'm telling," said Stefanie.

"That does it!" Zeek turned and aimed his gun at Stefanie's forehead.

"She's going! She's going!" Daniel grabbed Stefanie by the elbow and dragged her over the side of the trunk.

"Let her go home," pleaded Billy. "She's really sick."

"That's her fault. Next time y'all go on a midnight raid, choose a nicer night. Who knows? Maybe you'll get lucky and she'll lose her voice."

"What do mean, midnight raid?" stammered Daniel. "We didn't...."

"Sure you did," said Zeek with a satisfied grin. "Don't worry. Your secret's safe with me. Just as long as you keep your traps shut." Beacon waited for the youngsters to start their descent, then handed Billy two oil lamps, a handful of candles, and a half-empty box of matches. "You'll need these when your flashlight dies."

"What are you going to do?" asked Billy.

"Secure my situation." Beacon grinned as the four terrified youngsters slowly descended into the black unknown. When Billy's head was nearly out of sight, he called down: "Don't worry. I'll be back to take the tour later." Checking his watch, he closed and locked the lid of the trunk, gathered up the widow's artifacts and clothing, and tied them into the widow's bedspread. He barely noticed the banging and shouting coming from inside the trunk as he swept the shack clean of disturbance. Careful not to be seen, he slung the bedspread over his shoulder, snuck out the back door, and jogged toward his boat.

Billy climbed back up the ladder and pressed his ear to the inside of the lid. It was impossible to hear anything coming from inside the shack. "Zeek! Open up!" He banged several times on the inside of the lid, then yelled again. "Open the trunk, Zeek!" He stopped yelling and called down to the others who were gathered at the foot of the ladder. "Will y'all shut up? I can't hear." He tried banging again, then put his ear to the lid. "Zeek! Let us out of here!" He pounded a few more times, then listened again. "Open the trunk, Zeek! This isn't funny!" He pushed against the lid with his shoulder, but it wouldn't budge. "Darn you, Zeek! It's freezing in here!" After several minutes of silence, he gave up and descended the ladder. His flashlight was the only beam of comfort piercing the pitch-black cave where the four friends now huddled together.

"Zeek's gone. He left the shack."

"Good. Go back up and get us out of here," demanded Stefanie.

"I can't. He locked us in."

"He what?!"

"He locked us in."

Stefanie pushed her way past the boys and reached for the ladder. "I'm going up. Someone has to get us out of here."

"It's no use. The trunk won't budge. I tried."

"Then I'll try!" insisted the girl. She was only two rungs up the ladder when she started coughing and gasping for breath. "I can't breathe! There's no air down here!"

"Then stop using it up by screaming!" bristled Daniel. "We need to think."

"I can't think. I'm too scared, and too sick, and too annoyed to think."

"Then let the rest of us think."

"We're all scared," Billy confided as he helped her back down the ladder. "But at least we're down here together." He handed Daniel and Stefanie each an oil lamp, then fumbled for a match. When the lanterns were lit, the four captives surveyed their situation.

The handmade ladder descended about eleven feet below the widow's trunk. Just a few feet in front of the ladder, the ceiling dropped to six feet. Billy aimed his flashlight down the long, narrow corridor that faced the ladder, but the beam disappeared into blackness. There was no telling how long the corridor continued.

"Look, y'all. The walls are firing!" Daniel held his lantern up next to the tunnel lining made of sand and crushed seashell cement and watched as it twinkled like splintered glass against the flickering candlelight. The entire alcove surrounding the ladder looked like it had been sprayed in phosphorescent pink, purple, and green glitter glue. The similarity to the phosphorus firing at the bottom of the sea cast a wave of yearning over all four children.

"I want to go home," Stefanie said quietly. "What if Zeek doesn't come back for us? What if he just leaves us down here to rot?"

"He's not going to do that," Billy assured her. "You heard him. 'I'll be back to take the tour later.'"

"Well, I don't believe him. I think he locked us down here on purpose and has no intention of coming back for us. We're already running out of air. I can feel it." She wheezed dramatically. "See? What if we die down here? What if nobody ever finds us and we're down here for the rest of eternity?"

"You won't have to run out of air to find out," Daniel told her. "If you keep complaining, I'm going to kill you myself."

"Stop mommucking, y'all. We need to think things out." Billy thought for a moment, then snapped his fingers. "I bet there's another way out of here. I read a book once where this guy built a dungeon under his house with two entrances in case he accidentally locked himself into one. I bet this place has two entrances. It would have been suicide to build just one way in and out. I mean, what if you built only one entrance and it collapsed? You'd be trapped, right? So, you'd have to build it with a second way out just to survive."

"You think this place could collapse?" panicked Stefanie.

"That was just an example."

"Well, it was a stupid example. Besides, islands don't have dungeons. They're made out of sand."

"Islands don't have tunnels either, but we're standing in one," argued Daniel.

"What is this? Daniel-Has-To-Be-Right Day?"

"I'm just saying we can't say someplace doesn't have something when we're standing in a place that can't possibly exist, but does."

Mark moved closer to one of the walls and inspected it carefully. Turning to the others, he pointed to the unusual cement.

"I know. I recognize it, too," Billy told him.

"I know what this is. It's the cement used to plug up the hole in the Bobby Garrish tree!" Daniel's quick, green eyes soaked in the familiar mixture made from bits of crushed seashell and the soft, blond sand that lined every inch of Ocracoke Island from the ocean to the sound. An instant image of the four-hundred-year-old tree with the plug of cement in its bottom branch played like a welcomed movie. Visions of historic Howard Street, with its dirt path, tree-lined canopy, and rows of ancient family cemeteries transformed the black, claustrophobic tunnel into a dark, island night. But only for a moment.

"What's Bobby's tree got to do with getting out of here?" Stefanie wanted to know.

"Miss Theo made that tree cement about a hundred years ago," Daniel recalled as he tried putting two and two together. "Remember? She plugged up the limb so Bobby would stop throwing his homework and bow ties down the hollow. If she made that cement, maybe she made this cement."

"Get real."

"I don't know," said Billy thoughtfully. "It's not an impossible idea."

Mark nodded in agreement.

Stefanie suddenly laughed. "There is no way old Mrs. McNemmish emptied out that humongous trunk, came down that rickety old ladder, cemented the walls and ceiling, which she could never reach in a million years, then climbed back up that ladder, and put the stuff back in the trunk. Get a grip, y'all. She had trouble just putting out the cats."

"That's the point! She might have found another way out of here so she didn't have to go back up the ladder."

Stefanie wrinkled her forehead, feeling somewhat confused by the conversation. "Come on, y'all. I don't think even Mrs. McNemmish could have fit through the tiny hole in the Bobby Garrish tree."

"I know that, dimwitter! I'm just saying if she used the cement in the tree, and the matching cement is down here, maybe she put the cement down here and got out someplace else where she didn't have to climb back up the ladder."

"Oh. Well, I still don't know what that has to do with getting us out of here," griped Stefanie.

"It does if we find the other way out."

A sudden gust of wind from inside the tunnel whistled past the children, brushing against their faces. Both lantern lights and Billy's flashlight dimmed briefly, shuddered, went out, then came back on.

"That was weird," said Billy.

"*Carry on.*"

"Carry on what?" Stefanie asked him.

"What?" asked Billy.

"What did you say?"

"I said that was weird."

"After that. You said, 'Carry on.' Carry on what?"

"I didn't say, 'Carry on.'"

"Yes, you did. When the lights went out, you whispered into my ear, 'Carry on.'"

"Maybe Daniel whispered into your ear."

"Trust me. I didn't whisper into her ear. And I didn't hear anybody say 'Carry on' either. If you ask me, Stefanie's been hitting her cough drops too hard."

"Shut up, Daniel. I'm telling you, somebody whispered 'Carry on' into my ear, and since it wasn't Mark and there's nobody else down here, it had to be one of you!"

"Well, don't look at me," said Daniel. "I just want to know where that wind came from, because that's the way out of here."

"Well, I think y'all are mean teasing me because I heard somebody say, 'Carry on!' in perfectly good English, and all y'all did, too, and you're just saying you didn't to drive *me* nuts!"

"You're already nuts," groaned Daniel. "Can we please find the way out of here? This place is giving me the willies." Daniel was trembling from head to toe, more from feeling anxious than cold, and the closeness of the tunnel walls was making it worse.

Billy, being the oldest, stepped to the entrance of the long corridor opposite the ladder. "Stefanie, you and Mark hang behind me. Daniel, you stay in the back. And for heaven's sake, stay close."

Stefanie had every intention of staying close. She grabbed hold of the back of Billy's jacket with one hand and held the lantern with the other. Mark clung to her coat and shuffled behind, trying not to step on the backs of her shoes.

"I don't think this is a very good idea," Stefanie voiced after walking a mere fifty feet. "Maybe we should try the trunk again."

"Just keep walking," Daniel begged her.

"I am walking. I just think we should try getting out of the trunk again."

"I'm sure that wind came from someplace close," said Billy. "Let's just walk for a while and see if that's the way out." Billy aimed his flashlight up ahead as he braved farther and farther into the unknown. He couldn't help but take in the sparkling walls, low ceiling, and pounded sand floor. "Who do you think dug this tunnel, anyway?"

Daniel's eyes were still adjusting to the darkness and the flickering candlelight, but he considered the question. "You know what? I bet this tunnel was one of Blackbeard's hideouts. He had dozens of them on the island. Maybe Mrs. McNemmish figured out it was one of his and took care of it."

Billy stopped walking and turned so abruptly, he accidentally smacked Stefanie in the face. "Daniel! That's brilliant! If this was Blackbeard's hideout, then Stefanie was right! There might be another treasure chest down here and this might be where the key and the duck are hidden."

"Is that the key key?" Stefanie asked while rubbing her squashed nose. "Or is that the hint key? Because, if that's the hint key and not the key key, how are we supposed to know what it is when we don't find it? And what about the duck? Is the duck with the key a real duck, or is it a Snow Duck? Because, if it's a real duck, I'm not getting anything out of it! Hey, I know! Maybe it's the duck in Duck Duck Goose?"

Daniel clenched his teeth and counted to ten. "Do you think you could shut up for fifteen minutes until we either find the treasure or get out of here?"

"I did shut up for fifteen minutes, and we didn't find the treasure or get out of here."

"Maybe that wind we felt came from an opening behind one of the cemeteries," Billy thought out loud. "There's seventy-five of them on the island, and half of them are so far out of the way, no one would notice folks going in and out."

"Of a coffin?!"

"No! I'm just saying maybe there's an opening hidden behind one of the trees or something."

"That's ridiculous." Stefanie sneezed her opinion, then followed it with a chorus of coughing. "What kind of imbecile would put a tunnel entrance in a graveyard? It's bad luck."

"I don't care if it opens up into the Slushy Stand outhouse," said Daniel. "I just want to get out of here!" The farther he ventured into the entombed underground, the more anxious and angry he was becoming.

"It's shrinking down here," observed Stefanie. "If this hallway gets any skinnier, we're going to get squished to death."

Billy stopped walking and bent over to stretch his arms and neck. "Whoever built this thing was either really short, or loved seeing his own kneecaps." It was while he was bent over that he realized he was standing in front of a dead end.

"What do you mean, dead end? That's impossible!" freaked Daniel.

"That's just great!" sniffed Stefanie. "Now we have to go all the way back to Mrs. McNemmish's house and get out of the trunk like we should have done in the first place. I knew something like this would happen. I told you islands don't have tunnels with two entrances."

"And people aren't supposed to have two mouths, but that hasn't stopped you," quipped Daniel.

Billy waved his flashlight and saw the beam bounce off a wall directly to his left. When he aimed it to the right, the light was swallowed by the darkness. "I think the path goes down there. Follow me." With the others in tow, he followed the light into a second corridor, which happily opened to five feet across and over six-and-a-half feet high.

"That feels so good!" said Billy, standing up straight and waving his arms about. "At least we can walk together instead of single file." He aimed his light straight ahead, but once again, it was impossible to see how far the corridor went.

They had walked about a hundred yards down the second corridor when Daniel slapped a hand over his nose. "What's that smell?"

"I figured it was one of you guys," said Billy.

"No way!"

The pungent odor of decaying seaweed was so sickening, the kids huddled together and breathed in one of Stefanie's cherry-smelling cough drop wrappers.

"Can we go back now?" begged Stefanie. "This place is pukey. Maybe if we all push at the same time, we can break the lid open."

"I think we should keep going," suggested Billy. "I'm sure we're getting close to another way out. No one could have stood this smell for very long. Not even Blackbeard."

"I hear dripping," panicked Stefanie. "There's a leak down here. This whole place could cave in and we could all drown without even knowing it."

"I think we'd know it if we were drowning."

"We're not going to drown because it's not leaking!" Billy assured her. "It's just...sweating a little."

"Sweating?"

"Sure. Walls sweat all the time. Don't they, Mark?"

Mark gave him a curious look, then nodded for Stefanie's sake.

"See?"

But as the children moved forward, a single drop of water that had been threatening to let go took the daring plunge and dropped from the ceiling, landing with a splat on Stefanie's forehead. "I told you! I told you it's leaking! The ceiling's filling with water, and it's going to collapse right on top of us, and we're going to drown in soupy sand!"

"Stefanie, stop screaming!" hollered Daniel. He grabbed her ponytail and aimed her face toward the ceiling. "If you'll shut up long enough to look at the ceiling, you'll see that it's practically dry."

"It's damp."

"I said practically. Man alive! I should have let Zeek shoot you."

"If this tunnel has been here since Blackbeard's time, I don't think it's going to collapse on us now," Billy said reassuringly. "We just have to stay calm until we find the way out."

Mark looked up suddenly, snapped his fingers, and pointed to the cement with renewed enthusiasm.

"You're awfully chatty," Daniel told him.

"What about the cement?" Stefanie asked Mark.

"I think he wants to talk about the cement Mrs. McNemmish put in Bobby's tree," suggested Billy.

Mark nodded, then mimed hitting nails with a hammer.

"You mean the wooden planks on the bottom of the tree?" asked Billy. "It's always been boarded up like that."

Mark reached into his coat pocket and pulled out a piece of folded newspaper. He handed it to Stefanie, who handed it to Billy.

"What's this?" Billy examined the newsprint with his flashlight. "This is a photo of Blackbeard's outhouse. Where'd you get this?"

Mark pointed up.

"In the trunk? You found this in the trunk?"

The boy nodded.

"And you didn't show it to Zeek? You sneaky person, you."

Daniel and Stefanie crowded around him while Billy studied the 1938 newspaper clipping. "Look at this, y'all. Blackbeard's outhouse was on the exact same piece of property Miss Theo's shack is on."

"Then how come there's not a picture of the well?" asked Stefanie.

"He must have put the well underneath the outhouse. Then when the outhouse was destroyed, the widow and Arthur must have put their shack on top of the well. So that means," figured Daniel, "we're standing underneath the outhouse right now!"

"Oh, gross!" Stefanie slapped a hand over her nose and mouth. "No wonder it stinks down here."

"That was three hundred years ago, for heaven's sake. Besides, the outhouse was back over by the ladder." Billy thought for a moment, then added: "What if it wasn't an outhouse?"

"Of course it was an outhouse," said Stefanie. "He had a castle and an outhouse. Everyone on the island knows that."

"But what if it just looked like an outhouse, but was really the entrance to this tunnel all along? That would mean that Mrs. McNemmish knew about it the whole time she was living there. Maybe that's why she built her house there in the first place. That's why she never let anyone look inside the trunk! She was covering up the hole."

"So if she knew about the tunnel, and she made the same cement for down here as she did for Bobby's tree, and Bobby's tree has all that boarding on the bottom, maybe this path runs from underneath her house all the way to the tree on Howard Street! Maybe those boards are hiding a second entrance! Looks like Miss Theo was plugging up more than just a hole for Bobby's homework and bow ties. Maybe she was plugging up a spy hole," reckoned Billy.

"Mrs. McNemmish didn't cement these walls," insisted Stefanie. "She couldn't even reach the top of them."

"Maybe she could when she was younger. Maybe she shrunk after she cemented them." Daniel looked at Stefanie with a snide grin. "Told you there was another way out."

Billy slapped Mark on the back. "Way to go, Mark. Now we can say we went in one trunk and out the other."

"Gawd, Billy. That was pathetic."

"All y'all better be right," said Stefanie. "I have to go."

"We all have to go," said Daniel.

"No, idiot. I have to *pee!*"

"Oh!" Daniel looked around. "Go over there. We won't look."

"I will not!"

"Then let's get out of here," said Billy. "We're about a half-mile walk from a fried chicken dinner."

Have I told you of the night

That pirates came upon this sight.

They brought with them a magic spell

That hides beneath the cockleshell.

It lies in wait of blackened sky,

Then reaches out as you pass by.

The skull and bones have

had their laugh,

Now you must follow

Blackbeard's path.

C H A P T E R   X

The half-mile walk between Mrs. McNemmish's shack and Bobby Garrish's tree seemed to drag on forever. The children had already walked at least three or four miles of tunnel including dozens of twists and turns, and they still hadn't reached the end. Daniel walked with his coat sleeve up against his face and breathed in the welcomed scent of sea air and fabric softener. "You're lucky you have a cold," he told Stefanie more than two hours into the venture. "It really does smell like a three-hundred-year-old outhouse."

"It smells like our kitchen when my dad burns broccoli," gagged Billy. Mark agreed and walked with his nose flush against the back of Stefanie's coat.

"I stopped smelling ages ago," croaked the girl. Her voice was so coarse and nasal, she sounded like she had a head full of cotton. She held her lantern with one hand and fanned herself with the other. "It's so hot down here. I feel like I'm going to faint."

"Hot! It's freezing down here," chattered Billy.

"I'm so cold, my teeth are shivering," complained Daniel. "You're hot because you're sick. I told you, you should have gone home."

"Like I really chose to be locked down here with you three numbskulls. I hate dark places. I hate lantern light because it gives me a headache. And I hate Zeek. And I hate you three for making the stupid decision to bury Mrs. McNemmish and join her stupid treasure hunt. Not to mention, there's no food or water or telephone down here. And there's no bathroom! What kind of an idiot digs a tunnel without a bathroom?"

"This whole place is a bathroom. Besides, it's your fault we're down here. You're the one who kicked the trunk."

"I wouldn't have kicked the trunk if the treasure was in it."

As they talked and walked, the tunnel continued to make sharp turns every sixty feet or so. Most of the corridors were narrow and low, forcing the children to walk single file and stoop over, especially Billy, who had already reached the height of five feet nine inches tall. But then there were those corridors that allowed the children to walk side-by-side with Billy standing upright. Sometimes they were as wide as eight feet and as high as six feet. These corridors gave everyone a breath of relief.

"I really think I'm going to freak out if we don't get out of here soon," said Daniel.

"Try pretending you're outside," Billy told him. "That way your brain won't wig out as much."

"Who says?"

"I saw it in a movie. This guy was buried alive, so he kept thinking about being outside so he wouldn't go nuts. It would have worked, too, if he hadn't run out of air and suffocated."

"You think we're going to be buried alive and suffocate?" gasped Stefanie.

"No! Of course not. I just meant that we should think about being outside. It might work for tunnels."

Daniel imagined he was at the beach, looking up at the sky, but the seashell wall brushed against his coat sleeve and distracted him. "It's not working. I'm still going bonkers."

"I need to rest," whined Stefanie. "Can't we sit down for a while?"

"No! We have to keep walking. I'm serious," Daniel told her. "If we don't get out of here soon, I'm going to have a nervous breakdown."

"Rats. The flashlight's going out." Billy hit the metal cylinder with his palm, but unlike the time before, the light remained dim. "If this flashlight goes out, we're sunk. Those lanterns won't last forever, and we only have half a dozen candles."

"*Trouble's afoot.*"

"What's wrong with your foot?" asked Stefanie.

"Nothing's wrong with my foot," said Billy.

"You just said you were having trouble with your foot. I heard you."

"I didn't say I was having trouble with my foot. I said that the lanterns won't stay lit forever and we only have six candles."

Stefanie stopped walking and looked down at Mark, who was nodding in agreement with Billy. Taking a deep, frustrated breath, she said, "I heard you say you were having trouble with your foot right when that gust of wind blew by."

"What gust of wind?"

"I didn't feel any wind," said Billy. "And there's nothing wrong with my foot."

"My foot still hurts," Daniel informed everyone. "First I got it stuck in the folding chair last night, and then I smacked it when we got caught in the whirlpool."

"I wasn't talking to you."

"Well, who were you talking to?"

"I was talking to Billy. He said he was having trouble with his foot, so I asked him what was wrong with his foot."

"What's wrong with your foot?" Daniel asked him.

"Will y'all stop asking me what's wrong with my foot!" He put a tender hand on Stefanie's shoulder and looked down at her sympathetically. "Maybe your fever went up, because you're acting a whole lot weirder than usual. Not that you act weird a lot," he added immediately. "Maybe your ears are infected, and you're hearing things."

"My ears are just fine, thank you. I heard you say you were having trouble with your foot, plain as day. And I felt that gust of wind!"

"What gust of wind?" asked Daniel.

"Ohhhhhhh! I give up. This is taking too long. Can't we go any faster?"

"Sure, if you want to walk straight into a wall," grumbled Daniel. "Whoever dug this tunnel must have been out of his mind."

"Blackbeard," agreed everyone.

Billy had an idea. He traded his dying flashlight for Daniel's oil lamp and motioned for the other three to sit down for a while. "You guys stay here. I'm going up ahead and see if I can find the way out."

"Thank goodness." Happy to oblige, Stefanie, Mark, and Daniel sat down and leaned against the wall for their first real rest since their descent into the tunnel. Meanwhile, Billy summoned up the nerve to move forward, tiptoeing a few timid steps at a time. He was soon swallowed up by the darkness and out of sight. Only the flickering of his lamplight kept the others abreast of his movements. Suddenly, a blood-curdling yelp shattered the silence, followed by a loud thunk.

"Billy?"

"Are you okay?" shouted Stefanie.

"I think so. Ouch."

The threesome jumped to their feet and gingerly made their way toward Billy's swaying lamplight. They found him sprawled out on the ground with his right hand poised in midair. He had managed to hang on to the lantern, which was swaying back and forth like a wind-blown chandelier. The darkness hid his rose-colored embarrassment. "I slipped."

Stefanie covered her mouth and burst out laughing. Winking at Mark, she said, "Don't you just love it when somebody, besides yourself, does something really embarrassing?" Mark grinned as the two offered Billy a hand up. He refused the help on principle.

"Are you sure you're okay?" laughed Daniel.

"Great. Fine. Thanks for asking." Billy sat up, put down his lantern, and brushed off his hands. "I'm just glad I'm well padded." He wiggled around, intending to stand up, when he felt the very thing underneath his backside that had made him slip. He pulled out what felt like a cluster of sticks and held it next to his light. A moment later, he threw it back down. "Ooooooh, gross!"

"What?"

"I think I found a foot."

"A foot of what?" asked Stefanie.

"A *foot* foot! You know. With toes."

"Where?" Daniel turned the corner just ahead of Billy and aimed his dimming flashlight into the shadows of the widened pathway. The others quickly joined him and followed the light as it swept over the legs and hips of an adult-sized, human skeleton seated on the sand-packed floor. "Holy moly!" gasped the boy. His hand trembled slightly as he moved forward, continuing to run the flashlight up the spine and across the shoulders. The back of the large skull rested against the cement wall, tilted to one side. Its bottom jaw hung open as if it were about to speak. The entire skeleton was scantily dressed in tattered clothes with a faded red handkerchief hanging loosely around its neck. His arms hung down toward his thighs, while the fingers on one hand clung steadfastly to an empty bottle. "Now there's something you don't see every day."

Stefanie pressed forward for a timid peek and sank her fingernails into the back of Mark's hand. "Is he dead?"

Three heads turned and glared at the girl's beet-red face and glassy eyes.

"Is he DEAD?" asked Daniel. "No, he's not dead! He's sitting around in his bones and underwear because of the heat. What's the matter with you? Of course he's dead. And not in very good shape from the looks of it."

"Maybe he designed the tunnel," chuckled Billy.

"You shouldn't make fun of dead people," Stefanie warned him. "It's bad luck."

"It's not like you can hurt their feelings," Daniel pointed out.

Mark tapped Daniel on the shoulder and motioned for him to look up ahead.

"What's the matter?"

Mark motioned again.

Stefanie tugged on Daniel's coat sleeve. "Go look," she encouraged him.

Not thrilled with the assignment, Daniel closed his eyes and prayed. "Please be the way out of here." He gave the flashlight back to Billy, grabbed the brighter of the lanterns, and inched forward, careful not to step on anything else resembling a foot. "Whoa! Look at this, y'all." He was standing beside a second skeleton that was plastered upright against the wall with one of his fingers stuck in a hole. The bony remains were dressed similarly to the first skeleton, with the exception of the scarf. His was a dirty yellow.

"Hey, Stefanie. He's dead, too."

"Shut up, Daniel." Stefanie shivered as she shuffled behind Billy and Mark for a closer look. "That is so creepy. Why is it just standing there?"

"Don't you mean *how* is he still standing there," said Daniel. He examined the remains closer and added, "He's probably holding up the wall."

"What!"

"Knock it off, Daniel, you're scaring her. Maybe there was a leak when he was alive, but it's dry now," Billy assured her.

"Well, I think it's disgusting the way Mrs. McNemmish just left all these skeletons down here."

"What was she supposed to do with them? Stuff them in her backpack and take them home?"

"Uh, Mark, you might not want to do that," warned Billy.

Mark had wandered up to the standing skeleton and was pressing his face flush against the skull. His curious fingers fidgeted with the yellow handkerchief that hung loosely around the collarbone.

"Leave it alone!" shrieked Stefanie.

Mark shrugged.

"Because it's yucky, that's why. And it's disrespectful. That's his scarf."

Mark ignored both concerns and carefully untied the handkerchief. He slowly and gently slipped it off the skeleton's neck and wrapped it around his own.

"Can we go now?" begged Daniel. "It's hard to breathe down here."

Everyone agreed that now would be a great time to leave since Mark had his desired handkerchief, and both Stefanie and Daniel had a massive case of the creeps. But as the group turned to leave, a strange crackling noise emerged from the standing skeleton. Everyone watched in horror as the head suddenly began to nod and sway toward its right shoulder. A moment later, the sides of the skull twitched and shivered until the bottom jaw broke loose and fell against the collarbone. Billy jumped back and burst out laughing when the upper portion of the skull leaned farther toward the right shoulder and rolled off the neck, filling the tunnel with the sound of crunching eggshells.

"Don't breathe," whispered Daniel. But the warning was useless. The skeleton's head slowly peeled away from the wall completely, bounced off the collarbone, rolled off the rib cage, and landed on the ground with a muffled thud. It gurgled through a muddy spot, stopping at the tip of Stefanie's feet.

Stefanie went ballistic.

"For gawd sake, stop screaming!" shouted Daniel. "It's just a head!"

"Get it away from my foot!"

Mark slapped a hand over his mouth and shrugged modestly.

"Oops?! That's all you have to say? OOPS?!" screamed Stefanie.

Billy convulsed with laughter. "This is like reality TV, only better."

"Well, I think it's disgusting."

Billy reached over, picked up the skull, and carefully placed it back on top of the skeleton's shoulders. "See? All better."

"Sure," said Daniel. "He'll never know the difference." But the moment Billy removed his hands, the entire skeleton began to weave and shimmy. Parts of the arms and rib cage fell off and the backbone sagged. Bones from one part of the body dropped off and clacked onto other parts of the body. Within seconds, the entire skeleton caved in like a house of cards forming a giant heap. By the end of the calcium cave-in, the once-standing skeleton looked like an exploded stack of giant pick-up sticks. Only the single finger remained in the wall.

"Well!" chirped Billy. "That was exciting."

"I told you not to touch it!" screamed Stefanie with a smack to Mark's shoulder.

Mark just shrugged and giggled.

Billy looked at Daniel and winked. The two of them removed their hats and placed them over their hearts. "May you rest in pieces," they said in unison.

"That's not funny."

Mark was thoroughly enjoying the situation when he dropped to the floor and covered his head with his hands.

"Now what?" asked Daniel.

Before anyone could interpret, Billy let out another blood-curdling scream. Grabbing his head, he danced around in circles hysterically. "Get it off of me!" wailed the boy. His hands flailed wildly as he tried to smack a small, leathery bat out of his thick, blond hair. "Help me!" shrieked the boy.

"Stop flapping! You're making it worse!" Daniel told him.

"Help him!" shouted Stefanie. She grabbed the flashlight out of his hand, then yanked Mark over to the opposite wall.

Daniel scrunched up his face and inched closer to Billy, but jumped back nervously when he accidentally touched the bat.

"What are you doing? Get the bat out of his hair!"

"If you're so brave, you get it out of his hair!"

"Somebody get it out!" wailed Billy.

"Okay, okay." Daniel looked around the tunnel and remembered the empty bottle. He ran back and snatched the bottle out of the first skeleton's greedy clutches. Poised like a baseball player, he lifted the bottle and aimed it at Billy's head.

"What are you doing?"

"I'm hitting the bat."

"Not while it's still on my head!" Billy tried plucking the varmint out of his own hair, but the bat was too entangled. It squealed loudly as it dug its claws into his skull. "Just hit him a little bit," said Billy. "But do something! It's hurting me."

"I'll just stun him," Daniel promised. "Hold still." He inched toward Billy and once again raised the bottle into the air. But just as he was about to tap the animal, he recoiled.

"Just do it!" hollered Stefanie.

"Either shut up or do it yourself!"

"I can't. I don't believe in hurting animals."

"Then how come you don't mind if I do?"

"Will y'all shut up and help me!" yelled Billy.

"Okay, okay. Stand still." Daniel scrunched up his face, swung the bottle, and tapped the bat on its head. "Did I get him?"

The bat quieted for a moment, then fluttered and squealed even louder than before.

"Hit him harder!" Billy urged Daniel.

"If I hit him any harder, he'll squirt all over the place."

"Just do it!"

"Oh gawd." Daniel took a deep breath, aimed for the bat, closed his eyes, and imagined hitting a line drive toward second base. He slammed the creature so hard, he rendered it unconscious.

Daniel opened his eyes and peeked at his handiwork. "All right!" crowed the boy. "And the crowd goes crazy as Daniel Garrish hits his seventy-fifth home run for the season. Yay!!"

Billy staggered for a moment, started to say something, then slumped to the floor, out cold.

"Look what you did!" Stefanie leaned over and gently slapped Billy's face. "You were supposed to knock out the bat, not Billy. You know what? I should have done it myself. Oh no!"

"What?"

"You killed the bat."

"So what? It's a bat."

"You didn't have to kill it. You could have just tapped it asleep, then taken it out of his hair." She gave Daniel the most despicable look she could muster. "Murderer."

Mark shook his head and clucked his tongue in serious disgust.

"Oh shut up," Daniel told him.

Stefanie winced as she studied the poor animal. "Well? Aren't you going to take it out of Billy's hair so we can bury it?"

"You take it out of his hair. I killed it."

"I'm too sick."

"Fine."

"Fine!"

Daniel shuddered violently as he reached forward and plucked the bleeding varmint off his friend's scalp. "It squirted all over his hair," he said, gagging. He quickly tossed it onto the floor, then rubbed his hands on his pants. "I think I'm going to puke."

Billy moaned then stirred awake. "What happened?"

"Daniel knocked you out with the bottle."

"I killed the bat, didn't I?"

"Monster." Stefanie took the yellow scarf off of Mark's

neck and wrapped up the bat. She laid it down gently beside the mound of bones. "Poor thing."

Billy rubbed his head. It was bleeding where the bat had scratched him and there was yucky, sticky stuff in his hair. "What about me? I'll probably get rabies. Where'd that bat come from, anyway?"

Mark pointed up ahead.

"Good. If he can get in, we can get out."

Let me tell you of the sea,

I'll tell you tales of mystery,

Of fortune hunters 'round the world,

Who slip by night with greed unfurled

To pluck the fruits of sailors past,

Who lost their lives when

ships were cast.

The sea knows not if greed's to play,

Nor will it cry for yesterday.

CHAPTER XI

T he *Lucky Beacon* rocked as it sat anchored in Teach's Hole off Springer's Point. Resting below its hull, hidden by centuries of sand and sea wash, the lure of pirate relics rose with the mist off the water and seeped into Ezekiel Beacon's blood.

Zeek toyed with his beard as he pored over the crisp piece of ancient parchment known as the "missing Howard Map." A jar of Ocracoke sand taken from Blackbeard's Cove and hideout shared the galley table along with a set of lighthouse salt and pepper shakers he kept on hand for inspiration. He had stolen the set from a friend's galley after his first successful looting.

Today, there was no need for inspiration. Today, his hands held captive the real deal.

Zeek knew his history. Theodora had seen to that. He knew the value of this precious map. As he visually soaked in its curves and lines, he reminisced about Blackbeard's quartermaster, William Howard, who was not aboard the sloop the morning Blackbeard and most of his men were either killed or taken prisoner. It was that lucky turn of fate due to a bad back that brought this map into being. When Howard was pardoned by Governor Spotswood, he returned and purchased the island of Ocracoke. It was then that Howard set about constructing a secret map that would lead to a cache of sunken merchant ships in and around the infamous and treacherous Diamond Shoals. This map, it was said, had secret instructions for traversing the dangers. Several years after the creation of the map, it mysteriously disappeared and was never recovered...until now. There was no telling how long Theodora Teach McNemmish had had it, and except for a few tiny pieces of flaked parchment, the map was in perfect condition. Beacon looked up from the map and yelled for his hired hand to join him. "Birdie! Get down here!"

Beacon's man stomped out of the wheel room and playfully trotted down the galley steps. He was a short, stocky man with a pudgy, red face and childlike grin. His soft, brown eyes were chameleon-like and often worked individually of one another, making it impossible to tell whether he was looking at you or at the wall behind you. Beacon found this optical shortcoming annoying and forbade Birdie to look him straight in the eye.

"See this, Birdie? This is Mrs. Theodora Teach McNemmish's Last Will and Testament, and it's all mine."

Birdie removed his woolen cap and stared in the general direction of the parchment. "What is it, Zeek?"

"It's a treasure map, fluff brain. What does it look like?" Beacon returned to his prize. "We're gonna be rich, Birdie! I can feel it."

Beacon's first mate grinned. "Okay, Zeek."

Beacon opened his switchblade and delicately traced the key areas on the map. He then traced the same areas on the *Lucky's* navigational map. His hands quivered with excitement and anticipation, and he could hardly wait to get started. "Look at this, Birdie." He held a magnifying glass over a portion of the parchment that went from the northern tip of Portsmouth Island, southeast toward the Bermudas, then northwest, encircling the inland curl of the Gulf Stream. "You can see where there used to be a line drawn. Now look here." He again ran the glass over a faded line running southeast from Kill Devil Hills at Nags Head, then southwest, back to the same inland curl. "There used to be markings just above the northern bend of this curl here, but I can't make them out." He sat up and playfully punched Birdie on the arm. "These coordinates lead us straight to the Diamond Shoals, the largest deposit of loot on the face of this continent." He sat back and twirled his beard with the tip of his knife. "This is my kind of treasure hunting," he cackled. "They did the droppin,' and we'll do the shoppin.'"

Birdie scratched his head and stepped an arm's length away from his boss. "Now, I know I ain't as smart as you, Zeek. But don't that map put us right smack dab *on* them Diamond Shoals? I mean, there ain't a fisherman 'tween here and the moon can steer 'round them Diamond Shoals. That's why the ships with the loot went down, if you get my meaning."

Beacon got to his feet, grabbed Birdie by the throat, and thrust his bulbous nose onto the map. "I get your meaning, you pudgy-faced feather duster, but I don't remember asking your opinion. They're called Diamond Shoals, because the ships that sank there were full of diamonds!"

"The ships sank," gagged Birdie. "That should tell ya somethin' right off."

"Shut up! I need to think." Zeek released Birdie from his grip. "You're a moron. You're not supposed to make sense." The fact was, the man was right. Treasure seekers had been going after those shipwrecks for hundreds of years, but not one of them had ever lived to tell about it. No! There was something different about this map. The coordinates approached the shoals from an unusual angle. And there was that business about the map saying where and where not to sail. If only the lines were clearer. "Theodora knew what she had," he maintained. "This map is legit, I'm sure of it. It'll show us how to get in there."

Birdie backed up even farther. "Does it show us how to get out?"

Beacon didn't have time for word games. The wind was freshening. The Nor'easter had gained strength, and heavy rain splattered across the cabin windows. With the first rumbling of thunder, the lights in the *Lucky* blinked. Beacon switched on the Coast Guard channel. The approaching storm posed a threat to his plans if he didn't haul anchor soon. Besides, with Theodora's antiques in his stow, he couldn't afford to be boarded.

"Check the gear," he ordered Birdie. "I want to get out of here before we get socked in. And I sure don't want to be around when those blowfish come up missing."

"Somebody's missing their blowfish?" asked Birdie. "Who, Zeek? Who's missing their blowfish?"

Beacon moaned. "Never mind the blowfish. Just get the gear ready. And be quick about it." Beacon knew that in a few hours, when the four children were discovered missing, residents would be flitting about the island like a swarm of green-headed flies. He had covered his tracks well. No one would find the widow's things, so there would be no reason to check out her trunk. Not yet, anyway. And so what if he didn't go back and let them out? Someone would—eventually. By the time they squeal their puny heads off about him, he and his fortune will be long gone and across international waters. "I should have shot them when I had the chance," he thought to himself. He leaned back in his chair and chuckled. "What am I worried about? Daniel's probably strangled Stefanie by now, Mark's a total head case, and Billy's probably whacked Daniel for strangling Stefanie." After carefully returning the map to its protective cover, he left the galley and trotted upstairs to the captain's chair. "Hurry it up!" he yelled to Birdie. "We have riches to find!"

"Okay, Zeek." Birdie leaped onto the *Lucky's* bow and made ready to cast off. "Ready!" He called to his captain.

"Then cast off!" shouted Zeek.

"Casting off!" answered Birdie.

Beacon reached up and knocked three times on the ceiling panel for good luck. Hauling anchor, he steered his craft out of the sound, through the inlet, and into the open sea. He could no longer hide his excitement and lifted his bottle to his first mate. "To Mrs. Theodora Teach McNemmish, and to *our* fortune!"

Birdie grinned. "Okay, Zeek."

Mrs. McNemmish clapped her hands and squealed with delight. "That map is as useless as sails without wind," she told the pirate Blackbeard.

"Aye, mate. Y'ar startin' to think like one of me own buccaneers." Teach stood with his legs apart, a dagger in his right hand, and his worthy cutlass hanging by his side. Strapped across his massive chest, half hidden behind his thick, purple, upholstery frock, he wore an armory of holsters, guns, and knives.

"Y'ar a smart lass, McNemmish, but I would have been the smarter for running a dagger through that blasted Israel Hands when I had me chance. It's his blood flowing through Zeek Beacon." He strolled to the side of his ship and pressed against the polished perfection of craftsmanship born in his era. He gazed longingly over the forest of ghostly masts from unfurled sailing ships with rigging as taut and sound as a sailor's arms. In his world, where sunshine paled the images of ghost ships and pirate spirits, moonlight and stormy afternoons enhanced their glow, giving stature and essence to the time-lost travelers. Today, within the gray-purple aura of cloud, every ship that spirited the Graveyard of the Atlantic glowed.

"I miss the frolic and the daring of a good raid, Theodora. I miss the thrill of battle, the brawls, the bonfires that crackled 'til the crowing of the cock." He poured a mug of his special brew, peppered it with gunpowder, and lit it on fire. He handed it to the willing McNemmish.

"I remember a night not long before me unfortunate demise," recalled Blackbeard. "Me crew and I were sailing the Carolinas in a hurricane. We got past Hatteras safe enough but couldn't get a fix on Ocracoke. The lighthouse flame had gone out, and we couldn't navigate the coast. Suddenly, this great fire roared up into the sky and we could see well enough to steer inland. The following morn, I learned the fate of a poor lad, who when told to start a blaze for the lost souls at sea, burned all of his grandfather's handmade decoys. The young man was given forty lashes and a whittling knife and sent to sea on his uncle's shrimp boat." The pirate's booming laughter tickled Mrs. McNemmish.

"That lad was the great-great-granddaddy times three of my own sweet Arthur," recollected the widow.

"So it was. So it was," laughed Blackbeard. "Ah, the waters were alive back then, Theodora. Alive and colorful and exciting. McFife!" yelled the captain. "Bring your fiddle."

Captain Teach's large frame towered above his petite descendant. He waited for his fiddler to arrive, then gently removed the mug from Theodora's grip, placed his large, black-powder-stained fingers around her tiny waist, took her fragile hand in his own, and gracefully waltzed her around the deck of his beloved *Queen Anne's Revenge*. Old Mrs. McNemmish felt increasingly young and carefree as they danced ever so gently to the lilting tunes of England and Scotland and Ireland, then curtsied and bowed their finish.

"Thank ye, madam."

"Most pleased, kind sir."

"Howard!" bellowed Blackbeard.

Teach's quartermaster jogged across the deck and jumped to attention by his captain's side. "Aye, sir?"

"Are me cannons fit and ready?"

"Aye, Cap. Ready as a hot, sweet maiden." Howard winked at Mrs. McNemmish. "No offense, ma'am."

"No offense taken, sir."

Blackbeard rubbed his hands ruefully. "Come, Theodora. Let's have some fun with that overbloated leech Zeek Beacon. Let's mommuck him around a bit."

Mrs. McNemmish brushed back the light wisps of silky red hair that danced in front of her face. No longer bent with arthritis or ancient in wrinkled expression, her lilting voice quickened with the excitement. "I await your orders, Sir."

"Bravo!" cheered Blackbeard. "Then let the battle begin!" The captain led his lady to the gunwale, then beckoned his crippled sea mate to join them.

Israel Hands limped across the freshly swabbed deck. In the center of one leg was a giant, gaping hole where his kneecap used to be. Blackbeard put an arm around the man's shoulders and spoke earnestly. "That relative of yours has squid ink running through his veins. Beacon couldn't captain a standing fish bowl. He's an embarrassment to yer family, and to piracy!"

"Aye, Captain."

"Just so ye know," said Blackbeard.

"Aye, Captain."

"Good!" Blackbeard stood tall on the poop deck, his arms folded across his chest, his flag securing his presence. "To chase the enemy still boils me blood and brings a smile to me face. Come jolly fellows! See to the guns!"

Power is the sun that fuels our life,
Power is the sea with mysteries
still untapped,
Power is the storm that bends trees
to its will,
Power is the night whose stars are fixed
and certain.

Power is the bond that binds our souls,
Power is the hope that perseveres,
Power is your hand in mine and words
unspoken but understood,
Power is the courage to know that
we are less than powerful.

CHAPTER XII

S tefanie was grateful for the wider parts of the tunnel. Even though she would never admit the fact, it was a comfort being squeezed in between the three boys. Her body ached with fever and it was work just to breathe. "I'm so tired. Y'all said we were only half a mile from Bobby's tree. I could have walked to Kitty Hawk by now."

"She's right," said Billy. "We should have been there ages ago, but there are so many twists and turns down here, I don't even know which way we're facing."

"Maybe we should go back. This is getting us nowhere," complained Daniel.

Stefanie turned around and smacked him on his coat sleeve. "I told you that three hours ago. If you had lis-

159

tened to me in the first place, we would have been back there by now. And another thing..."

"Here it comes," moaned Daniel.

"This entire village is only one mile long and a half-mile wide. How do you get lost in a village that's only one mile long and a half-mile wide?"

"Look," barked Daniel. "I want to get out of here just as much as you do, but this tunnel didn't come with a map. And it's not like either of those guys back there are going to give us directions. Besides, we're not *in* the village. We're *under* it."

"Can't we just dig our way out?"

"With what, our fingernails? Besides, we'd flood the place."

"Man, my neck hurts from hunching over," said Billy. He stopped walking long enough to do a few of the neck and shoulder stretches he had learned in baseball clinic.

Mark bent down, rubbed his tired legs, and stretched as well, although his head was far from reaching the ceiling.

Daniel leaned against the wall and yawned, starting a chain reaction with the others. "So who do you think they were?" he asked, trying to keep up the conversation.

"Who do we think who were?"

"Those guys back there."

"What guys?" asked Stefanie.

"The guys selling popcorn," Daniel said mockingly. "I meant the skeletons! Who do you think they were before they were dead?"

Mark pointed to his neck where the yellow handkerchief had been before it was used to bury the bat.

"Mark says they were pirates," said Billy.

"They probably were," agreed Daniel. "They must have worked for Blackbeard."

Stefanie surveyed the narrow corridor they had just turned into and shivered. "They must have done something pretty awful to be stuck down here long enough to petrify."

"Of course they were awful," remarked Daniel. "They were pirates."

"That doesn't mean they were awful," said Billy. "Some pirates were just pirates. It made them richer than privateering."

Stefanie shook her head in disagreement. "Those guys back there had to have been really bad. They were probably stuck down here because they were being punished. If they were only a little bit bad, they would have been shot and buried instead of being stuck down here until their bones turned into skeletons."

"Bones are skeletons. Besides, I don't think Blackbeard meant to keep them down here until their *bodies* turned into skeletons. He probably just forgot about them."

"Forgot about them! Daniel, you are so stupid. What do you think they were doing down here? Having a class picnic? No. Did Blackbeard come back for them? No. Did he say, 'Oh my, we left Harry and Joseph in the tunnel eating their chicken. We better go back and get them out?' I don't think so. Is Zeek coming back for us? No. Are we being punished? Yes."

"Ooh, chicken," sighed Billy. "Couldn't y'all just sink your teeth into some hot, crisp, batter-fried chicken right now?" His stomach gurgled and he looked at the girl desperately. "Did you have to mention food?"

"I haven't eaten since last night," she informed him. "And now I have a lump in my throat from taking a boat out at midnight in the middle of a rainstorm."

"Stop complaining. At least you have cough drops. I'm dying of thirst. What I wouldn't give for some hot chocolate," dreamed Daniel.

Mark wrinkled his eyebrows and nodded.

"Well! That's not going to happen, is it?" croaked Stefanie, who was getting hoarser by the minute.

Daniel sighed as the foursome continued down the long corridor. "I was thinking about those skeletons back there. Those men were actually people before they were pirates. They could have been somebody's husband, or father, or brother before they got stuck down here."

"Why would somebody marry a pirate?" asked Stefanie.

"They probably became pirates after they were married."

"Why would someone want to be a pirate if they were already married?"

"It was just a question, for crying out loud! I don't know. Maybe they married somebody like you and just wanted to get away from her mouth! Besides, if the pirates didn't marry and have kids, who'd be living on Ocracoke?"

Mark halted the conversation when he stopped walking and shot his hands toward the ceiling.

"Oh, gawd. Not another bat," wailed Billy.

The answer came in a muffled boom that sent vibrations throughout the tunnel. Bits of sand and seashell rained down from the ceiling.

"We're under the ocean!" panicked Daniel.

"That's not the ocean, it's thunder," said Billy. "The storm's right on top of us."

Stefanie lifted her foot off the ground. The bottom of her shoe was dripping. "It's leaking down here. Didn't I tell you it was leaking down here? I bet those pirates drowned, and that's why they turned into skeletons."

"Well, it can't be much of a leak," Billy assured her, "or the walls wouldn't hold."

"What!" Stefanie shrieked hysterically. "This is awful! First it's a little leak. Then it's a bigger leak. Then it's a puddle. Then the whole place is a tidal pool. And then it falls through. I knew it. I knew we'd die down here. Didn't I tell you we'd die down here? We'll either drown, or rot, or get crushed. We are standing in the middle of a huge sandcastle built by mad pirates and it's about to start gushing water. By the time anyone finds us, we'll be unidentified puffballs floating on saltwater and seashells. Our parents won't even recognize us. The only good thing about it is, I won't have to pee anymore because I'll be dead!" She ended with a fit of coughing and wheezing, rendering her speechless, which delighted Daniel to no end.

"Finished?" he asked her sarcastically.

"Yummmm. Unidentified puffballs floating on saltwater and seashells," Billy thought out loud. "Sounds like something they'd serve at Teach's Takeout."

"Will you kindly stop talking about food!" hollered Daniel.

Another loud clap of thunder sent everyone cowering to the floor with their hands pinned over their ears. "Crimminey!" moaned Billy. "That did not help my headache."

Mark pointed to one of the lanterns and shrugged regretfully.

"Are you nuts? We are not putting out one of the lanterns," Stefanie told him under no uncertain terms. "It's already too dark down here with both lanterns lit. I can't see if I'm stepping on anything. What if one of us steps on another skeleton? I might trip over a foot or something. Besides, I'm scared and hungry and thirsty, and I have to go to the bathroom, and I want to see better so I can find my way out of here before I go CRAZY!"

"Mark's right. The flashlight is dead and if we use up both lanterns now, we're not going to have enough light for later. And trust me," warned Daniel. "Six candles and a half a box of matches aren't going to last very long."

"There's nothing to be scared of," said Billy, "except for maybe another bat."

"Oh, yeah? What if there's a hurricane going on up there? Or a tornado? What if the Coast Guard evacuates the island and they just leave us down here? I could die of pneumonia or the plague or something."

"I vote for leaving you down here."

"Shut up, Daniel."

"Maybe we should turn around," confessed Billy, following another half-hour of walking. "Maybe we can break the lid. Sure! We can use some of the bones like baseball bats and ram our way out."

"That's disgusting! You don't go around borrowing people's bones."

Daniel grimaced. "I kind of agree with Stefanie on that one."

"Well, maybe we could all yell at the same time. Someone might hear us."

"What if that doesn't work? What if everyone leaves the island like they did during the last hurricane? No one knows we're down here, and we could get left down here without any food or water or a bathroom? It won't matter which end of the tunnel we're stuck in. We're going to look like Mr. Bones back there and the only way they'll identify us is by our teeth. Achoo! Did you hear that? I have to get out of here. I'm really sick. See? Cough, cough. I have no voice left, and if I don't get out of here RIGHT NOW, I'm going to have a NERVOUS BREAKDOWN!"

"So will the rest of us!" Daniel told her.

Mark put his finger to his lips. He gripped Stefanie's arm as the concussion from a burst of thunder shook more cement from the ceiling and walls.

"Oh, God, it's collapsing. Help!" shouted Stefanie. "Somebody help!"

"Knock it off, Stefanie! There's no one else down here, and you know it."

"At least I'm trying to get help. This whole place is collapsing and we're down here looking for a stupid key! We're being punished," she said, fighting back tears. "We did something awful to Mrs. McNemmish, and now we're being punished. We wrecked the church, and we're looking for a treasure that doesn't even belong to us because we didn't find the duck and key. AND IT'S ALL Y'ALL'S FAULT!"

"Please, can I kill her now?" implored Daniel.

"Maybe later," whispered Billy. "You might need something to look forward to." He took Stefanie's hand and walked beside her as the corridor took another sharp turn and widened. "The Coast Guard's not going to evacuate the island without finding us first," he promised her. "If there's a hurricane or tornado going on up there, we're probably safer down here. This is probably where Miss Theo came when everyone else evacuated. Maybe that's why those pirates were down here. Maybe this was their hideout during a storm."

"That's true," agreed Daniel. "It's not likely they'd be invited into the lighthouse to wait it out with the rest of the islanders."

The words were barely out of his mouth when there was a deafening crack of thunder and rush of air. An uneasy silence followed, then, from somewhere deep in the pitch-black distance, an eerie sort of creaking noise crept along the corridor, tickling the children's ears and touching their deepest nerves. Like the creaking of tree limb against tree limb in the densest part of Blackbeard's Cove, the sound gripped them by their throats and hearts, and no one breathed a word or moved a muscle. Then BANG! And with it, a startled squeal from Stefanie's lips. A moment later, she crumpled to the floor in a dead faint.

Billy's stomach was in his throat and he could barely speak. "She passed out," he managed to whisper. He bent down and with trembling hand, tried to wake her, but she was out cold. He lifted his quaking lantern light in the direction of the noise but was afraid to look. "What in Sam Jones was that?"

"Ghosts," quivered Daniel. "I think this tunnel is possessed or something." His eyes suddenly flew open and he shot a glance at Mark. "I bet it's one of those skeletons back there. You never should have taken his scarf. Maybe he liked that scarf."

Mark scowled back.

"I do not sound like Stefanie. I'm telling you, there's something spooky going on down here."

"You know what that banging noise sounded like? It sounded like a door slamming shut in a really old person's house. Wait a second! That's it!" shouted Billy. "That's the door out of here! It must have slammed shut from the wind! Sure! It has to be the other entrance! We must really be close. How else could we have heard the thunder?"

"I thought we said the way out was through the planks on the bottom of the Bobby Garrish tree," said Daniel.

"Well, maybe they came loose in the wind and then slammed back into the trunk!"

Stefanie stirred awake and sat up. "What happened?"

"You fainted. But guess what? I think that noise was our way out of here." Billy took Mark's advice and blew out one of the lanterns, then lit candles for Daniel, Stefanie, and Mark to hold. With the flashlight gone, he held onto the only remaining lit lantern. "I'm going up ahead to check things out. Y'all stay here with Stefanie." Taking a deep breath, he held the lantern out in front of him and bravely tiptoed forward.

"Don't trip!" teased Daniel.

"Very funny."

"Oh my gosh, Daniel, I just thought of something," whispered Stefanie.

"Why are you whispering?"

"Because Zeek might be down here. What if Zeek made that noise when he came down here to kill us? No one would ever find out. We'd be missing for life!"

"How can you be missing for life if you're dead?"

"You can be missing for life if you're dead. Amelia Earhart was missing for life, and she's dead. Mrs. McNemmish is missing for life, and she's dead."

Daniel rested his head in his arms. "You're giving me

a migraine."

"Serves you right for getting me stuck down here."

No one said anything for a while, then Daniel looked up, hoping to catch Billy returning with good news. "Shoot! I don't see his light. He must have gone around another corner. Billy!" hollered Daniel. "Hey! Meehonkey! Meehonkey! Where are you?"

When there was no response to the island call of hide-and-seek, Stefanie panicked all over again. "I told you Zeek was down here. He came down through the other entrance and killed Billy. And we're next!"

"No one killed anyone. Now, be quiet, I think I heard something." Daniel listened intently to see if he could hear Billy's voice, when all three heard what sounded like a cry for help.

"It's worse!" gasped Stefanie. "Zeek's torturing him!" She grabbed Daniel and Mark forming a tight huddle. "What do we do now?"

"We're going after him, that's what." Daniel took his first daring steps, dragging Stefanie and Mark with him. "Billy? Meehonkey!"

"How can he answer if he's dead?"

"He's not dead. You can't yell if you're dead."

The tightly interlocking huddle inched along the pathway. Stefanie grasped her candle, bathing in the only warmth and comfort that existed in the underground labyrinth. "Please don't go out," she prayed to the candle. "Please, please, please don't go out." The third "please" blew the candle out.

"Stefanie, I told you to be quiet." Daniel tipped his candle over hers, relighting it. "No more 'pleases,'" he said, covering his own mouth.

"Sweet maiden."

Stefanie put a hand over her mouth so as not to blow out the candle for a second time. "What did you call me?"

"I didn't call you anything. I told you to be quiet."

"After that," said Stefanie, "you called me a sweet maiden. What kind of stupid remark is that?"

"Why in the world would I call you a sweet maiden?"

"That's what I just asked you."

The huddle inched forward another few feet, then turned a corner. "Trust me," said Daniel. "I wouldn't call you a sweet anything."

Mark giggled.

"Then what did you say?"

"I said for you to be quiet. So be quiet!"

"You know what," Stefanie told him bluntly. "You have issues."

"I have issues! You have a new one every time you open your mouth. That's the third thing you've said you've heard that no one else has heard. I think your antenna needs a tune-up."

Mark tapped Daniel's shoulder, making him jump a foot off the ground. "What!"

Mark pointed up ahead.

"Oh, thank goodness. It's Billy's light! And for heaven's sake, don't tap me on the shoulder like that. You scared me to death!"

Stefanie clutched Mark's coat sleeve and hid behind both boys. "Is he okay?" she asked Daniel.

"I don't know. I can't see him."

"Is he dead?"

"I don't know."

"Did Zeek kill him?"

Mark reached forward to stop Daniel from choking her when all three heard a muffled crunch emerge from underneath the younger boy's shoe.

"Oh no. Not again." Stefanie flinched as Daniel's light illuminated a slovenly dressed skeleton who was seated on the floor with a dish and cup resting on his thighbone. A few feet away, facing the skeleton, a second skeleton sat with his fingers petrified to a spread of ancient playing cards. That skeleton was wearing the remains of a South American sombrero, faded blanket, and empty holster. On the floor next to him, stacked like a pile of leftover chicken bones, were the glistening digits from his other hand, which had apparently rolled in phosphorescent shell dust.

Stefanie backed away. "Somebody should have buried them," she said quietly. "It's not right just leaving them down here like this. Even if they were pirates, they were people. It's disrespectful."

Daniel sighed in agreement. "Maybe we should come back down here and bury them after we find the way out of here. What's a few more dead bodies in the ocean?"

"Don't be disgusting."

"Who's being disgusting? I'm just saying, by the time this is over, we will have buried more pirates than Captain Kidd."

Daniel held his candle next to the skeleton holding the playing cards. "Not a bad poker hand for a dead guy." He looked around, then carefully picked up the cards and stuck them in his pocket. The skeleton's fingers fell apart. "Oops. Sorry." He looked at Mark and Stefanie and shrugged. "I guess someone forgot to tell these guys their boss was dead."

Mark and Stefanie looked back at him and shook their heads disapprovingly.

"Hey. People don't get attached to their playing cards," he explained. "They get attached to their clothing."

"They also get attached to their fingers."

"I told him I was sorry."

Stefanie grabbed his coat and pointed. "I just saw something move." She indicated the flickering candlelight wiggling against the wall. "See? There it goes again."

Daniel gritted his teeth and mustered up all the bravery he could manage. "Billy," he squeaked. He cleared his throat. "Billy! Meehonkey!"

"I'm over here! Hurry up!"

Daniel dropped his shoulders and breathed. "I told you he wasn't dead." He scurried toward the light, lugging the other two with him. "Boy, am I glad to see you."

"We thought Zeek killed you!" Stefanie told him.

"I didn't," said Daniel. "Did you find the way out?"

"Not exactly," said Billy. "But get a load of this." He led the way up the tunnel and around another corner. "Voila!"

"Holy cow," gasped Daniel.

"Whoa!" Stefanie let go of Daniel's hand and swept across the wide corridor as if an invisible tractor beam were pulling her toward a daydream. Her hot, feverish eyes and ready fingers led the way to a million possibilities. Maybe more, if she were lucky. "Now, *that's* what I'm talking about!"

Mark moved closer to the hub of activity and squeezed all the sight he could muster through his thick lenses, but the light from just one lantern and three candles did little to help him see what all the commotion was about. Finally, putting his hands on his hips, he announced his presence with glaring expression.

"It's the treasure!" shouted Billy. He grabbed Mark by his hands and danced him around in circles. "Isn't the chest a beauty?"

The massive treasure chest was carved out of mahogany wood and was completely outlined in polished brass. The initials E.D.T. were etched on the front latch, which was unlocked and had fallen open. On the wood beneath the lock, the words "For the Devil's Eyes Alone" were carved with a knife. The strangest thing, however, were the two skeletons that were shackled to the brass handles on either side of the trunk.

"More skeletons," groaned Stefanie. "They could have started their own village down here."

"Why are they handcuffed to it?" Daniel wondered. "It's not like they could have snuck this chest out of here."

"Snuck it *out* of here?" chuckled Billy. "How did they get it *in* here? Even if they pushed it the whole way, they couldn't have gotten it around the corners."

Stefanie rolled her eyes to the ceiling. "Y'all are so stupid. You think they shoved my great big bed through my itty-bitty doorway? No—they put it together in my bedroom. I swear, I don't know how y'all manage to figure anything out on your own."

Daniel raised his eyebrows. "No wonder no one ever found any of his trunks. He hid them before he made them."

"Well, it's going to take all four of us to open it," said Billy. "I tried on my own, but it's too heavy. Come on, y'all. Spread out."

Mark examined the trunk with his hands. A slow grin spread across his face as he thought about the widow and her promise of riches and wealth.

But Stefanie couldn't take her eyes off the skeletons. "What's wrong with their bones?"

"What do you mean?"

"Look at them. They're all tumbled."

"What?"

"They're put together weird."

"They're dead. That's about as weird as it gets," said Daniel.

"I know they're dead. But they're weird dead."

"Stefanie, they've been down here for three hundred years. Maybe their bones shifted. Come on, let's open the trunk," Billy encouraged her.

"We need to hurry it up," insisted Daniel. "I don't know how much longer this lantern is going to stay lit, and the other one has less oil in it than this one."

But Stefanie's mind had turned elsewhere. "I bet there's a million dollars' worth of diamonds in there. And emeralds, and pearls, and gold pieces, and rubies."

"Doubloons," said Billy. "All pirate treasures have doubloons. Come on. Help me with the lid."

Daniel dug his heels into the dirt. "On the count of three, everybody push."

"Wait!" Billy pulled away.

"What's the matter?"

"What if somebody's in there?"

"Somebody who?"

"I don't know. Another Spanish maiden."

"Sweet maiden." Stefanie whispered the words under her breath. It was true. The words she alone had heard were clues to things they were to do or things they were going to find. A sudden chill swept through her body and she shivered. She was starting to act as weird as Mark, and that scared her. Maybe it was the fever. But then again...

"If Billy's right, she could be loaded with jewels!"

"Stefanie!"

"What?"

"I don't mean to be crude," interjected Daniel, "but who cares if there's a skeleton in there? We've seen more skeletons in one day than half the medical students at the university. Let's just open it."

Mark nodded enthusiastically.

Billy's hands were trembling with fear, but his heart was throbbing with excitement. "Okay. On the count of three, everybody push. One...two...three!"

"Ugh. It weighs a ton," grunted Stefanie.

"Keep pushing," groaned Billy.

"Almost," heaved Daniel.

"Almost..."

"Got it!"

Stefanie let go of the lid and plopped down onto the ground. Her head was pulsing.

"Are you okay?"

"I'm fine. Stop staring at me and see what's in the trunk!"

"Aye, aye, Captain."

Daniel took the lit lantern and was about to lower it into the chest, when Stefanie staggered to her feet. "Let me do it." She took the lamp and gently dropped it inside. An antique-lace tablecloth lay stretched over whatever treasure awaited their discovery. Without hesitation, she pulled off the tablecloth and shattered the near silence with an ear-splitting scream.

"I hate her! I hate her!" she wailed as she turned and kicked the wall. "I hope Mrs. McNemmish ends up on the wrong ghost ship, with the wrong captain, in the wrong era, fighting on the wrong side!"

Billy, Daniel, and Mark also jumped back, but burst out laughing.

"I told you there might be a body in there," giggled Billy.

Daniel stared down at the beautifully dressed remains of a lady. "He sure liked collecting women."

"Not a bad hobby," admitted Billy.

Stefanie wandered back to the trunk and examined the female resident. "I don't believe it! She's not wearing one piece of jewelry! What kind of a Spanish maiden doesn't wear jewelry?"

"One that's been stuck in a trunk for three hundred years."

"I've been stuck in this horrible tunnel for a whole day. I don't care if she's been in that trunk for six hundred years. She could at least be wearing a necklace."

Billy looked down at the remains, somewhat confused. "I thought the widow said she buried the Spanish maiden."

"That's a different Spanish maiden," said Daniel, quite convinced that Mrs. McNemmish had given the woman she spoke of a burial at sea.

"Then where's this one's jewelry?" Stefanie wanted to know. "And how come she didn't bury this one at sea? She run out of ocean?"

"She probably ran out of help."

"Maybe we should take her out before we go digging around in the trunk," suggested Billy.

He and Daniel tried lifting the maiden out of the chest in one piece without disturbing her dress, but her fragile remains fell apart as soon as they touched her. The two boys stacked her remains in a pile next to the pirate on the left side of the trunk.

"If we find a box, we should probably bury her in it," suggested Daniel.

"Excuse me?" asked Stefanie. She placed her hands on her hips and scoffed. "Why are you going to bury her and not the others? Because she's a girl skeleton?"

"Yes, because she's a girl skeleton."

"Oh. Well, that's okay then."

Stefanie sat down for a rest while Daniel, Billy, and Mark dove into the trunk. Suddenly, her feet began to rock back and forth and she drummed on her legs with her fingers. "Well, did you find anything good yet? I want to go home."

Daniel gave her a nasty glare, then went back to rooting. "We just got started two seconds ago. Give it a minute."

"Well, find something quick. I'm tired and dirty and hungry and my throat hurts."

"And you have to pee. Like we haven't heard that before," grumbled Daniel.

While Stefanie waited, she studied the two shackled skeletons. She had the greatest urge to rearrange their bones. "Can't y'all look any faster? We can't stay down here forever, you know." She rustled through her coat pockets. "I'm out of cough drops."

"Stop complaining and chew on a wrapper."

"Funny."

Billy reached down and lifted out the shelf that had supported the Spanish maiden. The rest of the massive trunk looked promising.

"There's lots of stuff in here," he told Stefanie. "Oh, wow! Look at these guns! They're gorgeous! There must be a dozen of them." Billy brought out several of the guns and laid them on the ground. The long-nosed pistols were brightly polished, some with wooden handles, some with silver and gold filigree. All were in perfect condition. "These definitely belong in our museum." He lifted them out one at a time and laid them on the ground. Each gun was beautifully preserved and looked like it had been plucked out of a pirate book. "There's some smaller chests in here that are filled with gold and silver dinnerware," he told Stefanie. "That must be worth a fortune. These are real antiques, not just old stuff."

Before the boys continued with their rooting and treasure hunting, they took one of the larger mahogany boxes and gently placed the maiden's bones inside. Removing their hats, they said a small prayer, then went back to the trunk.

Stefanie gave them five minutes, then sighed and rolled her eyes to the ceiling. "Have you found any diamonds yet?"

"Not yet."

"Gold?"

"Uh-uh."

"What about emeralds, or pearls, or diamonds, or gold necklaces, or diamonds?"

"You said diamonds three times," said Daniel. "Don't you think we'd give you the diamonds if we found any diamonds, just to shut you up?"

"Listen to me, Daniel Garrish."

"Now you did it," grinned Billy.

"A treasure always has diamonds. Diamonds and gold. That's what the word *treasure* means. Just ask anyone. They'll tell you. You can't have a treasure without diamonds and gold! Miss Theo knew that. A treasure's supposed to have rings and necklaces and earrings and gold pieces, not to mention jeweled goblets and diamond whatchamacallits for your hair. This is a stupid treasure! This is the only treasure in the entire world that doesn't have any treasure except for the treasure in the widow's shack, which also didn't have any treasure, unless you want to call the hole in the floor a treasure, which it isn't. And another thing," she said followed by a string of sneezes. "I don't think there is a key. I think she made it up. I think her brain sopped up so much cement and seaweed she only dreamt there was a key. That's it. Either you all get me out of here now, or I'm going to start tearing these walls apart with my coat buttons. And then, I'm going back out to the ocean, haul up Mrs. McNemmish, drag her back to the church, and bury her next to Lizzy Spencer, who will talk her ear off for the rest of eternity! And another thing. I will never, ever, EVER listen to any of y'all again for the rest of my life!"

"Does that mean we don't have to listen to you either?"

"Daniel Garrish..."

"Yeah, I know. Shut up."

"Stop mommucking, y'all," said Billy. "There's probably some really good stuff in here. We just haven't found any of it yet, that's all."

"There'd better be," wheezed Stefanie. She helped Billy root through more layers of stuff that had little or no value, at least to them. There were empty leather holsters, galley cups and plates, a brass telescope and seafaring compass, and tin cans. Lots of tin cans.

Daniel pocketed the compass, then hauled out several of the larger tins and placed them on the floor. The first two cans were filled with gunpowder. The rest were filled with an assortment of walnuts, pecans, almonds, and hazelnuts.

While Daniel occupied himself with the larger cans, Billy opened some of the smaller cans and peeked inside. "Look at this, y'all. There must be a billion of Mrs. McNemmish's white seeds in here."

"Well, at least we can eat the walnuts and pecans," said Stefanie.

"I don't think so." Daniel shook one of the walnuts and listened to the strange rattling noise. "I don't think they're supposed to sound like that. I think they're rotten."

"Figures. The first food we find, we can't eat!"

"We could eat the bat," suggested Daniel. "We could roast it over one of the lanterns."

"We are not roasting the bat," gagged Stefanie.

"I was just kidding." Daniel emptied one of the tin cans and offered it to Stefanie.

"What's that for?"

"To pee in."

"I'm not peeing in that!"

"You said you had to go."

"I'd rather hold it for a year than pee in that." She blew her nose into the last of her tissues. "And another thing."

"Oh, gawd."

"Your ankle looks really disgusting."

"Oh gross!" gasped Billy. "It's humongous!"

Daniel looked down. His right pant leg had pulled up over his sneaker, revealing a bright-red grapefruit where his ankle should be. Up close, he found a single raised circle on his skin. "Something bit me!"

"It looks like a spider bite," said Billy.

"What kind of spider?" panicked Daniel.

"I don't know. Something southern."

"I thought you were a Scout."

"I am a Scout. That doesn't mean I know about spiders."

Mark picked up a handful of mud and slapped it on Daniel's ankle.

"Am I going to die?"

Mark looked blank for a moment, then shrugged.

"Fifty-fifty," said Billy. "That's better than yes."

"Can we go now?" begged Stefanie. "There's no duck and no key and I'm tired."

Mark shook his head no, then walked over to the trunk and began rooting around in it blindly. He was practically hanging upside-down in the giant chest when he stood up, turned around, adjusted his glasses and grinned.

"Money!" screamed Stefanie. She rushed over and relieved Mark of the large potato sack brimming over with Spanish and English currency. "It's about time!"

"Bingo!" hollered Billy. "Mark! You did it!" He and Daniel ran their fingers through the gold pieces when Stefanie turned to Daniel with renewed determination.

"Give me the can," she told him. "We're staying."

I believe in the sun that warms my back
and nourishes the earth.
I believe in the moon that tides our
oceans and grounds our souls.
I believe in the stars that guide my
journey on land and sea.
I believe in this place that was, and is,
and always will be.

CHAPTER XIII

B illy scooped up a handful of coins and rained them down onto Mark's head. "I've never seen this much money! I wonder if it's enough to retire?"

"This isn't just a good treasure. This is a great treasure!" Daniel tilted back his head and envisioned heaven through the thick layers of ceiling sand. "Thank you, Mrs. McNemmish. Thank you, thank you, thank you!" Heaven itself answered back as a rumble of thunder reminded the boys of their perilous situation.

Stefanie darted back into the lighted part of the tunnel to find Billy, Daniel, and Mark emptying cans of assorted nuts into the trunk. "The bag is all dried up, so we're going to put the coins in the nut cans," Billy explained as he hurriedly began the process. Daniel assisted by scooping up large fistfuls of coins from the bag and dropped them into the empty tins. The sound amused Mark.

"You know what I think," said Stefanie.

"No. But you're probably going to tell us anyway."

"I think leaving the money down here was the stupidest thing Mrs. McNemmish ever did. It's worse than leaving the skeletons down here. What would have happened to all those coins if the tunnel had collapsed, or if we never came down here to rescue them? It's not like any of the skeletons were going to spend the money. And she sure never did. I would have been living in a castle if I had found these coins." She watched the boys filling the tins for a few moments, then turned her attention back to the shackled skeletons. "They are *so* weird."

"For crying out loud, Stefanie, get over it already."

Mark had gone back to rooting around inside the chest. He climbed out, gave a sharp squeal of delight, and displayed a small, folded blanket that had been lying near the bottom of the trunk.

"Whatcha got?" Stefanie asked him.

Mark motioned for Stefanie to bring her candle nearer to his. Stefanie understood and helped him illuminate the blanket. But Mark's excitement was hard to interpret. It was plain that he knew something about the blanket, but it would take some time to figure out exactly what it was he did know.

No one on the island understood *what* Mark knew, or how he knew things. No one understood *how* he could always be two steps ahead of everyone, such as looking at the phone right before it rang, or answering a question in school by writing it on the board half a second before it was asked. Everyone simply took for granted he could and left it at that.

Mark looked at Stefanie, beseeching her to take an even closer look at the blanket.

"It's a baby quilt," she told him.

Mark nodded enthusiastically. He dropped down to the ground where he pressed open the quilt, then reached up and pulled Stefanie down to the ground with him.

"You can look at that later," said Billy. "We have to get out of here. The ceiling's starting to break apart every time it thunders. We'll come back for the cans of money when we find the way out."

Mark shook his head defiantly. He wanted everyone to look at the quilt.

"Look," Daniel told him urgently. "I might really be sick. I might be dying from a poisonous spider bite. Look at the size of my ankle!"

"Oh! So your sickness is worse than my sickness," objected Stefanie. "How come you weren't so worried about me getting out of here?"

"I was worried about you," admitted Billy.

"Thank you, Billy."

Mark took Stefanie's arm and pulled her closer to the quilt. He insisted she take a better look.

Stefanie crawled over to the trunk and borrowed the lantern. Turning it up slightly, she rested it on the ground beside the small, handmade blanket. "Well, I don't see what's so great about it. It's not very pretty. The church quilts are much prettier than this one."

Mark pressed his hand against her shoulder, pushing her closer to the quilting.

"Mark, I don't know what you want me to see. Can't you just tell me? I mean, they're just lines and dots and simple pictures."

Mark outlined several of the quilted squares with his finger, then forced Stefanie's hand to do the same. He then lifted the lantern and held it closer still.

Stefanie sighed. She felt really bad for Mark, but sometimes, like now, his silence was just plain frustrating. Stefanie tried harder. She looked over each hemmed and decorated square one by one. "Well, the three squares in the middle all have trees crocheted on them. The bottom two squares on the right have sand dunes and water. I think the triangles in the middle of those squares are supposed to be sailboats." She moved the lantern to the upper left of the quilt. "These squares over here look like mountains because they're green, and the sand dunes are yellow. This here is a sprig of lavender. Must be someone's favorite flower, or something. Anyway, these stitches in the center squares here are just rows of stitches. Then the top three squares across have more stitches, and a flag."

Mark pointed to the squares with the plain rows of stitches.

"I don't know what they are. They're just two parallel rows of stitches."

"Wait a minute! I know what that is!" Billy leaned over the quilt and examined it quickly. "That's a slave quilt!"

"A what?"

"A slave quilt. Daniel, look at this."

Daniel joined the others and was less enthused about examining the blanket while being locked somewhere underneath a sandbar that may or may not hold under the storm outside. "Can't we look at it when we get home?" he asked Mark. But Mark once again shook his head stubbornly.

Billy squatted down and looked over the lines and quilting with great interest. "This tunnel is turning into a history lesson," he said appreciatively. "But if this was a pirate tunnel, what was a slave quilt doing in the trunk? It doesn't make any sense."

"None of this makes sense," objected Stefanie. "What's so special about this quilt, anyway? My mom's quilts are much prettier than this one. My baby quilt had ducks and a giraffe and..."

"No, no. This is a really special quilt," explained Billy. "It's supposed to be plain. It's supposed to look like a handmade baby quilt any mother or grandmother could make. Plain and simple. Nothing special to look at."

"They got that right."

Daniel took his candle and limped over to the trunk and sat on the front, right corner. "See those flat tins over by the wall? Well, we found hard tack, and deer jerky, and dried fruit inside them while you were peeing. We can't eat any of it because it's petrified. But that's the food Civil War soldiers carried with them into the fields, or while marching to a new camp. Well, during the war, union soldiers and some confederate soldiers snuck the food out of the camps or stole it from their officers and gave it to the people who were helping runaway slaves. We learned about this stuff in history class last year."

"This tunnel must have been used to hide runaway slaves!" Billy interjected. "How cool is that? They must have used that trunk to hide their stuff!"

"You are so not right," argued Stefanie. "First of all, if this was a pirate tunnel, how did Blackbeard's girlfriend end up on top of the Civil War quilt instead of under it? And second of all, if there were Civil War people down here, they would have stolen all the stuff out of the trunk and taken it with them and sold it like anyone smart would have done, which proves Mrs. McNemmish wasn't too sharp. And third of all, we're southern, so Mrs. McNemmish must have put this stuff down here for storage since she didn't have an attic."

"Are you finished?" asked Daniel.

"Yes."

"Good. Because it all makes perfect sense," said Daniel. "Anything having to do with runaway slaves would have to be hidden, in case the people were found and sent back. That way, the stuff would still be here for the next runaways. No one would think to look under a pirate skeleton. This tunnel must have been part of the Underground Railroad!"

"Railroad? Ocracoke doesn't have a railroad. It doesn't even have a bus."

"It wasn't really a railroad," explained Billy. "Well, some of it was, but not in the South. Down here, it was a pipeline of houses and farms and hideouts where people helped slaves make their way north. Then they could take the train to safety. The boats and trees on the quilt were landmarks to show the slaves where they were. Then these stitches here told them which direction they should go. The people that made these quilts would wash them and hang them out to dry, just like regular people would do with their baby quilts. Then the slaves would run up and read them like road maps. Runaway slaves must have used this tunnel the same way Blackbeard did. Man! This is a really important tunnel. No wonder Mrs. McNemmish took care of it."

"Mrs. McNemmish must have figured all of this out," said Daniel. "She must have kept this place as a memorial or something."

"We have to do that," said Billy.

"What?" Stefanie squawked so loudly, she started another coughing fit.

Billy slapped her on her back. "We have to come back down here and take care of the tunnel and the trunk just like Mrs. McNemmish did!"

"Are you out of your mind? We can't do that. We are out of air, out of food, out of bathrooms, out of patience, and not even out of here yet, and you want to come back? Let me tell you something, Billy O'Neal. You are a couple of colors shy of a rainbow. I can't even eat chicken any more because of all the bones I've seen today. No. All y'all can come back down here and bury the skeletons if you want to, but if y'all think I'm coming back down here to keep an eye on the place, y'all are nuttier than she was."

Mark suddenly jumped to his feet, turned toward the corridor, and pointed.

"Really?" Billy was delighted. "Mark thinks that if this tunnel was a hideout for slaves, it *had* to have two entrances. They'd need one way to sneak in and one way to sneak out."

"They sure did a lot of twisting and turning in between," complained Stefanie.

A crack of thunder sent a strong vibration throughout

the tunnel and several large chunks of ceiling broke loose, hitting Daniel on his shoulder.

This time Billy panicked. "Quick! Stuff your pockets with whatever you want to take and leave the rest down here. We'll find the way out, then come back down with help and get the rest of it."

"But it's still our stuff, right?" asked Stefanie.

"You bet it is." Billy looped his pinky finger around Stefanie's. "We split everything four ways."

"Four ways!" she repeated. Mark nodded enthusiastically, then folded up the quilt and tucked it under his arm. With the aid of his candle, he reached into the trunk and pulled out two pockets' worth of assorted nuts and white seeds, then reached into one of the smaller chests and pulled out a gold spoon for his mother. He filled his other two pockets with coins.

Billy filled his pockets with coins and seeds, then blew out the candles and stored them in his inside pocket in case they were needed later. With the lit oil lamp at his fingertips, he motioned for everyone to follow him out of the corridor. The foursome had barely moved three feet away from the trunk, when an eerie creaking noise rose up from the chest, chilling the backs of their necks. Daniel was positive that if he turned around, he would be greeted by a ghost, or walking skeleton, or worse—Zeek Beacon. Billy slowly turned his head, inching the rest of his body around until he faced the trunk full on. "The lid's closing by itself," he whispered.

One by one, Daniel, Stefanie, and Mark turned around until all four faced the slowly creaking trunk lid. Their eyes remained glued as the lid stopped and hovered, undecided whether to close the rest of the way.

Stefanie's nose tickled. Her eyelids narrowed as the unwelcomed sneeze blossomed to its fullest and burst forth before she could cover her face. The trunk lid quivered and dropped another three inches, creaking like an old, rusty door hinge.

"Nobody move," muttered Billy.

Stefanie pinched her nose and held her breath.

Daniel stood paralyzed in place, his right hand gripping Mark's elbow. He could hear his own heart beating in his ears.

Mark's cheeks moved involuntarily. Then came the grin. Something in his chest stirred and the giggle spewed up and out of him like an unruly fountain. The second it emerged, the treasure chest lid shuddered so violently, the entire trunk shimmied and rocked. Stefanie backed up against the wall, half expecting the thing to walk, much like her washing machine did on the spin cycle. Then there was a long, painful moan, one last quake, and the chest slammed shut spraying cold air across the width of the tunnel and onto the four stunned and terrified faces. Stefanie let out a shriek, grabbed the wall behind her with her hands, and slid to the floor like melted wax.

Billy thought if he opened his mouth, his heart would fall out. "Not again," he managed to squeal.

With his heart banging out of his chest, Daniel reached over and whaled on Mark, smacking him on his coat sleeves. "You had to giggle! I swear, Mark, if we get out of here alive, I just might have to kill you."

"Me first," said Billy.

Stefanie blinked her eyes open. When they focused, she pointed toward the side of the trunk. "Look."

"What?"

"The skeletons."

"Uh-oh." Billy slapped a hand over his mouth as he ogled the two pirate skeletons that had guarded Blackbeard's hidden treasure for nearly three centuries. Until today, they had remained unscathed—a still life in history. Now, their remains lay in two matching heaps on either side of the trunk. The two skulls sat upon the toppled bones like the cherry topping on an ice cream sundae. Only their wrists stayed intact, still shackled to the sides of the chest.

Three scowling faces turned toward the youngest boy. "Quiet, but deadly," sighed Billy. He took the lantern and gingerly approached the skeleton on the right. Something caught his eye.

"Hey! Look at this, y'all." He reached over the bony rubble and picked up a giant conch Snow Duck that had been hidden behind the seated skeleton. A quickening of electricity shot through his body and he eked out the words: "This is it!"

"No way!" Daniel hobbled forward and lifted the duck out of Billy's hand. "It's the Snow Duck!" He turned it upside down to see if there was a name taped to the bottom and heard a faint clicking noise coming from inside one of the conches. He shook it up and down several times and watched in amazement as a tiny skeleton key, no bigger than an inch long, dropped onto the tunnel floor.

"Well, I'll be a slug bait worm hook." Billy squatted down and placed his lantern beside the small, brass item that brought Mrs. McNemmish's words off the page of her notepaper and into the real world of four treasure-seeking children. "It's a key!"

"It really *is* a key," said Daniel.

"But it's a *key* key," Billy stated emphatically. "And it came from inside a shell!"

Daniel cocked his head and looked at Billy wearily. "I *know* it's a *key* key. I can see it's a *key* key."

Stefanie led Mark to the tiny spot of ground where the key lay and squatted down for a better look. "Well! All I can say is, it's a pretty small key for all the stuff we had to go through to find it. And I'll tell you something else. That had better be the right key, because I didn't come down here to get pneumonia, and get dripped on, and step over skeletons, and pee in a can for nothing. There had better be some diamonds in whatever that key opens because if there aren't any diamonds and there isn't any treasure, I'm going to take that key and shove it up the widow's..."

"Stefanie!" Billy laughed gleefully as he picked up the key and examined it in his palm. "It's a skeleton key! Must belong to one of them."

"Give me that." Daniel grabbed the key and stuck it in his pocket. He shook his head at Stefanie. "You make me nuts, you know that?"

"That's my job."

"See if there's anything else in the duck," said Billy.

"Like what? Another body?"

"I don't know. Mark keeps looking at it like there's something else inside. Ooooh. Maybe there's something inside that tells us what it opens. "

Daniel sighed wearily. Rather than argue, he stuck two fingers up into the large conch shell and felt around. "There is something," he said struggling. A piece of coarse paper rubbed against his fingertips. He closed his eyes and squeezed his fingers further into the conch. When he withdrew his hand, he had two, four-inch long pieces of the handmade paper pinched between his fingertips.

"Bookmarks?" asked Stefanie.

"I think they're some kind of tickets," Daniel guessed. He held them closer to the light for examination. "The writing's kind of wacky, but I can read the dates. They both say 'June 25, 1718.' This one has the word 'stick' or 'sticks' on it. And this one has 'silver t' something on it. There's some kind of markings on the back of both of them, but I can't make it out."

"I wonder what they're tickets for?" asked Billy.

"Well, if they're for a movie, we're late." Daniel studied them for another few moments, then carefully stuck them in his coat pocket along with the key. "Come on, y'all. We need to get out of here." He took hold of Stefanie's arm and followed behind Billy and Mark as they left the trunk and corridor. When they returned, it would be with help and plenty of light guiding their way to their treasure.

The search for the way out began with eager chitchat about the key and the mysterious tickets, then grew silent as the corridors seemed to once again stretch on endlessly.

"The tunnel shrank again," sighed Billy.

Daniel's stomach growled. "Man, I'm hungry."

"I'm so tired," whispered Stefanie.

Mark yawned, then leaned his forehead on Billy's shoulder as they walked in tandem.

When Billy reached the next dead end, he held the lantern to his left to see if the corridor continued in that direction. When it didn't, he turned to the right. He was confused to see that that corridor also ended within just a few yards.

"Wait a second!"

"What's the matter?"

Billy walked forward, then lifted his lantern toward the eleven-foot-high ceiling. Letting out a huge sigh of relief, he turned toward the others. "We're here! We're at the end of the tunnel!"

Daniel reached for the box of matches and quickly lit the second lantern. "Amen," heaved the boy. He was too exhausted to actually get excited.

Stefanie walked toward the dead-end wall and saw that the ceiling was the same height as the one below the widow's shack. "I don't see a ladder out of here," she said frantically.

"It's got to be here someplace," said Daniel.

"Stefanie, get on my shoulders," said Billy.

"What?"

"Get on my shoulders and hold the lantern up toward the ceiling."

Stefanie straddled Billy's shoulders and held the lantern above her head, revealing a cluster of giant tree roots sprouting from where the ceiling and far left wall came together. Partially hidden and wedged into the cement behind the roots was a rope and wood-beam ladder.

"Good. Now all we have to do is dig it out," said Billy.

"Dig it out! With what?"

"Our bare hands, if we have to. Once we dig out the ladder, we can punch through the ceiling where the roots are sticking out."

Mark reached into his coat pocket and pulled out the gold spoon he had collected for his mother. He walked over to Billy and held it out.

Billy smiled graciously. "Thanks, Mark. We'll come back and get your mom another one."

"We'll get her the whole set!" said Daniel, grateful for the aid. Daniel had just finished thanking Mark when a deafening crack of thunder accompanied by a bright flash of lightning dropped a spray of sand and seashell onto the children's heads.

"I saw light!" screamed Daniel. "I saw light through a crack in the ceiling!"

"Thank goodness," heaved Stefanie. She leaned against the wall and slithered to the ground for a much needed rest. Mark sat down beside her, hugging his precious slave quilt.

Stefanie smiled weakly. "Me, too," she told him. "I just want to go home, be sick in my own house, be in my own bed, and be under my own cover. And I want to use a real, live bathroom, with a sink, and water, and toilet paper, and a window. And I won't even care if Matt comes into my bedroom and acts like a dork."

"I'm going to go home and sleep for a week," said Billy. "Then, when I wake up, I'm going to eat an entire fried chicken dinner, one of Jason's pizzas, three slushies, a sub from Styron's Store, and four baskets of hush puppies from the Island Inn. That's before I start on onion rings and shrimp jammers at the Pub." He dreamed about sitting on a rocker at Howard's Pub, playing cards, and eating himself into oblivion. "Change that. I'm going to eat first, then sleep."

"All I want is a hot shower and a doctor," said Daniel. "Then I want a huge bowl of clam chowder, a basket of fritters, and about a gallon of soda. Then I'm going to sleep for a month. What do you want, Mark?"

Mark thought for a moment, then made a circle with his hand, including his three friends and himself.

"You already have us," Daniel told him gently.

Stefanie looked up at Daniel and Billy, her eyes swollen, red, and pleading. "Can we go home now?" she asked quietly.

Billy nodded. "You and Mark rest. Daniel and I are going to dig the rope ladder out of the wall so we can punch through the tree boards."

Daniel was the first to dig. Climbing onto Billy's shoulders, he chopped at the wall and the first few rungs of the ladder with Mark's spoon. The bottom two rope-tied boards broke loose quickly, taking bits of ceiling with it. Sand and rain dripped onto Daniel's head. It wasn't long, however, before his left shoulder, which had been injured in the boat the night before, was in too much pain to continue. He climbed down off Billy's shoulder so Billy could take a turn.

Because Daniel's ankle was unsteady, Stefanie support-ed him while he supported Billy. But Billy could only dig a few minutes at a time because of his injured wrist. It was nearly an hour before the third rung was loose enough to pull free. Billy ducked when a large chunk of cement dis-lodged from the ceiling and dropped onto his head. "Why is it always my head?" yelped the boy. But it was hard to be angry. Welcomed raindrops showered onto his face, bringing new life into his tired body. "I can see one of the boards!" he called down.

"Can you see anything else?" asked Stefanie.

"I can see the sky, but it's too dark to see anything else." Billy wet his mouth with the rainwater, then traded places with Daniel, Stefanie, and Mark, who thirstily drank in the drops. Billy and Daniel traded places several more times before two more rungs were detached from the wall.

"Two more rungs and I can climb up," said Billy when it was his turn. He turned his face to the ceiling and let the rain splash onto his face. "Gawd, it's delicious." He got down off of Daniel's shoulders and let Mark and Stefanie each have another turn at drinking.

After a short rest, Billy got back onto Daniel's shoulders. He had just reached up to loosen the next rung, when a searing streak of lightning split the sky like a luminescent whip shooting straight to the heart of the Bobby Garrish tree. The tree crackled and snapped, filling the hole in the ceiling with fire and igniting the tree roots and ladder, momentarily blinding both Daniel and Billy. The blast of energy from the thunder hurled both boys and Stefanie to the ground almost at once.

"It's caving in!" screamed Billy. He scrambled to his feet, grabbed Stefanie, and lunged for Mark, who sat paralyzed against the wall. He dragged both of them back into the tunnel, then returned for Daniel.

Daniel tried to get up on his own, but his body felt like lead. He dragged himself partway back toward the opening of the corridor as bits of fiery ash and timber poured down around him.

"Daniel, your hair's on fire!" Billy ripped off his coat and covered Daniel's head until the flames were out, but it left Daniel's hair singed and smoking.

Billy grabbed Daniel underneath his arms and dragged him out of the way just as a flaming tree root, the size of a five-foot log, dropped onto the spot where he had been lying. Both lanterns were crushed. The rope and plank ladder they had worked so diligently to free had burned clear through and hung by a fiery thread. Billy raced back into the alcove to see if more of the ceiling had opened up, but the fire and smoke engulfed the place. Suddenly, a huge chunk of ceiling dropped to the ground, bringing with it a torrent of sand. Like an hourglass, a dune began to swell and grow inside the tunnel, blocking the tunnel exit. Gripped with fear and choking, Billy ran back to the others and dropped to the floor.

Stefanie's eyes grew enormous as she peered into the distance and watched the glow of fire play off the dead-end wall. Trembling, with terror written across her stunned, rigid features, she stared at Billy who was seated on the ground. "What are you doing? Why are you sitting here? You have to go back in there! You have to keep digging the ladder! We're almost out, you said so yourself!"

Billy coughed into his coat sleeve and motioned for everyone to move farther back. "It's no use. The whole place is on fire. The walls and the ceiling are caving in." He closed his eyes and breathed in the faint smell of smoke that was rapidly following them back into the tunnel.

"We have to go back to the shack!" said Daniel.

"What? No!" shouted Stefanie. "No! I'm sure the fire will go out and then we can climb out of the tree. I can't go back!" she panicked. "You can't go back," she told Daniel. "Mark can't go back!"

"She's right," said Billy. "Y'all stay here. We only have a few candles left, but you have the light from the fire. Keep moving back away from the smoke. I'll go back and get out of the trunk somehow. If the fire goes out and y'all get out, send somebody for me." He took Stefanie by the shoulders and held her gently. "I'll run the whole way. I promise. I'll break through the trunk if it takes all night. I just need to rest for a minute."

"No!" Stefanie shook her head vehemently. "No!" she screamed again. "You have to go back in there and get us out! Please!"

"Stefanie, the tree's on fire!"

Stefanie's eyes shifted back and forth from her three friends, to the smoky corridor in front of her, to the pitch-black tunnel behind her. The sound of rain, fire, and thunder seemed to pin her powerlessly against the wall. "You don't understand," she sobbed. "I didn't say good-bye to my mom. I have to see my mom and tell her good-bye because she was at the school meeting today and I wasn't, so I have to get out of here and say good-bye to her so she doesn't worry. I never go anywhere without saying good-bye to my mom, but I did today. I just left the house when I wasn't supposed to, and I know she's up there waiting for me." She stood against the wall crying as she looked down at Daniel, who was doubled over in pain. "We have to help him. Please, please, can't we go back in there and try? Maybe we could use the rungs you've already dug out. Or maybe you're right. We could all go back to the shack. I don't mind walking. I'll help Daniel, and you can help Mark." She gasped for breath as her crying and coughing gripped her throat and chest. "Please, Billy. If that entrance is on fire, can't we go back to the widow's house together?"

Billy slowly rose to his feet and gathered Stefanie into his arms. He hugged her tightly. His eyes and throat were scorched and he was exhausted, but tears streamed from his eyes as he listened to Stefanie's sobbing. "The ladder's gone," he told her quietly. "I am so sorry I got you into this. I swear I didn't know all this was going to happen."

Daniel sat up coughing. The smoke was getting to him as well. "I bet your mom is looking for you right now. The whole village is probably out there looking for us. Maybe when they put out the tree fire they'll find us." He pointed to Billy. "I'll bet Drum knew something was wrong the second Billy didn't show up for a meal."

"Sure. And I'll bet the ranger and Teddy squeezed the truth out of Zeek and they're halfway through the tunnel by now." He looked at Stefanie and smiled weakly. "You should be really proud of yourself. You did a really good job down here. When we get out of here, you'll be really glad you did this. I bet that key we found opens up a really amazing treasure chest with tons of diamonds in it. You'll be rolling in jewels by Thanksgiving! You'll see."

He grabbed Mark and motioned for Stefanie and Daniel to move further back into the tunnel as thicker smoke made its way down the corridor. "Daniel's right," he told Stefanie. "I bet the whole village is out there looking for us. I'll probably run into someone on the way back to the widow's shack. But you're going to have to take care of Daniel and Mark," he told her. "Can you do that?"

Stefanie looked over at Mark, who was huddled up in a ball with the quilt in one hand and a white seed in the other. She suddenly thought about Zeek and how he held a gun to them and forced them down the ladder and into the tunnel. She wished herself and her friends back in the widow's shack before everything had changed, when Snow Ducks and treasure stories were everything, and nothing. She remembered the day Teddy showed them the four Snow Ducks that were on the widow's mantle. Four, worthless Snow Ducks that sent them on a scavenger hunt that would probably cost them their lives.

"This was all for nothing," she blurted out. "The church, the boats, the tunnel, the treasure. We did it for nothing! We buried Mrs. McNemmish and found all this stuff for nothing!"

"Not for nothing!" said Daniel. "We did it for Mrs. McNemmish. We buried her at sea because it's what she wanted us to do and because we loved her! Stefanie, you did a really great thing. You risked your life so that someone else could have something they really wanted. That's everything! I'm really proud of you. I'm proud of all of us. And no one's going to let us die down here. Someone will find us. You know your mom and dad are trying. So is my dad, and Billy's dad, and Mark's dad. And you know Teddy is looking for us. He's really smart. He'll know what to do."

"You don't know that," wept Stefanie. "How? How are they going to find us? They don't even know this tunnel exists. We might as well be on the moon." She leaned against the wall and wiped her stinging eyes. She loved the moon. Sometimes the moon was so big behind the sand dunes, it looked like all you needed was to hop onto your bike and ride right onto it. "We'll never see the moon again," she said quietly. "Or the ocean. Or the dunes. Or the pelicans." She looked at Billy with tired, sad eyes. "I'm not really going to see my family again, am I?"

Mark tapped her on the shoulder and pretended to write.

Billy smiled. "See? Mark's just glad he's not in school."

"We're going to miss the Halloween carnival at school," sighed Stefanie. "We never even got to decorate the island."

"Or egg anybody's car," admitted Daniel.

"Or camp out in the graveyards," reminisced Billy.

"You never made it for a whole night, and you know it," said Daniel.

"I lasted a couple of hours. Once."

"Well, I love school, and I love Halloween, and I love every place on this island except for down here," said Stefanie. "No!" she screamed suddenly. "This isn't right. We're getting out of here, now!"

"Stefanie, what are you doing? Where are you going?" shouted Billy.

Daniel lifted his head and strained to see Stefanie moving back toward the entrance of the tunnel. "Stefanie, get back here. You'll get burned!"

"I'm getting the ladder down!"

Billy rushed to stop her. "You can't go in there! There's smoke everywhere, and the wall is falling down. I'll go back to the widow's house. I'll leave right now!"

"Get off of me!" yelled Stefanie. She broke loose from Billy's grip and dove into the dense smoke that led to the base of the mounting sand pile. "Where's the hole? I can't see the roots or the hole out of here! Where's the hole out of here?"

Mark also panicked. He was terrified that Stefanie would get burned or killed if she didn't return to the tunnel. Climbing to his feet, he inched along the wall using her voice as a guide, hoping to take her back with him. But when he felt the heat of the fire, he began to flail his arms about. He wanted desperately to call out, but his own voice remained a memory. Tears streamed from his eyes as he reached out, hoping Stefanie would see him and pull him to safety. No one noticed him as he walked into the dense smoke and raining sand. He continued to move farther and farther toward the voices, but still no one noticed him. Growing increasingly frightened, he traced his steps back in the direction of the tunnel where Daniel was lying on the ground. Suddenly, a swarm of frightened and confused bats flew out of hiding and rushed past Mark's head, startling the youngster. Mark whirled around and shooed them away, but his right foot got caught on Daniel's outstretched leg. An agonizing cry and muffled crunch left Mark face down on the ground. Daniel tried lifting him and called for help. When Billy and Stefanie got to him, the youngster's thick eyeglasses were shattered and pressed into his face. Hearing his name, he lifted his head for one brief second, just long enough for Billy to see the large shard of glass that was sticking out of Mark's forehead just above his right eye. Blood poured down his face and onto the ground. A moment later, he passed out.

Stefanie's eyes fixated on the youngster. She wrung her hands and stammered, "I did that. I did that to him."

"It's all right," said Billy. He stepped over Daniel and pulled Mark deeper into the tunnel. "Get me the quilt," he told Stefanie. He waited while Stefanie came out of her stupor and grabbed the quilt, which was on the floor a few feet away. She gave it to Billy, who held it to Mark's face.

"Daniel, sit up and hold this over his eye."

Daniel, dazed with pain and inhaled smoke, scooted over and held the blanket securely over Mark's eye while Billy pulled the chunk of glass out of his forehead.

"You need to hold the quilt to his head to try and stop the bleeding. Whatever you do, don't let go."

"I'll try," said Daniel.

"What should I do?" asked Stefanie. "This was my fault. What should I do?"

"Help me light the candles." He gave Stefanie four candles to hold while he secured the box of matches and lit them. He then placed them on the floor throughout the tunnel corridor to see if there was enough oxygen. The candles flickered, but stayed lit. "There's enough oxygen for now," he told everyone. It was their own carbon dioxide that would become poison if they weren't rescued soon.

Stefanie gazed down at both Daniel and Mark. Her eyes burned too badly to cry anymore, but inside she was screaming. "I'm so sorry," she told Billy.

"You had a good idea, Stefanie. That was really brave."

"Stupid, but brave," Daniel teased her gently.

"Brave? I'm not brave. I'm scared, and I want to go home!" She sat down on the ground and leaned back against the glittering cement. "I'm so tired. I just want to go home and see my mom and go to sleep." She caught her breath as if letting go of the day and rested her head on Billy's shoulder. Daniel looked over at her and smiled sympathetically. "No one's ever going to believe you peed in a can," he told her with a bit of a chuckle.

"That's the bravest thing I've ever done," she said smiling back. Closing her eyes, she went limp.

Billy reached over, untied Daniel's shoes, and slipped them off his feet. "You owe me ten dollars."

"For taking off my shoes?"

"We split an order of crab legs last Thursday, and you said you'd pay me back."

"And you want it now?"

"I just remembered." Billy sat back and rested. "You know," he told Daniel, "If we survive, we're going to have to write about this in English class."

"Forget that. Mr. Fulcher's going to turn this tunnel into a field trip."

Billy laughed. "Yeah. Biology. The whole class can collect the skeletons and bury them."

"That's archeology." Daniel pressed the cloth to Mark's head until it stuck on its own. Hot embers had replaced Daniel's contact lenses and his leg was numb all the way up to his thigh. "My mouth is so dry, I can't swallow." He looked at Billy with half-open eyes. "Are you scared?"

Billy shrugged. "I think I'm too tired to be scared."

Daniel sat quietly for a moment. "I don't want to die. I don't think Mrs. McNemmish thought we would. If we don't, I'll pay you back." His words were slurred at the end of the sentence, and then there was silence.

Billy yawned. If he died, he wouldn't be able to come back and take care of the tunnel. Too bad. Mrs. McNemmish would have liked that. If only he weren't so tired, he'd go for help. "We did good," he told his sleeping friends. He smiled down at Mark, Stefanie, and Daniel. Then closing his eyes, he slept.

Close your eyes and listen well,

And you will hear the tale I tell.

Of Blackbeard's men and

ghostly lights

That shine upon the sea at night.

They say that Blackbeard lingers on

And visits Ocracoke each dawn.

"Oh, crow cock!" you'll hear him sing,

For Blackbeard is the Pirate King.

CHAPTER XIV

High, breaking waves and dense rain pounded the *Lucky Beacon* as she rocked and pitched toward the infamous and dangerous Diamond Shoals. Birdie clung to the arms of his copilot's chair, swaying in time to a pencil as it rolled back and forth across the console. "Maybe we should go back," he reckoned, his plump face paling to a dull gray-green. "It's not like anyone's gonna steal the stuff before we do." He burped.

Zeek Beacon laughed as he battled the wheel. The wind wailed across the bow, rattling windows and shifting squeaky planks as his craft slammed head on into high breakers. "What's the matter, Birdie? No guts for a little adventure?"

"No guts is right. This rockin' is makin' me seasick."
He burped again.

"You're the only fisherman I know who can get
quamish standing still in a puddle of rainwater." Beacon
spoke as he strained to see out the window. The colorless
sky, pelting rain, and choppy water blended into a dull
slate gray, creating a seamless horizon with no point of reference. His years of experience and the ship's instruments
were his eyes and ears.

"Tell me, old Bird. What are you going to do with your
share of the treasure? Buy yourself a fancy car, then clam
onto a couple of hot mermaids to ride around with?"

Birdie wrapped his legs around the base of his chair
and stared blankly out the front window. His petal-pink
cheeks were slowly returning to their natural glow as a
wide, cheerful grin spread across his face. "I'm gonna buy
me a parrot!"

"A parrot?"

"Sure. I love parrots. I had me a parrot once. He was
green and yellow and red. Only he was busted. All he
could say was, 'Sit. Go ahead. Sit. Go ahead. Sit. Go
ahead. Sit. Go ahead.'"

"I get the picture," said Zeek.

"After a while, Granny's hound got this nervous condition, 'cause every time she'd go and feed the dog, the
bird would yell, 'Sit. Go ahead. Sit. Go ahead. Sit. Go
ahead. Sit. Go ahead.'"

"I get it!" shrieked Beacon.

"Poor dog kept stoppin' and startin' and sittin' and
standin' every other bite of food, 'til one day all his fur fell
out. So Granny got her pellet rifle and shot the parrot

dead. Weren't wasted, though. She plucked 'im, and dipped 'im, and et 'im with her stew."

"Granny sounds like a real winner."

Beacon had sailed silently and uneventfully for several hours when he checked his craft's nautical instruments. He realized at once that the *Lucky Beacon* had blown off course. "This can't be right," he told his man. "We can't be this far off course." He checked and rechecked his instruments then referred to the William Howard Map. "Blast! We'll have to make up time when the storm blows over." He did have one comforting thought. Like Birdie said—it wasn't like anyone was going to steal the stuff before he did.

"I'll tell you what," Zeek told Birdie several hours later, referring back to the conversation. "When you're rich, you can buy all the parrots you want. You can buy a flock of them, for all I care. And Granny doesn't have to know a thing about it. You and I are going to a place where people mind their own business and keep a distance from everyone else's. That's the way I like it."

Birdie grinned. "Okay, Zeek." He was about to add something cheery, when the boat began to lurch as if the keel were dragging through sand. A moment later, there was a loud thunk followed by a metallic, grinding noise.

"Sounds like we're in the shallows," Birdie reported nervously. He grabbed his slicker, stumbled through the doorway, and plowed headlong into the raging downpour. He skidded across the waterlogged planks, slamming into the portside railing. His thick waist and weighty thighs acted like sandbags and kept him from flipping overboard. "I don't see any markers!" he shouted above the roaring sea. "But it feels like a sand bar!"

"Impossible!" Beacon glanced down at his depth finder. It read forty feet. He cupped his hands and yelled to his assistant. "We're nowhere near a sandbar. Get back in here and check out the engine room." Beacon's attention was brought back to the wheel when it developed a strong shimmy and pulled to the starboard. He was struggling against the high waves that continued to smash against the side. Water spilled onto the decks and roof, causing the cabin ceiling to drip through a series of small holes.

"This storm's getting out of control!" thundered the *Lucky's* commander. The winds had swelled to gale force. With it, blinding sheets of rain painted the windshield, making it impossible to see. Birdie blew back into the cabin just as the boat lurched forward with such force, the engine squealed to a stop. Smoke rose up from the engine room into the wheelhouse, filling the cabin with a noxious odor. The *Lucky Beacon* had run aground.

"Blast! Bloody engine!" screamed Beacon. He smacked his fist on the console, cracking the wooden frame at the very moment the cabin lights flickered and died. "This is impossible! Birdie, get a light and check for damages. And get me some power!"

Birdie stumbled and thunked his way down into the hold and worked quickly to engage the emergency power. Restoring the rest of the power would take time. When the red lights came on, Zeek again studied his coordinates.

"Look at this!" he raved as if Birdie were standing close enough to smack. "The map, the radar, and the computer read clear of any land mass. According to my readouts, the *Lucky Beacon* has eighty miles to go before we hit Howard's entrance to the shoals and over a hundred miles before we hit low water. According to the blasted boat, we're right smack dab on a sandbar! Where in Sam Jones are we?"

Birdie was out of hearing distance. He was inspecting the rest of the craft during his captain's tirade and didn't join him in the wheelhouse until the main power grid was restored.

"She's okay down below, but I can't check her outer hull 'til daylight," Birdie panted, trotting up the stairs. He stood silently for a moment, nervously wringing out his cap. "Uh, Zeek?" Beacon's mate grappled for the right words. "You think maybe we should call for some help?" He finished his question, backed up two spaces, and covered his face with his hand, fully expecting to be smacked. "We could say we was fishin' and run aground, so it weren't our fault exactly." A huge wave slammed the craft broadside, and Birdie fell forward into his boss's bench-pressed arms. Beacon growled loudly and shoved his pudgy shipmate backward into his chair.

"No, I don't think we should call for help, you twit-brained feather fluff! What kind of moron except you would believe we went fishing in a Nor'easter? Besides, I don't want anyone knowing we're out here." Beacon shook his head. "I'm beginning to think Grannie shot the wrong bird." He sat down and tracked the progress of the storm on his radar screen. "According to radar, we're just getting the outermost edge of the hurricane. Then again, according to this idiot piece of equipment, we're somewhere in the middle of the ocean instead of being stuck on some God-forsaken sandbar. I'll call some buddies of mine to come and haul us out of here when the storm dies down. Until then, *shut up!*"

Birdie slapped a sopping-wet, gloved hand over his mouth and nodded. "Okay, Zeek."

Ezekiel Beacon returned to his study of the Howard Map, protecting it from the droplets of water raining in from the ceiling. He was deep in thought when he looked up and growled in the direction of Birdie, who was staring over his left shoulder. "What in the world are you looking at?"

"Can I talk?"

"Yes, you can talk. What are you looking at?"

"'Cause you told me not to talk."

Beacon grabbed Birdie's face and shifted it to the right so at least one of the man's eyes would actually face him straight on. "What were you looking at?" he repeated louder and angrier.

Birdie gulped. "I was lookin' at you, Zeek. Sorry."

Beacon smacked him. "The first thing I'm going to do with your share of the money is have your headlights aimed!"

"Granny says my nose and heart are in the right places."

"Granny's a moron."

Troubled, Zeek left the wheelhouse, raced down to the galley, and poured himself a cup of strong coffee. A tilt of his flask gave it the flavor and punch he needed. "I've waited my entire life for a break like this," he scowled at Birdie. "I hunted whelks for that old lady too many times to let a storm and a grounding keep me from what's right-fully mine." He took a sip of his beverage and relaxed his stature. "I need that loot, Birdie. I'm going to buy myself an island somewhere in South America and never come back to this backward island." The truth was, if the *Lucky* had to be dredged, which now seemed inevitable, his whereabouts and his mischief would be discovered and more than likely reported. Not to mention, the second those four yapping beach butts were found, they'd shoot off their mouths about him and the Howard Map. Brainless imps, they were probably still standing on the rungs of the ladder screaming their tonsils out. A second cup of his brew began to work its magic, and Beacon perked up.

"You know, Birdie. A few extra divers might not be a bad idea." He twirled his fileting knife with the ease and dexterity of a baton twirler. "Sure! We could collect twice the loot in half the time. This dredging thing might turn out in our favor."

"Won't they find out about the map?" fretted Birdie.

"Well then. We'll just have to arrange a little detour on their trip back to shore."

"Detour?"

Beacon reached up to smack Birdie, then changed his mind. It wasn't worth the effort. "An accident, you molting, cross-eyed peep tweet. I'll arrange an accident on their way home."

"Oh! Okay, Zeek."

Beacon laughed. "Wouldn't old lady McNemmish pitch a fit if she knew I was the one with the treasure map?" A wave of coffee spilled over the cup and onto the parchment, reminding him of the storm outside. He quickly mopped up the liquid and placed the valuable piece of parchment back into its protective covering.

"The widow gave me somethin,' too," said Birdie, enjoying his captain's good spirits. He reached into his pants pocket and pulled out a tiny, black velvet bag. Two plump fingers opened the bag and pulled out a handful of perfectly shaped white seeds. He displayed the seeds in front of Beacon, drinking in their mystery and beauty, then put them back in their bag. "See?"

For a single moment, Beacon envied Birdie. Anyone who could get that excited about seeds had very little in life to worry about. His envy faded, however, when he glanced over the tabletop a few minutes later and watched his pink-cheeked assistant dip a cold fish stick into his cup. The thought of spending the next several hours eating and conversing with this tubby, cross-beamed trash recycler was unbearable. "Birdie!"

Birdie looked up, remembered the "eye" rule, and quickly looked down. "Yes, Zeek?"

"You're making me sick!" He yanked the fish stick out of Birdie's hand and tossed it into the trashcan. "Finish your coffee, then get your bulbous bottom down to the hold and get our diving gear in order. And don't bug me 'til I call you. I need to think."

"Yes, Zeek." Birdie grabbed his cup of brew, a loaf of white bread, and a can of chocolate syrup on his way out of the galley. This time, it was Zeek Beacon who turned green.

By midnight, the storm began to recede, but the combination of a rocking boat and the warmth of his drinks had lulled Zeek into a deep sleep. Pages of notes charting out his first few dives lay strewn across the galley table and floor. Beacon was dreaming of his new life in South America when Birdie bubbled into the room.

"Whatcha want, Zeek? Ya done thinkin'?"

Beacon jumped up startled, then quickly settled back down into his seat. Grabbing his bottle, he took a swig and squinted in Birdie's direction. The faint outline of chocolate syrup highlighted Birdie's lips, and he smelled like brew and brass cleaner.

"Moron," grumbled Beacon. "What do you mean, what do I want? You're the one who came in here."

"I know, Zeek. But you're the one who came down to the hold and told me to get my butt up here."

"No, I didn't."

Birdie scratched his head. "Well, somebody with your voice came down the ladder to the hold with the diving gear and yelled for me to stow the stuff and get my butt into the galley. I figured since you're the only one on the boat 'cept for me, and since it was your voice, it must'a been you."

"You been sniffing that brass cleaner again?"

"No, Zeek."

Beacon gathered his notes and stood up. He shoved Birdie away from the doorway. "I'm going up on deck. Make me some fresh coffee. And make it strong."

"Uh, Zeek?" Birdie spoke timidly with his hand perched and ready to protect his face from a sudden smacking. "You still didn't tell me what you want."

"I told you. I don't want anything! Now, make me some coffee!"

"But Zeek, I heard you. You called, 'Birdie!' That's me. 'Get your butt up here!' So I got my butt up here. Did you finish thinking?"

Beacon closed his eyes and took a deep breath. "I swear, if you don't shut up and get me a cup of coffee, I'm going to glue your beak shut!"

"Yes, Zeek."

Beacon stormed upstairs and began a systematic check of his instruments. "Blast it! Nothing's working right!" The magnetic pull in the part of the Atlantic Ocean known as the Bermuda Triangle was playing havoc with his boat's instruments. Beacon had heard legends about missing ships, disappearing aircraft, and the mysterious tampering with ships' instruments in that part of the Atlantic, but this was the first time it had affected him. Now here he was, in the center of the triangle that ran from the Bermuda Islands, west of the Carolinas, and over toward Puerto Rico, and the only fixed points for navigating were the stars, which were hidden by storm clouds.

Zeek reached into his coat pocket for his cell phone. It was time to call his buddies and have the *Lucky Beacon* dredged out of the sand. Poised to pull his hand out of his pocket, he stopped abruptly and turned when he felt Birdie's crossed eyes glaring over his left shoulder. "You're driving me nuts!" exploded the captain.

"Sorry, Zeek. *But ain't that an unusual sky?*"

Beacon turned and glared out the console window. Through the rain and darkness, he could see a single, illu- minated, swirling cloud connecting sky to water. It seemed to loom larger than life as it spiraled through the thick air toward the tip of the *Lucky's* bow. Beacon rose out of his chair, his eyes fixated on the stealth-like plume. He was also aware of a chilling stillness in the air, and his color paled. "That's a funnel cloud," he informed his first mate. "And we're sitting ducks!" He tried moving away from his chair, but sheer panic pasted his boots to the floor. His eyes widened as the dancing funnel stepped up and onto the bow. The accompanying tap on his shoulder sent his arms flailing wildly.

"What?" screamed Beacon. His heart pounded so hard, it made the ballpoint pen in his pocket jump. "Are you trying to kill me?" He turned to smack Birdie across the face, but the man had wisely gone below. "Get back up here, you coward!"

Birdie rushed up from the galley with a steaming mug of coffee. "I'm right here, Zeek. You told me to get your coffee and be quiet before you glued my beak shut."

"That was before you told me about the funnel cloud and tried to give me a heart attack!"

Birdie scrunched his eyebrows. "What funnel cloud, Zeek?"

"What funnel cloud? That funnel cloud, you fluff-feathered bird twit!" He turned and pointed, but the cloud had disappeared as quickly and mysteriously as it had first appeared. In its place, a storm cloud charged with flashes of flat lightning began pulling apart like a clump of dirty cotton, revealing an aura of twinkling white lights.

"Look at that, Zeek. There's a boat out there with their Christmas lights already turned on!" Birdie clapped his hands enthusiastically. "Maybe it's a cruise ship, Zeek. Maybe we could flag 'em down and they'll rescue us and we can be passengers for a couple of days. Wouldn't that be fun, Zeek? It's not even Thanksgiving, and they've put up their Christmas lights. You think they'll let us on board for a few days?" Birdie glanced over at Beacon and became suddenly overwhelmed with concern. "Golly, Zeek. Are you okay? 'Cause you don't look okay. Come to think of it, you don't sound okay. I mean, first you're yellin' at me to hurry my butt into the galley, then you're askin' me to get your coffee, then you come back into the galley and ask for your coffee on the poop deck as if we were on some kind of pirate ship instead of havin' run aground out here near them shoals you're so fond of, and then you want me to look at a funnel cloud that ain't there, and you don't say anythin' about those pretty Christmas twinkle lights."

Beacon reached out as if he were about to strangle Birdie, changed his mind, and took the steaming mug of coffee. He sniffed it to make sure it had all its proper ingredients. He then reached up and aimed his assistant's head so that one of the man's eyes faced his own. "Do you know what I think?"

"No, Zeek."

"I think the good Lord let the air out of your scuba tanks too soon. In the first place, I didn't tell you to get out of the hold and go into the galley. Secondly, I never followed you into the galley because I was already there. And I didn't ask for my coffee on the poop deck because we don't have a poop deck! Not to mention, you're the one who told me about the funnel cloud when your eyeballs crisscrossed out the console window. You're also the one who tapped me on the shoulder and nearly gave me a coronary! Does any of this sound familiar?"

Birdie stood frozen and trembling for a moment, then broke into a playful grin and giggled. "Aw, you're just teasin' me to cheer me up, ain't ya, Zeek? How could I tap you on the shoulder all the way from the galley? I'd have to have pretty long arms to tap you on the shoulder all the way from the galley. I like clouds and ships with twinkle lights, though."

Beacon stared at the plump, simple-minded lug nut standing before him in stunned silence. "Unbelievable!" ranted the captain. "Hey! What's that hissing noise? Birdie, go check the boiler room. Hurry!"

"Yes, Zeek." Birdie climbed down into the hold and looked around. "It's coming from outside," he panted as he raced back up the stairs. He grabbed his slicker and went out onto the deck. As he stood leaning against the deck railing, a strange quieting came over him. He turned and looked toward Beacon with a blank expression. "It's okay," he told his captain. "That sizzlin' noise is the ocean putting out the sun."

"Excuse me?"

Birdie looked down so as not to break the eye rule. "Excuse you for what, Zeek?"

"No, you trip-wit. I said excuse me, because you said that hissing noise is the ocean putting out the sun. What kind of insane babble blurb is that?"

Birdie scratched his head. He was very worried about his captain. "I'll go check the engine room again," he told Beacon. "Hope you feel better."

"Me? You're the one who's cracking up!"

"Uh, Zeek?"

"Now what?"

"I think that boat with the Christmas lights is aimin' for us."

Zeek turned quickly. Birdie was right. The cluster of lights was rapidly approaching his craft. "Blast it all! If they find us, they'll report it and we'll get towed in. Birdie, get into your gear and see how much sand we're sitting in. Hurry! If we're towed in now, it's all over." To himself he thought, "If those kids spilled the beans, it'll be their word against mine." He had to think fast.

"Birdie! Stow the extra diving gear and throw that duffle I brought on board into the water. Hurry, man!" He turned and watched the spray of lights growing closer. But because the heavy rain and thick storm clouds obscured his view, it was impossible to make out the kind of ship that was pursuing him. The height of the approaching lights made him think it was either a small cruise ship or a large Coast Guard cutter.

Beacon grabbed his coat and raced outside. The ship's lights were growing closer at a daring and frightening speed. "Hey! What's wrong with you?" He ran back inside and to the helm. "Those imbeciles are headed straight for us!" He ran to the steps and yelled down into the hold. "Birdie! Get back up here and sound the bell! Now!"

Beacon turned on his floodlights and flashed them in the direction of the oncoming craft. Birdie scurried back up the stairs and into the wheel room half-naked and half-dressed in diving gear. He reached for the horn and blasted it three times, warning the approaching ship to turn, but the brilliant, diamond-like lights sailed closer still.

"What's wrong with those morons?" Beacon shoved Birdie to one side and blasted the horn himself. "Turn, you imbeciles! You're headed for a dead boat!" He flashed his lights using Morse code. "You're going to run aground!" flickered the lights. "Who's at your helm—Pickles the Poodle?" screamed the irate captain.

Both Beacon and Birdie watched in silent horror as the lights from the approaching ship loomed before them. Just as the ship grew close enough for the men to see the hint of a hazily sketched outline, the twinkling cluster slowed down. It stopped a scant five hundred yards away. Beacon let out an audible sigh of relief along with a few choice words for the boat's captain. "I'm putting you on report!" he screamed through the window. "Birdie! Get me a drink!"

"Yes, Zeek."

Birdie finished dressing in the cabin, trotted down into the galley, then back up again with an open bottle sloshing over the rim. He handed it to Beacon, then grabbed the pair of binoculars that were hanging on a hinge beside the outer cabin door. He pressed his left eye to the right eyepiece, covered his right eye with his baseball mitt of a hand, and peered into the distance. "Wow! That's a really nice boat, Zeek. You think they'll let us ride on that boat, Zeek?"

Beacon took a swig from his pint and rechecked his instruments. "What are you babbling about?"

"The boat, Zeek. Do you think they'd give us a ride?"

"For crying out loud, Birdie, you've been on a cutter before."

Birdie continued goggling through the binoculars. "The lights look really pretty up close, Zeek. And they've got their sails out even though it's storming."

"Sails?" Beacon put down his bottle, stood up, and smacked Birdie on the head.

"Whatcha do that for, Zeek?"

"It's been awhile." Beacon pushed Birdie aside and snatched the binoculars out of his hands. He aimed the glasses at the cutter, jumped back startled, then peered through them again. "What in Sam Jones is that?" He ran out onto the deck and gawked at the three-masted schooner, shrouded by cloud and faintly outlined. The ship's sails were unfurled and its midmast loomed fifty feet high. Light from the whale-oil lamps illuminated the black flag high atop the crow's nest, which swept the bottom of the quilted, black thunderclouds floating above it. Beacon stood in stunned silence as he watched the awesome ship turn its starboard side parallel to the *Lucky Beacon*. Stretching across the schooner's gunwale, a row of cannons stood open-mouthed and primed for firing.

"Told ya it was a nice boat," said Birdie.

"That's not a boat, you twit-brained bird turd! That's a bloody building!" He glared at the eighteenth-century vessel, wondering if he was totally out of his mind (easily explained from having spent so much time with Birdie) or, by some freak accident, he had sailed into an area of the Bermuda Triangle, which evoked phantom ships from bygone eras.

Beacon aimed his binoculars at the ship's crow's nest only to find someone staring back at him through a hand-held telescope. "What the devil? Birdie! There's someone up there pointing a glass eye at us! Hey! You hawking me or what?" yelled Beacon. He shifted the aim of his binoculars to the forward deck of the massive ship just in time to see the hazy form of a man draw his sword and aim it toward the mainsail. The man was of enormous stature and the weight of his power seemed to catch a ride on the wind, hitting Beacon square-on. "They *are* spying on us!"

"Aye!" boomed a voice rich with thunder and peppered with laughter. "Spying on ye is the least of yer worries, mate."

"Who said that?" Beacon ran his binoculars back and forth over the sea and above the starboard rail of the giant apparition. A rush of hazy images was gathering behind a row of cannon tubes. In the midst of the activity, Beacon heard a voice coming from the direction of the ship's crow's nest—a booming, devilish voice that roared like a volcano, growling and belching from the depths of the earth.

"The *Lucky Beacon's* in range, sir!" hollered Israel Hands.

"In range for what? Who are you?" shouted Beacon. He remained focused on the twinkling phantom ship. He barely had time to lower his binoculars when a loud bang shook the *Lucky Beacon* with such force that both he and Birdie tumbled onto the railing. Starry bursts of yellow and white light flashed across the sky, arched against a background of long, drawn-out whistles and pops. "What is this? Some kind of a joke?" spewed Beacon.

A second explosion shattered the cabin-door window. Beacon dropped onto the sloshing planks as luminescent blues, reds, greens, and yellows streaked overhead.

As the third explosion erupted atop their heads, Beacon grabbed Birdie by his coat collar, dragged him into the cabin, and shoved him below the console. "What in the name of all that is holy was all that?"

"Th-thunder?" quivered Birdie. His head was buried beneath his arms while his backside loomed up behind him like a mountaintop. Beacon popped up and smacked Birdie on the side of the mountain. "You ever see thunder spewing danger flares? That was cannon fire, you tweak-beaked snail bait."

"Well, once..."

"Shut up."

"Okay, Zeek."

Before Zeek could think what to do, another string of explosions followed by brightly colored lights and whistles rained down upon the stranded *Lucky Beacon*. Plumes of yellow smoke flooded into the wheelhouse, forcing the men back outside.

"You trying to kill us or what?" Beacon screamed across the pounding waves.

His answer came in a bombardment of cannon fire and explosions. Golden embers fluttered down from the sky like luminescent snowflakes, turning the *Lucky Beacon* into a glowing, deep-sea nugget. A resounding whistle, boom, and splintering of floorboards sent Beacon and Birdie scampering aft and down the flight of stairs leading to the rear hold.

Beacon stretched his neck and peeked up over the top step to get a better look at the scoundrels who were attacking him. The cloud cover and yellow haze made it impossible. "What kind of backward, landlubbing dingbatters are you people!" shouted the enraged captain. "Don't you know a dead boat when you see one? Birdie! Get up here!" He grabbed his man by his suspenders and hoisted him back onto the deck. "What did you do with my rifles?"

"I stowed 'em, like you said," twittered Birdie. "But you can't shoot 'em back, Zeek. What if it's a cruise ship full of people, or the Coast Guard, or the ranger, or the sheriff?"

Beacon grabbed Birdie with such force, he practically lifted the man out of his boots. "When's the last time you saw a cruise ship, or the Coast Guard, or the ranger, or the sheriff in a three-masted schooner? Duck!"

Both men hit the deck as a cannonball whizzed passed them, disappearing into the thick, gray nowhere. Birdie looked up, his crossed eyes desperate to focus on his boss. "Maybe they got themselves a new boat."

"That was a cannonball, you imbecile! Were you born this stupid, or did someone sit on your head at birth, because you've got the brainpower of a beached jellyfish. Those idiots are firing on us! Do you understand that? Whoever that is out there, they're firing on us! I want to shoot back! Now, go get my rifles! Duck!" Beacon shoved Birdie onto the floor as a four-pound cannonball ripped through the cabin, out the side window, and through the starboard rail.

"Did you see that? They're attacking us! They've declared war on my boat! You'll pay for that window and rail!"

"Who, Zeek? Who's gonna pay for that window and rail?"

"If I knew that, do you think I'd be down here kissing my toenails?" A cannonball whistled overhead, nicking the *Lucky Beacon's* antennae. "That does it! Birdie, go over to the rail and see who's firing on us."

"I'm not going over there. You go over there. You're the captain."

"You're bloody right, I'm the captain. And I just gave you an order. Go over there and see who's firing on us." Birdie popped his head up just as another cannonball whizzed overhead, landing on the deck twenty feet away from the stunned treasure seekers. Zeek pulled Birdie back into the hold. "Forget that. I have something better." Zeek remembered his cell phone and pulled it out of his coat pocket. "Blast it! No cells!"

Time is but a moment passed,

Future, thus, a moment lasts.

Illusion breeches time with "now,"

Proven by a touch or sound.

When hearts are full and rage is high,

We cross the boundaries "now"

did bind.

Think not that time alone does stand,

But intertwines when given hand.

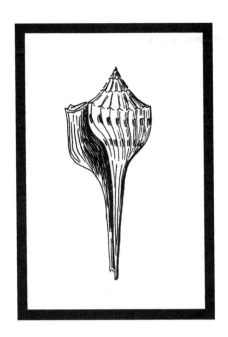

CHAPTER XV

Mrs. McNemmish and Blackbeard roared with laughter as cannonballs flew from the starboard side of the *Queen Anne's Revenge.* "This is wonderful fun," shouted a giddy Theodora.

"Aye, mate. Y'ar earning yer rank among The Brethren of the Coast, Theodora. I'm proud to have ye as a brother pirate, standing on me side. Keep the cannons firing, mates!" Mrs. McNemmish blushed. She stood a little taller along the gun deck as she watched Teach's crew load and reload the cannons. Pride swelled inside her each time Teach's voice thundered across the sky. "Fire!" he would bellow. And his men would jump into action.

After the guns were loaded, Pirate First Class McNemmish gleaned the privilege of yanking back the lanyard. She then jumped back and covered her ears as she watched the cannonball spew from the tube, fly through time, and split Beacon's night with a whistle and boom. Each precious explosion filled her heart with glee and the knowledge that Zeek Beacon was terrified and confused.

"BANG!" roared a cannon.

"That's for my Arthur's favorite pipe!" yelled the widow.

"BOOM!" exploded a cannonball.

"That's for the bully you've been all your life!"

BANG! BANG! BOOM!

Blackbeard clung to his mug with one hand, and with the other grabbed hold of a dangling rope and swung himself onto the outstretched arm of the bowsprit. Three hundred years earlier, following his violent and bloody death in Teach's Hole, his severed head dangled from a similar yardarm. But today, he looked down in awe at his newest recruit.

"Huzza, Theodora! Well done, mate!"

Israel Hands pulled a large, wooden belaying pin out of the gunwale and handed it to Mrs. McNemmish. "There ain't a speck of decent family piracy left in the scourge," he admitted about his great-grandson times three. "Have at 'im, McNemmish."

Theodora Teach McNemmish smiled graciously and took the wooden pin. "Thank you, Mr. Hands."

Theodora held the pin at its tapered end, stepped up to the rail, and wound her arm like a giant windmill blade. Letting go, the pin whirled away through the mist of time, above four centuries of tall-masted ghost ships, beyond the spirited *U.S.S. Monitor* and beyond the haunting *Carroll A. Deering*, two ghost ships seen by generations of O'cockers, beyond the two hundred sailing ships that sank or simply disappeared into memory, finally hitting its target squarely on his head.

"Bull's-eye!" crowed the lady. She alternated between throwing belaying pins and firing cannonballs until her ghostly arm was about to drop off from exhaustion. "I haven't had this much fun in nearly a century."

Blackbeard straddled the yardarm and toasted his company of men and one splendid lady. "To me crew!" hailed the buccaneer.

"To the Pirate King!" hailed his crew.

Zeek crawled out of the hold and raced across the deck on his hands and knees. Birdie was closing in behind him when a belaying pin appeared out of thin air and whacked Beacon on the back of his head. Beacon continued crawling until he reached the wheelhouse, then greeted Birdie with a smack on the head. "What did you hit me for?"

"I didn't hit ya, Zeek. It was a baseball bat."

"Baseball bat?" Beacon hit him again. "Very funny." He looked up in time to follow the trail of a cannonball that overshot the *Lucky* and plummeted into the ocean fifty feet away. "Ha! Missed me!" He never saw the wooden stake that soared through the open door and bopped him on the head. "Ow! What the...?" He grabbed his head and turned, when he got clobbered a third time. He grabbed Birdie by the throat. "Stop that!"

"Stop what, Zeek?"

"Stop hitting me!"

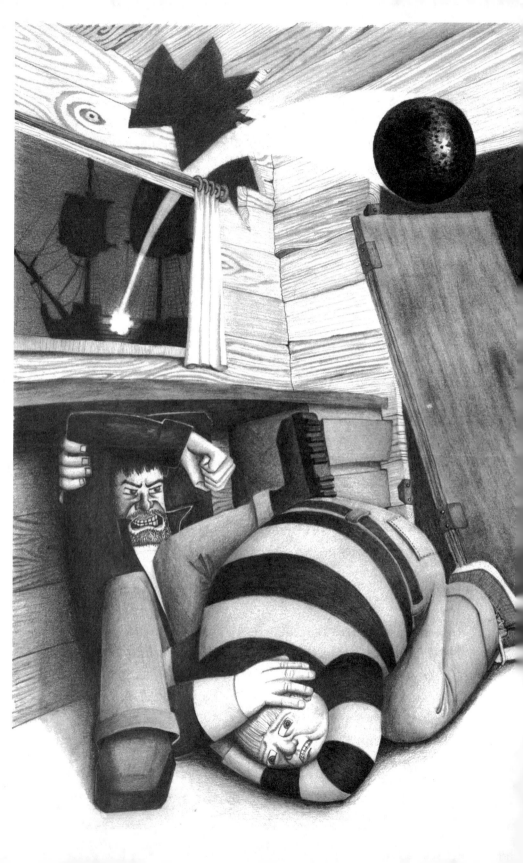

"I ain't hittin' ya, Zeek. It's them flyin' baseball bats!"

"What baseball bats? Blast it, Birdie, get me a rifle."

Birdie waddled eagerly down into the galley hold, quickly returning with an armload of weapons. Beacon's fingers trembled as he loaded his rifle and returned fire in the direction of the assault. "Grab a gun," he ordered Birdie.

"Who we gonna shoot, Zeek? 'Cause I don't see anybody to shoot. Just that big boat."

"Shoot anybody! I don't care who!"

A cannonball whistled overhead, then seemed to disappear. A second later, the sound of splintering floorboards sent both men scampering back outside.

"They are trying to kill us!" Beacon crouched behind the side rail and poised his rifle in the direction of the last cannon fire. Birdie knelt bravely beside him, poised with his rifle in the same direction. "Tell me who to shoot, Zeek."

"I don't know who to shoot. Just shoot at whoever's shooting at us."

"But I don't know who's shootin' at us, Zeek."

"Ahhhh!" Beacon growled something incoherent. "I'm in the middle of the ocean, my boat's being attacked, and Mustard the Wonder Dog is my first mate! Just shoot, for crying out loud! Shoot anything and anybody! There!" He pointed. "Shoot there!"

Both men loaded and fired weapons in between ducking and dodging rounds of cannonballs and rocketing belaying pins.

"We're gonna run out of ammo, Zeek. What do we do when we run out of ammo?"

"Offer you up as a sacrifice," he told the dimwit beside him. "If that doesn't work, pray. Duck!"

A stream of cannonballs blasted their way toward the *Lucky Beacon* as the stormy night sky brightened with swirling color. Whistles and booms shook the very foundation Birdie and Beacon clung to. Birdie grabbed the binoculars, peered through them briefly, then looked down at the floor in front of Beacon, having remembered the eye rule. He reached up and tapped him on the shoulder as more floorboards splintered around him.

"What?" screamed Beacon. Across the bow, he yelled, "You'll pay for that!"

"Uh, there's another boat coming, Zeek. It's coming straight at us from the other direction. What do we do, Zeek? Should I fire at them, too, Zeek?"

Beacon jumped up and grabbed the binoculars out of Birdie's hand. "Oh no, you don't!" he ranted. "You are *not* starting with me!" He leaned out over the railing and with his last few rounds fired in the direction of the oncoming boat. He then raced to the opposite deck and fired at the schooner. "Birdie!" he commanded. "Break out the pistols!"

"But Zeek, I think that's Rudy's boat." Birdie jumped up and down and waved at the approaching Coast Guard cutter as it came into full view. "Rudy! Over here, Rudy!"

"Get down!" screamed Beacon. "It's a trick! They're trying to draw our attention away from the other ship so it can finish us off!"

"Zeek Beacon! Throw down your weapons!" blasted a voice over a loudspeaker. "This is the Coast Guard. We're coming aboard!"

Keith Cutler and Pete Scarborough stood beside Rudy Howard as their cutter pulled up to the back of the *Lucky Beacon*.

"Don't listen to them!" Beacon told Birdie. "Just keep shooting at the ship."

"What in the world is he shooting at?" asked Keith.

Rudy rotated his searchlight, but saw that the *Lucky Beacon*, though shrouded by cloud, was in no threat of danger. He pulled the microphone off the wall clip and held it to his mouth. "Stop firing!" he ordered Beacon. "Throw down your weapons and stand with your hands above your heads. We are going to board your boat!"

Zeek Beacon crawled aft and peeked over the top of the back rail. "Go away!" he called out. "Can't you see they're trying to kill me? They'll kill you, too! Get down! Get down!" He waved his arm as one would do to tell someone else to hit the deck, then crawled back to Birdie and continued firing at the schooner.

"What has he been drinking?" said Pete.

Keith took the microphone. "Zeek! This is Keith Cutler. There is no one firing on you. Just put down your weapons and stand up!"

Beacon and Birdie dropped to the deck as another cannonball screamed past them, landing with an explosion on the starboard side of the *Lucky Beacon*.

"Did you see that? Did you see that?" Beacon yelled hysterically. "They're firing cannons at a grounded ship! Don't just stand there, fire back!"

"Grounded ship? Cannons?" Keith aimed the light at the *Lucky's* waterline. "He's floating in the middle of the ocean and firing at a storm cloud!"

Rudy shook his head. "He's lost his mind and taken Birdie with him."

"That wasn't a far walk," chuckled Pete.

Rudy cut the engines and told Pete and Keith to get

ready to board the *Lucky*. "Zeek! Listen to me! There is no one firing at you. There are no other boats anywhere around. No one's going to hurt either of you. Now put down your weapons, stand up, and wait for us to board your craft." He waited a moment, but neither man moved. "I'm warning you, Beacon. Give it a rest!"

"It's a trick!" hollered Beacon. "You just want us to think you really don't see anything so we'll get blasted!" He turned to Birdie. "They're trying to trick us."

"Okay, Zeek. I think I know who's shootin' at us, Zeek. It's those folks we can't see, on the ship that ain't there no more. And those people on Rudy's Coast Guard cutter ain't really tellin' us to surrender to those folks on that other boat, neither, because they only think they're here talkin' from their boat about the boat that ain't here because they really aren't, they only think they are, like you said."

Beacon paused for a moment, then reached over and smacked Birdie on his head. "Didn't I tell you never to think?" He knelt behind the sidewall and waited for the next round of cannon fire to attack his craft. He waited for the flash of light, the whistle, and the explosion. But a minute passed, and no cannonballs split the sky with yellowing smoke or blasted their way through levels of wooden planking. No belaying pins appeared and disappeared, or bopped him on the head. No colorful starbursts rained golden snowflakes. Now, except for the very real Coast Guard cutter, the grounded *Lucky Beacon* was the only craft in the water, swaying to the rhythm of the storm-tossed waves.

Beacon shook his head with bewilderment. He motioned for Birdie to lay down his weapon and stand up.

"I ain't standin' up. You stand up."

"You stand up first," said Beacon. "That's an order."

"Right. So if it's a trick and they blow my head off, you'll know to stay down."

"Exactly."

Birdie smiled. "See? I ain't as dumb as I look." Birdie put down his gun and slowly rose to his feet. When no one shot at him, he attempted surrendering, only he didn't know who to surrender to first. He raised his hands above his head and turned in the direction of the cannon fire, but no one was there. But when he turned in the direction of the Coast Guard cutter, he wasn't sure they were there either, so he turned back in the direction of the cannon fire. Then he turned back to the Coast Guard so as not to get into trouble in case they really were there. He continued to turn back and forth until Keith Cutler jumped aboard the *Lucky Beacon* and secured Birdie by his shoulders. "You can stop surrendering now," he told him gently.

Birdie put down his hands and grinned. "Okay, Keith."

Rudy jumped aboard and grabbed Zeek. "You're under arrest," he said as he locked him into handcuffs.

"For what?" growled Beacon.

"At the moment, for unlawful target practice. Do you want your rights read to you, or do you know them by heart?"

"You should be arresting them, not me!" argued the man. "They tried to kill us! They've been firing on us for hours. Look at my boat! It's a wreck! I came out here to do some fishing and ran aground in the storm. I get fired on, and I'm the one arrested?"

"I wasn't aware you needed an armory to go fishing," said Rudy. "Besides, look around. You're not grounded, and there's no one else out here. I don't know who you think you were firing on, but they're not here now."

"You mean, you don't see them either?" asked Birdie. "Well, that's good, 'cause they kept shootin' those cannonballs at us, boom, boom, boom, and we never even saw who they were. And they threw baseball bats."

"Belaying pins," Beacon corrected him.

"Belaying pins?" retorted Rudy.

"Yeah, belaying pins," recounted Birdie. His eyes grew large and animated as they wiggled around from all the excitement. "Those pins came flyin' through the air like my granny's pie roller when she had a burr up her skirt and hit Zeek right smack in the middle of his head. Wanna see his bump?"

"That's quite all right," said Keith. He left Beacon and Birdie and strolled around the *Lucky*, carefully checking it both inside and out. "Cannonballs? Belaying pins? Give me a break." He returned to Zeek, disgusted. "There's absolutely nothing wrong with your boat a little less fist and some engine repair won't fix. There's not a scratch on her, as far as I can see. And what's this business about being grounded? There's not a sand pile for eighty miles of here."

"What?" Beacon's eyes blazed. He was furious. He ran from one side of the boat to the other, examining the floors, side rails, and ceilings. With the clouds beginning to clear, and the cutter's lights aimed directly at his craft, he could see for himself that the *Lucky Beacon* was in good condition. And it was rocking! "I am telling you, I ran aground and there was a ship right out there that has been firing cannonballs at us since midnight! They attacked my boat!"

"Well, there's no one attacking you now," shouted Rudy. "Look. Drop anchor and we'll send for a tow in the morning. Maybe they'll find something. What did the boat look like? I can't believe I'm asking this," he said with a roll of his eyes.

Beacon was hesitant. "I'm not sure. I only got a quick look."

"Well? What did it look like?"

"I told you, I'm not sure!"

"I know," said Birdie.

"Shut up, Bird twit."

Rudy took Birdie to one side. "That must have been some boat that was firing on you guys. Are you all right?"

"I'm really hungry," said Birdie.

"Well, we'll make sure you get something to eat as soon as we get to shore. Uh, listen, Birdie. Why don't you tell me about the boat that was firing on you? That way, we can find it and arrest those scoundrels. It's okay. You can tell me. I'll clear it with Zeek later."

"It looked like them boats up in Jamestown. All them fancy sails just breezin' around like Granny's bedsheets. With all the fire and smoke, it was hard to see for sure. But Zeek had a hissy fit. 'Cause we didn't know who to shoot. Zeek told me just to shoot in the direction of anybody shooting at us."

"And you're sure you heard these shots?" asked Rudy.

"Sure I did. They were shooting cannonballs that went straight through the floor."

"But the floor's just fine. Look for yourself." Rudy pointed a finger at the floor that wrapped around the outside deck. "See?"

"Oh. Well, maybe when we were seeing whether your cutter was really here, the people from the other boat that was here came aboard and fixed it before they weren't here anymore."

Rudy puckered his lips, trying hard not to smile. "Thank you, Birdie. You were a big help."

"It was a three-masted schooner," Beacon murmured disgustedly.

"A what?"

"You heard me. It was a three-masted schooner. Must have reappeared in the Triangle, or something. I want them held responsible for damages!"

"Have you lost your mind? The Coast Guard is not putting out an A.P.B. for a three-masted schooner that reappeared in some ghostly apparition. The county would lock me up alongside of you."

Keith returned to the top deck and pulled Pete and Rudy to one side. "I haven't a clue what's gone on here, but the galley's fully stocked, and there's enough diving equipment to last them a month. And look at this." He pulled the ancient map out of its sleeve and showed it to the men. "I think this thing's for real." He put it back into the sleeve and tucked it under his arm. "I checked the stow. He's got some of the widow's things, but no sign of the kids."

Pete grabbed Beacon by the arm and shoved him onto the Coast Guard cutter. Rudy escorted Birdie. With the *Lucky Beacon* anchored and locked down, the cutter was turned back toward the island. He prayed the children were still alive.

I am the bird who flies on high,

I am the cloud, the rain, the sky.

I am the life that bears new fruit,

I am the song upon the lute.

I am the soul who tasted life,

I am the sailor, the pirate, the wife.

I am the smile upon your face,

You are the future, so full of grace.

CHAPTER XVI

R anger Garrish hung up the phone and turned to the family and friends who were nervously pacing throughout his house. "That was Wilson. They're *not* going to evacuate the island, but they are shutting down the ferries until the storm passes."

"Did he say anything about the kids?" asked Elizabeth. "Did anyone see them leave the island?"

"No one has seen them since the meeting."

"That was hours ago! What about the other ferries? Maybe they took the Cedar Island or Swan Quarter ferry. They were really upset about poor old Mrs. McNemmish disappearing. Daniel could hardly speak, he was so upset. Did Wilson check with the other ferries?"

"I did," said Teddy. He and Mustard stepped into the house, bringing a gust of wind and rain with them. "There hasn't been a walker or a biker all day." He grabbed Mustard and dried him off before the dog had time to shake. "It is *really* coming down out there. Wherever they are, I hope they're inside."

"I can't stand this," cried Marylee Austin. "Somebody has to have seen them somewhere. It's an island, for heaven's sake." She rearranged the Garrish's sofa pillows for the fourth time in five minutes. "The entire village of Ocracoke is only one mile long and a half-mile wide. How do you lose four children in a village that's only one mile long and a half-mile wide?"

"The *village* is one mile long," Todd reminded her. "The island is *thirteen* miles long and has about a million places to hide."

"Why in the world would they want to hide?" asked Elizabeth.

Todd and Teddy glanced at each other. "Let's just say, we have some pretty good ideas," said the sheriff.

Jeffrey Tillet sat quietly in a corner of the room. His long, gentle fingers sanded the delicate neck of a hand-carved heron. "Mark will know we're looking for him," he said calmly and without looking up. "He can't see two feet in front of him and he's as silent as a shadow, but he'll know we're looking for him."

"I don't understand any of this," cried Marylee. "Why don't they call? Stefanie loves to talk on the phone, and she would never go anywhere without telling me."

"Billy must be starving," said Drum O'Neal. "He's usually on his sixth or seventh meal by now." Drum had stopped by the Pony Island Restaurant on his way over and brought enough food to feed everyone, including the children if they should happen to return. "If Billy can smell the chicken and hush puppies, he'll find his way here."

Marylee dabbed her eyes with a tissue. "Billy could stand to miss a few meals. But poor Stefanie will wilt away to nothing."

"This is getting us nowhere." Teddy bounced up off the sofa, grabbed his rain gear, and called for Mustard. "I'm going over to the widow's shack. Maybe some of Mark's pirate sense will rub off on me."

Todd kissed Elizabeth and grabbed his parka. "I'm going with you."

The biting wind and rain slowed their pace as they walked west along the giant loop that ran from Styron's Store, past the Ocracoke Lighthouse, and back around toward Miss Miller's house. Mrs. McNemmish's shack was at the far west bend of the loop that jutted out into the sound, halfway between the ditch at Silver Lake and Teach's Hole. Mustard was the first to reach the shack. He ran back and forth from her side lawn to the street, barking excitedly.

"What is it, boy?" Teddy and Todd trotted behind Mustard to the side of the house where they spotted the four bicycles stashed behind a thick row of prickly yucca.

"Thank goodness!" said Todd. "They must be hiding inside." He raced to the door, but when he reached for the key, he discovered it missing from his key chain. He knocked several times, but when no one answered the door, he rammed it open with his shoulder. "Daniel! Billy! Are you guys in here?" He and Teddy searched every inch of the tiny house, but realized immediately that the shack was empty.

Teddy called his office and reported that he and the ranger had located the four bikes, but that no one was inside the shack. Todd followed up with a call to his house.

"We haven't found them yet," he told his wife disappointedly. "But I think we're onto something."

"Hey, Todd. Look at this." The sheriff was in the widow's bedroom pointing down at her bed. "Her bedspread is missing." He looked up and gawked at the ranger incredulously. "Lordy! You don't think they took her out of the coffin and wrapped her up in the bedspread, do you?"

"No! Why would they do that? And why would they leave their bikes here and go somewhere else?"

"None of this makes any sense." Teddy strolled across the shack looking for other things that might be missing or out of place, but the rest of the house looked intact. He stopped beside the widow's trunk and picked up a single, white seed that was lying on the floor beside it. "This wasn't here this morning. I swept the place clean myself."

"That's a Snow Duck seed."

Teddy glanced up at the mantle. The eight Snow Ducks—the last ones ever to be made—stood silently waiting to go home with their assigned child. Each duck still possessed its single, white belly-button seed. "This is getting us nowhere," said Teddy. "I want to go over to the Coast Guard station and see if Rudy's found out anything." He led Mustard and the ranger out of the house, then fought the storm back to Todd's house where he called for his car. The sheriff had just finished a hot cup of coffee when his assistant arrived with the vehicle.

"I checked out all the rental cottages and mobile homes," he whispered to the sheriff. "No one has seen the kids since they left the school. Sorry."

Teddy dropped off his assistant, then he and Todd headed toward the Coast Guard station on the other side of the creek. Silver Lake had swelled over the top of the sandy street surrounding the tiny harbor and was already spilling onto front lawns and store paths.

Teddy steered toward Oyster Creek and pulled into the parking lot that faced the harbor just as a streak of lightning flashed with such power, the entire creek side lit up. The ear-splitting crack of thunder shook the car with such force, the motor shut down and the car alarm went off.

Teddy reached for the ignition key to turn off the alarm when a bolt of blue-white lightning flashed directly in front of the car, connecting sky to water. The simultaneous explosion sent both men cowering beneath their arms while the car alarm continued to blare. Neither man saw that for one brief moment, night had turned into day.

"Todd!" Teddy whispered so low, the ranger could barely hear him above the overhead rumbling and wailing alarm. "Todd! Look at the ignition key. It's firing!" The ignition key looked like it had been dipped in glow-in-the-dark paint, held under a light, then brought into a dark closet where it lit up like a Christmas bulb.

"That's the weirdest thing I've ever seen," the ranger exclaimed, his eyes glued to the glowing object. "Is it hot?"

Teddy's quivering fingers reached out and timidly touched the key. "It's stone cold!" He waited several minutes for the glow to wane, then cautiously touching it a second time, turned off the alarm. "How weird was that?"

"No weirder than the rest of this week. My mom would say 'twas a week of upside-downs and backwards.' Only with a Southern-Irish-Australian accent."

Teddy pulled the key out of the ignition and turned to step out of the car, when he stopped abruptly and looked back at the ranger. "What did you say?"

"When?"

"Just now. You said we were having a week of upside-downs and backwards. Oh, my lord!" He slapped a hand to his head, put the key back into the ignition, and started up the car.

"Where are we going?"

"It's on backward!" shouted the sheriff. He careened out of the parking lot and flew back onto the flooded street toward the widow's house. "I can't believe I didn't see it! Todd, you're a genius!" Swerving around the harbor, he hydroplaned back onto Lighthouse Road, glided across Styron's front lawn, sloshed past the white, stucco lighthouse, and fishtailed around the top of the loop. "I knew something was bothering me about the lock, but I couldn't figure it out. It's on backward!"

"Teddy, slow down! What lock? What are you talking about?"

Teddy threw the car into third gear and sailed onto the widow's front lawn. The car slid sideways, then backward, bumping to a stop between the giant limbs of a three-hundred-year-old cedar.

Both men jerked forward, catching themselves on the dashboard. Mustard fell off the back seat and onto the floor with a loud thud. "Nice landing," Todd spit out sarcastically.

"Come on!" Teddy jumped out of the car and opened the door for Mustard. "Hurry up!" He ran into the widow's house and threw on the kitchen lights.

"What is wrong with you?" panted Todd.

Teddy grabbed the trunk lock in his hand and showed it to the ranger. "See? It's on backward! Todd, I put this lock on myself. Somebody took it off and put it back on the wrong way!"

"So you think the kids opened the trunk and closed it back up again? What for?"

"I don't know. I don't even know if they're the ones who fooled around with the lock, but it's a start." He quickly opened and removed the lock, then he and Todd pushed open the heavy lid. Todd nearly fell in.

"Whoa!" Teddy grabbed the back of Todd's coat and yanked him backward. Gasping in shock and amazement, the two men got onto their knees and gaped into the black void.

"If that's not a whale with two heads!" declared Todd. "Did you know about this?"

"No, I didn't know about this. No one knew about this." Teddy stared into the bottom of the trunk, blinking as if he were trying to awake from a comical dream. "Do you know how long this chest has been sitting here?" he asked, speaking too fast to expect Todd to answer. "This chest has been sitting here with the lid closed since Noah's Ark was christened! I don't think one person on this island has ever gotten a look inside."

"Theodora used to tell us there were bodies in it. Oh, my God! *Bodies!*" Todd shot a horrifying glance at Teddy. "The kids!" He leaned over the ladder and screamed at the top of his lungs, but the response was as silent as the bottom was black. "I'm going down."

"Wait a minute. How could they be down there if the lock was put back on?"

"I don't know. But I'll tell you this. Those four kids have been missing all day, their bikes are outside, and this trunk has been tampered with. There's no way I'm not going down there to check it out. Are you coming?"

"Just a second." Teddy rushed to the telephone and called Elizabeth Garrish. "Tell Drum and Jeffrey to meet us over at the widow's house, and to bring ropes, water, flashlights, and a first-aid kit."

"Did you find them?" asked the voice on the other end of the phone.

"Not yet. But you're not going to believe what we did find. If Rudy calls, let him know where we are."

By the time Teddy hung up, Todd had climbed down the ladder using his small keychain flashlight as a guide.

"You are not going to believe what's down there," he panted as he climbed back up. "It's a tunnel. And there are footprints down there. Lots of them. And look at this!" He handed Teddy a small piece of paper that had been dropped onto the ground. "It's a cough-drop wrapper. And it still smells like cherry, which means it can't be too old. Didn't Marylee say Stefanie was sick?"

"That could be hers. We'll have to ask Marylee."

Drum and Jeffrey flew through the front door, soaked to the skin and reeling from a jolt of earsplitting thunder. Mustard jumped to his feet and greeted them.

"What a mess," said Drum, shaking off the rain. "Did you find them?"

"No. But we think we know where they might be. Take a look at that." He pointed toward Mrs. McNemmish's treasure chest.

Drum walked over to the trunk and stared into the gaping hole. "Well, I'll be a fly-fishin' worm hook! If that ain't the dangburndest thing I've ever seen. What do you make of that, Jeffrey?"

Jeffrey took a long, hard look. "You think the kids are down there?"

"We don't know. All we do know is that the kids' bikes are outside, and someone opened the trunk and put the lock back on backward. So either they went down there and came back up, or they're still down there and somebody locked them in."

"Locked them in?"

Before Teddy could explain, Todd hung up the phone and joined them. "I just spoke with Marylee, and that *is* Stefanie's cough-drop wrapper. That at least proves they were down there."

"Wait a minute! Why would somebody lock them in?" asked Drum.

"We don't know. But I have a really bad feeling it has something to do with the widow's disappearance." Teddy hesitated for a moment, then spoke with some embarrassment. "I probably should have said something sooner, but Theodora left the kids a letter before she died."

"A letter? What did it say?" asked Todd.

"I never got to see it. I just thought it was one of her stories. But when I asked the kids about it after the school meeting, I couldn't get a straight answer from any of them. Now I think it had something to do with why they took her body and why they disappeared."

"Why they took her body!" asked Drum. "What makes you think they took her body?"

Teddy rolled his eyes. "I know when a duck's flown over my car, Drum. The kids left their calling cards all over the island."

"We're wasting time," said Todd. He wrapped several coils of rope around his shoulder and filled his coat pockets with water bottles, flashlights, and the first-aid kit. "Drum, you and Jeffrey stay up here in case we need you. And for heaven's sake, don't let anyone in. Especially the mothers."

Teddy followed Todd into the trunk, told Mustard to mind his manners, and headed down the ladder. He turned on one of his high-powered flashlights halfway down.

When the men reached the bottom, both Todd and Teddy were forced to stoop over as they proceeded into the low-ceilinged tunnel. Todd called out the children's names as he came to the first sharp turn. A few minutes later, Teddy called out. They alternated calling every few minutes, but with the same unsuccessful result.

Todd took the lead and sped through the first several corridors. Unfortunately, the reflection from his flashlight was so strong against the glistening walls, he ran smack into two of them. He stopped so abruptly, Teddy rammed into him.

"Will you either slow down or let me lead?" barked Teddy.

"You don't move fast enough."

"I don't slam into walls, either."

"No, you just slam into trees." Todd hurried through the next few corridors, stopping suddenly when he turned a corner. "Shoot! The ceiling lowered again. I'm not going to have any hair left on the top of my head if I keep scraping it off."

"These walls are amazing," huffed Teddy, finally stopping to catch his breath. "All those years of shell collecting, and this is what she did with them."

"Theodora did not make this tunnel," said Todd.

"She may not have made it, but this is the same cement that's on the Bobby Garrish tree, and she did make that."

"One mystery at a time," Todd told the sheriff. "Come on. You can rest after we find the kids." He was about to turn another corner when his right shoe rolled over something that was strewn across the floor. He caught his balance by grabbing hold of the corner wall. In doing so, the beam of his light and corner of his eye picked up the outline of a sleeping figure. "Daniel?" he called out hopefully. He lowered the beam of his flashlight and let out a surprised yelp. "Oh, my God!"

"What's the matter? Did you find them?"

Teddy caught up with Todd, and the two of them stared down in utter horror at the unfortunate being in the ragged clothes and red handkerchief. "This is awful! What if the kids saw this? Lordy, can you imagine Stefanie's reaction? She must have gone ballistic!" He envisioned all four children coming across this obvious display of death and desertion and being totally scared out of their minds. "Teddy! You don't think Theodora and Arthur..."

"No! Of course not! Besides, it takes forever to turn into a skeleton. And look at the way he's dressed. Not exactly beachwear." A moment later, Teddy turned toward the ranger, his face elated. "I think this guy was a pirate!" He thought for a moment then grabbed Todd by his shoulders. "This is the tunnel! Our kids found the tunnel!"

"What tunnel?"

"*The* tunnel. Remember when we were kids and someone wrote a story about Blackbeard having a tunnel somewhere in North Carolina, but no one believed him because no one ever found it? I think this is the tunnel! Todd! This is great stuff!"

"Do you think we could find the kids before you get all emotional on me?"

"Sorry."

Less enthused than his friend, Todd carefully stepped around the skeleton and continued his search. After finding the second skeleton in a heap against the wall, he chuckled to himself. "I wouldn't want to be in Daniel's shoes right now. Stefanie and skeletons can't be good."

As the men walked on a little farther, the pungent odor of rotten seaweed began making Teddy nauseous. "What's that smell?"

"Seventh-grade science class," grunted Todd, breathing into his coat sleeve. "Sorry. It's the first thing I thought of. Uh-oh. Teddy, look." He flooded the pathway with light surrounding a yellow handkerchief and an old bottle. When he lifted up the handkerchief, the body of the bludgeoned bat fell out. "There's still damp blood on it," he said, rubbing the congealed fluid between his fingers. He lifted the bottle and examined it closely with the beam of his flashlight. "There's blood and hair stuck to the bottle. It looks like Billy's hair." He cupped his hands and screamed into the darkness. "Billy! Daniel! Hey! Meehonkey! Can you guys hear me?" But once again, a disappointing silence was the only response.

The men stopped walking when the muted rumble of thunder sent a vibration throughout the tunnel that was so powerful, sand rained down from the ceiling. "I don't know what went on down here, but I don't trust this tunnel," said Teddy, brushing off the flecks of cement that had dripped onto his head and shoulders. He aimed his flashlight down the corridor and saw that it was about to make another sharp turn. "I'm sorry Todd, but we have to go back."

"What? No! If the kids came this far, they probably kept on walking."

Teddy felt another vibration and looked around urgently. "Todd, we've been down here almost an hour and it's going to take that long to get back to the shack. We need help. If the kids are down here and these walls collapse, we'll get buried along with them if we don't have the right equipment."

"I'm not leaving without the kids."

"They may not be down here! They might have gone back upstairs and locked the trunk themselves."

"I'm not leaving until I find out. You can do whatever you want."

A new look of panic rushed across Teddy's face when the floor began to vibrate and small rivulets of water began to bleed from the walls. "We're out of here, Todd."

"I'm not leaving without the kids! There's no way this tunnel goes much farther. And look! More footprints. Maybe they're looking for another way out. They probably fell asleep for a while. That's why they're not answering."

"We need help, Todd. We can't get the kids out if we're buried alive with them. Now, let's go!"

Dejected, Todd was forced to agree. If the kids had gone on ahead, they might be running out of air and would need oxygen. After a few more unrewarded calls, the men reluctantly turned back.

"Dear God," prayed Todd. "Please let them be alive."

Dreams of riches ruled their hearts,

Golden trinkets, sassy tarts.

Ships with plundered goods were seen

As easy prey, in pirate dreams.

Dreaming takes us for a ride,

Our hopes and prayers are

locked inside.

We dream of things like peace

and love,

Then ask for guidance from above.

CHAPTER XVII

T he good news is, we know they were down there," Todd told Drum and Jeffrey as he stepped out of the trunk and back into Mrs. McNemmish's shack. "The bad news is, we don't know where they are, or if they're still down there, or whether or not the tunnel will hold."

"We're going to need help finding them and getting them out of there," Teddy added quickly.

"I'll go down," said Drum.

"I'll go with him," volunteered Jeffrey.

"Not without oxygen and some shoring tools. It's too dangerous. If the tunnel collapses, we're going to need shovels and picks to dig them out. Drum, call B.J. and have her meet us here with the fire truck. And tell her to bring all the help she can round up. In the meantime..."

"B.J.'s on a call," Drum interrupted. "Elizabeth phoned here and said that lightning hit the Bobby Garrish tree. The whole tree caught fire. There's sparks all over the Toothache Tree, The Village Craftsmen, and the Methodist Church!"

"Was anyone hurt? Are the cemeteries all right?" asked Todd.

"Seems so. But you know what's weird? When they went there to put out the tree fire, the boards on the bottom of the tree had caught fire, too. They burned right through the ground and fell into some kind of ditch or shaft underneath the tree. Elizabeth said that B.J. said that Chris said the drop looked to be about eleven feet deep."

"Eleven feet?" Todd's stomach did a sudden flip-flop, and he grabbed Drum's arm. "Are you sure they said eleven feet?"

Drum nodded. "That's what she said."

Teddy and Todd looked at each other and shouted in unison. "There's a second entrance! Quick! Grab the ropes and lights and let's go!" Teddy had everyone gather up the equipment, then shoved them out the door and into his car.

"Where are we going? What about the kids?" asked Drum. "If Billy's down in that tunnel, I want to go down and look for him. I don't care how dangerous you think it is."

"We think Bobby's tree is another way into the tunnel," Todd explained as Teddy pulled back onto the flooded street. He quickly described the cement tunnel, the footprints, the skeletons, and the dead bat. He left out the part about Billy's hair being on the bloodied bottle. He figured Drum was upset enough, and the information wouldn't help the situation. He stopped talking and grabbed hold of the dashboard as the car skidded and slid down the flooded, one-way street the wrong way. "You could get a ticket for this," he told the sheriff.

"I'll write myself one in the morning. You want to get there, don't you?" He careened down Schoolhouse Road and onto the Howard Street parking lot a mere minute and a half after leaving the widow's shack.

Todd, Drum, and Jeffrey jumped out of the car and said a quiet prayer of thanks for having survived the harrowing trip. Teddy and Mustard slipped out of the car unscathed and ready to go to work.

"Todd, you check out the hole underneath the tree while I talk to Chris and B.J.," called Teddy, already jogging up the waterlogged dirt path alongside of Mustard. "Drum, you and Jeffrey follow me."

Todd sloshed through three inches of fallen rain while still fighting the torrential downfall. As he neared the Bobby Garrish tree, it was immediately apparent that the fire was out, but the air was thick with smoke and soggy ash. The bottom of the tree had burned away, leaving a giant, triangular hole that hollowed upward and into the first spread of branches. The opening of the shaft below the tree between the widespread roots and burned-up boards was four feet wide. Without light, it was impossible to see anything below. Todd stood up and pulled a piece of dry bark off the underside of a tree branch that kept watch over one of the nearby cemeteries. Reaching into his pocket, he pulled out a lighter and lit the bark. He dropped it into the shaft and was rewarded with enough firelight for enough time to see that the shaft dropped down a good ten or eleven feet, but mounds of sand and chunks of cement blocked any wider view. It was easy to see the confusion in measuring its depth, but it didn't change the fact that it looked to be a second entrance into the same tunnel. "Daniel! Billy! Hello! Can anybody hear me?" The disappointing answer came in silence just as the bark died out and the shaft turned as black as the soot surrounding him.

Meanwhile, Teddy, Mustard, Drum, and Jeffrey ran after firefighters B.J. Howard and Chris Gaskill as they were backing out of the opposite end of Howard Street, just shy of John Ivy's chicken pen.

"Hey! Stop the truck!" Teddy whistled and flailed his arms as he ran. "Hey, y'all! Stop the truck!" He caught up to the hook and ladder as it turned onto Firehouse Road where it would be put to bed for the night. "Chris, we need your help," gasped the sheriff. He bent over to catch his breath but put a hand up to show he wasn't finished talking. "You have to bring the truck back over to the Bobby Garrish tree."

Chris opened the window and glared at Teddy. He was tired and irritated from having just put out a major fire. "What for? It's almost midnight!"

"I know what time it is." The sheriff spoke quickly and urgently. "I need you to lower me down the hole into that shaft."

"You what?!"

"We have to hurry!" added Drum, as he caught up with Teddy.

Jeffrey nodded agreement while heaving for air.

Chris frowned. "Look. We're not lowering anybody

down anything," he objected. "Whatever it is, it'll have to wait until tomorrow."

"The kids will be dead by then!" said Teddy.

B.J. leaned over and spoke to her friends through the window. "What kids? The missing kids?"

"We think they're down that shaft," explained Teddy. "And if we don't get them out of there now, they're going to either drown or suffocate. God help us. I hope they're still alive as it is."

Todd ran up to the truck and tapped Teddy on the shoulder. "Look at this," he said, breathing heavily. He held out a piece of cement that was an exact duplicate of the stuff used on the walls and ceiling in the tunnel.

"That's the plug from the tree," said B.J. "Miss Theo put it there about a century ago."

Todd shook his head. "That piece is still over by the tree. This came from inside the top of the shaft. I'm telling you, it's another way in!"

"Another way into what?" asked Chris.

"Please, y'all. We don't have time to explain. Those kids could be under all that rubble."

"Wait a minute, wait a minute!" halted Chris. "No one knew that shaft was even down there until the tree caught fire."

"Someone did," said Jeffrey, pointing to the cement lining.

"Look. The kids got locked into a tunnel that starts underneath the widow's shack. We think this is a second way in," explained Teddy.

"When we went down to look for them, they had walked so far ahead, we had to double back." Todd looked and sounded frazzled. "Listen, y'all. The tunnel is starting to collapse, and if we don't get down there soon and get them out, we're going to lose them."

Chris put his head in his hands and groaned. "I'm not even sure the shaft will hold up if I lower you down. If you haven't noticed, there's a hurricane going on. It would take days to shore it up safely."

"We don't have days!" yelled Drum. "Just do it!"

Teddy appealed to both of them. "If we're wrong about the kids being down there, we're wrong and you can sue us. But if we're right, those four kids down there could be dying."

"This is nuts!" Chris waited an instant, but then reached for his walkie-talkie. "Wade, get back over here. And bring Alton. Never mind why, just get over here." He turned to the four men awaiting his answer. "I can't believe I let you talk me into this. Okay, tell us what to do."

B.J. pulled the truck back around Schoolhouse Road and began unloading equipment with the help of Chris, Teddy, and the three parents. In less than ten minutes, Todd and B.J. were strapped into rescue harnesses. One at a time, they crawled underneath the remainder of the tree and were slowly lowered down into the shaft. Chris and Drum anchored themselves using nearby trees and lowered the climbers on belaying ropes. Jeffrey and Teddy latched high-powered flashlights off the lowest branches of the tree and aimed them down below.

"Can you see anything?" called Drum. "Can you see the kids?"

"There's too much sand and smoke!" shouted B.J.

"We still need more light!" Todd yelled up to Chris. He

squinted through the smoke and rain at the mound of sand, cement, and burnt wood that was blocking the entrance into the main tunnel. "It looks like part of the ceiling collapsed. Wait a minute! I see a broken lantern! Send somebody over to the widow's house and see if any of her lanterns are missing!"

"I'll send Alton!"

B.J., still suspended from her rope, swung and grabbed hold of a large shell that protruded from the shaft wall that was farthest from the tree. She shouted the children's names, but her voice was muffled by the storm and mounds of sand.

"If we can dig a hole big enough to get through the entrance, we might be able to see the kids, or at least yell to them," said Todd. He stopped talking and coughed into his coat sleeve. "I can't breathe down here. We need oxygen masks and headlamps." He closed his eyes and silently agonized over what the children, if they were still alive, were going through. With luck, the storm put out any tunnel fire they might have endured. It would have also provided the kids with much-needed water. He yanked on the rope, signaling to Chris and Drum to pull the two of them back up. When he was out of the shaft, Todd rinsed the smoke and soot out of his scorched eyes and mouth.

B.J. gulped down a bottle of water. "I really hope the kids aren't down there. We were only down there for fifteen minutes and couldn't breathe."

"I know the situation," snapped the frustrated ranger. He was tired and scared and angry with himself for not continuing his search from the widow's side while the others searched the shaft.

Wade Jackson and Alton Scarborough returned to the scene of the fire and cave-in, having just left a half-hour before. They were quickly filled in, and Alton sped over to the widow's shack to check on the lanterns. Within minutes, it was confirmed that the widow's antique lanterns were both missing from the shack.

"You're going to need handpicks down there," said Wade. He pulled them off the truck, and then followed Teddy into the shaft. Extra oxygen masks, shovels, backboards, and a trauma kit were set out and ready to be lowered at a moment's notice.

Teddy and Wade chopped at the cement and sand mound, removing as much debris from the tunnel entrance as possible while hanging from their harnesses. After half an hour of digging and hacking, they were lifted out of the shaft, replaced by Chris and Drum.

As the night and hours dredged on, the wind and rain continued. The belaying ropes were slick and difficult to manage, and the sand was soaked to ten times its normal weight. Each time the pickaxes were passed on to the next crew, someone would call out the children's names, but with the same, silent result. Sometimes, only the sound of the pounding rain and the chopping of axes filled the silent void. Nobody spoke about their concerns for the children, but everyone had them.

Todd and Teddy were close to breaching the barrier when word got out about the possibility of the children being trapped down the mysterious shaft. It wasn't long before villagers began to congregate on Howard Street and Schoolhouse Road. They brought food and coffee for the rescuers and lit candles for the children, hoping the flames would carry their prayers to heaven. Many people told stories about the kids and about Mrs. McNemmish. Eventually, the Coast Guard was alerted and sent over two men with extra masks and more rescue equipment. Two helicopters were made ready and were waiting to take the children to the hospital in Elizabeth City just as soon as they were found.

Todd chipped at a piece of cement that fell away, taking several feet of cement with it. The tiniest spark of light, no bigger than a speck of dust, flickered from the other side. "I'm through!" he called up. He aimed his headlamp through the opening and pulled cement and sand away with his hands. Teddy climbed up and helped dig. Within minutes, Todd's head and arms were through to the other side. He quickly swept his flashlight back and forth. "I can't see anything."

Teddy signaled for slack in the rescue line, then climbed through the breach next to Todd. He aimed his flashlight in the same direction. "Daniel! Billy!"

Todd let out an exhausted sigh. He wondered if he had really seen the flicker of light, or had the hours of work and hope played a trick on him? He slipped off his mask and called out, "Daniel! Stefanie! Meehonkey! Can you hear me? Keep digging," he told Teddy. "Mark! Billy? Hello! Can y'all hear me?"

Daniel stirred in his sleep. He was dreaming he heard voices. He tried to open his eyes, but his lids weighed a ton. "Am I dead?" he wondered. But the throbbing in his leg was as real as last week's math test. "Guess not," he thought to himself. "Well. That's good. I can't breathe very good. I need to keep breathing. Breathing's good. Keep breathing. In, out, in, out...I need to get up. I need to get some help." He slipped away again, but brought himself back when Mark's hand twitched and jumped off his lap. "I can hear him breathe. Good. He's not dead. Ouch! My chest hurts. It's whistling when I breathe." He tried swallowing. "That hurt. Why does my throat hurt?" He tried to lick his lips, but they were too parched and dry to separate. Besides, his tongue was swollen. "My lips must have welded together from the heat," he told himself. "How can I drink if my mouth is welded?" He dreamt about drinking water from a bottle, but his throat was too dry to swallow. He raised his right eyebrow and forced his eye to open, but it slammed shut again. "Lid's too heavy." He tried moving. "That hurts too much. But that's a good thing, right? You can't feel pain if you're dead." His limbs were dead. They fell asleep supporting Mark. "My hand feels enormous! Hey, it turned into a baseball mitt." He wiggled his fingers. They were stuck to a cloth of some kind that was pressed against Mark's forehead. Why was that, exactly?

Mark jumped in his sleep. His right hand reached up to touch his forehead, and he winced in pain. Daniel heard him moaning and forced his swollen, thick hand to gently stroke Mark's head. He should have taken better care of Mark. He should have seen him take off after Stefanie and stopped him. A hot tear rolled out of his eye, down his cheek, and onto his lips. "The sea is full of tears," Mrs. McNemmish once told him. "That's why it's so salty. The sea will always be full of salty tears as long as people make each other cry." He forced his one eye open and looked down. Mark's face had relaxed, and he had stopped moaning. Daniel continued to stroke his hair, but the feeling had long gone out of his hand.

Mark was having a vision. He was dreaming that a big ship had overtaken Ezekiel Beacon's boat, and cannonballs were flying through the air. He could see Blackbeard and Mrs. McNemmish laughing. He startled Daniel when he giggled in his sleep. Daniel felt Mark's body give way when the boy's dream was over.

Daniel took a deep breath and pressed his swollen tongue against the inside of his lips. He pressed harder and harder, finally breaching the top and bottom with a tiny space. "Billy." He heard his own voice, but only in his mind. He thought about biting into a whole lemon and salivated enough to lick his lips, making a wider opening. He tried swallowing again, even though it hurt as much as the last time. "Billy," he whispered hoarsely. "Wake up."

He couldn't remember where Billy was sitting, but he could hear him coughing in his sleep over by the wall. "Good. He didn't die either." Billy's cough was a dry cough. "That's right!" he remembered silently. "Billy's sitting against the wall with Stefanie." He listened as hard as his brain would allow. "I don't hear Stefanie breathing." He listened again, putting all of his attention in her direction. "I can't hear her." Something grabbed him in the pit of his stomach and tears welled in his eyes. "Stefanie," he thought, trying to find the will to call her name out loud. Tears fell across his cheeks and onto his lap. "God, please don't be dead. Please don't be dead. No! She's not dead! She's fine. I know she's fine. She has to be fine. I should have been nicer to her. If she wasn't such a pain in the butt." He smiled weakly. "Stefanie was born a pain in the butt. God, please don't let her be dead."

He was sorry he hadn't found any diamonds for her. He'd buy her a diamond with his share of the money they'd found if she'd just stay alive. "Please be alive, Stefanie, please be alive," he silently willed her.

Teddy slipped off his mask and cupped his hands. "Billy! Daniel! Hello! Can you hear me?"

Daniel slowly lifted his left hand off of Mark's forehead where it had been plastered since the boy had fallen. A piece of the precious slave quilt remained stuck to his fingers. Slave quilt. A road map to freedom. He wondered how many different people had used this tunnel or had hidden in this tunnel on their way to freedom. He could almost hear their voices, as if their spirits still haunted the corridors. No. The voices weren't in his head. They were coming from somewhere outside of himself. He shook his head and wiggled slightly in an effort to stay awake. It was so hard. His eyelids wanted to stay shut in the worst way. "Was that you, Billy?" That voice would never do. He needed to try again, louder this time. "Did you say something?" he asked, directing the question toward his friend.

Teddy grabbed Todd's arm. "Stop digging! I heard something. Billy! Daniel! Can you hear me?" He aimed the flashlight over the mountain of sand and stretched his neck to see farther into the tunnel. "There! Up against the wall! Daniel! Stefanie! Are you in there?"

"Daniel?" called Todd.

Daniel smiled. He could relax now. "Over here," he called quietly, then turned his head and slept.

High above the bowsprit,

Hangs the bloody head of Teach,

A pirate of the cutthroat kind,

Who stormed both sea and beach.

But never will he flinch, not he,

Nor feel the guilt inside,

For Blackbeard was the Pirate King

Of pirates far and wide.

CHAPTER XVIII

The children were twenty-five feet from the entrance. Todd clawed his way through the remainder of the wall, then scrambled through to the other side. Teddy handed him the large searchlight, then called for oxygen, water, blankets, and backboards to be lowered down into the shaft.

Todd grabbed the light and made his way to the children. He checked on all four to make sure they were alive and breathing, then quietly squatted down beside his son. "Daniel, can you hear me?" He pulled off his oxygen mask and slipped it over his son's face. The air in the tunnel was thick and vile, and all four children were sitting in damp sand and soot with water and bits of ceiling falling around them.

Daniel stirred. He fought with his eyes until they suc-
cumbed and opened, but the light from the lamp was too
much, and he let them fall shut again. "Can I...can I have
some water?" he asked in a dry, raspy voice.

Todd lifted the mask and held a bottle to Daniel's lips.
"Just a sip, son. You can have more after the Coast Guard
medic checks you out." He glanced down at Mark, who
was still lying on Daniel's lap. The blanket smelled of
damp smoke.

"Stefanie..." whispered Daniel. "Is she..."

"She's alive," Todd assured him. "Shh. We'll talk later."

"Dad?"

"What, Daniel?"

"Are you going to kill us?"

Todd smiled for the first time all day. "We'll see."

Daniel breathed in the cool, clean air. He couldn't
remember if it was day or night. He thought maybe it was
night. Ocracoke was amazing at night. Sometimes there
were so many stars, it looked like someone had thrown a
black blanket over the sky, littered it with pinholes, then
shone a light through it. On other nights, when small
wisps of cloud fluttered across the sky, it made the stars
flicker like little white moths flitting around in the moonlight. If you stood anywhere at all on South Beach and
twirled around in a circle, you could see the star-filled
horizon touching the earth on every inch of sand dune or
ocean. Being on South Point at night was like standing in
one of those glass bubbles with shaker stars falling all
around you but never really landing. Daniel couldn't wait
to go back to South Beach. He wondered if being grounded for life would include not going to the beach.

As breathing became easier, some of his strength began to return and he was able to raise both eyelids without having them slam shut right away. It was then that Daniel became fully and fearfully aware of Mark's breathing. It sounded like crackling eggshells. He turned his head toward Billy, who was snoring. He still couldn't hear Stefanie, and the pit of his stomach gripped. But he trusted his father that she was alive. He needed to trust his father. He couldn't bear the alternative. He closed his eyes and surprised himself with a giggle. Boy, was Stefanie going to be mad if that little key didn't open up the biggest treasure chest on the face of the earth. And it had better be filled with diamonds. He thought about old Mrs. McNemmish and the key they found inside the giant Snow Duck. The key's the key, thought Daniel. The key's the key. The key belongs to the C, so let it B, and we'll yell G, and have some T, so Stefanie can P.

Ouch. Somebody turned on more lights. Daniel tried to cover his eyelids, but he couldn't move his arm and wondered if it was dead. He chuckled out loud, remembering Stefanie's reaction to the first skeleton they had encountered.

Teddy had just come into the tunnel and was relieved to hear Daniel quietly chuckling to himself. "Hey, kiddo. What's so funny?" he asked Daniel, while slipping an oxygen mask over Billy's face.

Daniel thought for a moment. "I forget. But I think it was funny."

"I think we better get you some fresh air," laughed the sheriff.

Daniel suddenly realized that there was no one resting on his lap, and he forced one eye slightly open. The light hurt. "Where's Mark?"

"They're taking him out on a stretcher. Your dad and Chris will be back in a minute, and we'll get the rest of you out."

"How's Stefanie?"

"Well, we put a mask on her, but we need to get her to the hospital as soon as possible. She and Mark are pretty bad off."

"I'm sorry, Teddy."

"You can be sorry next week. Right now, we need to get y'all out of here."

Daniel rested until his father returned, then questioned him. "Where are we? How did you find us?"

"You're at the other end of Mrs. McNemmish's tunnel. There was an entrance under the Bobby Garrish tree that opened up when it was hit by lightning."

"That's what we thought," he told the ranger. "We tried to get out that way, but the tree caught on fire, and the ladder caught on fire, and then the tunnel caught on fire."

"Actually, it was Chris, B.J., Wade, and Alton who found the second entrance when they put the fire out. Teddy and I tried looking for you underneath the widow's shack, but we were afraid the tunnel might start caving in when the storm hit. Daniel, do you know who locked you in?"

"Zeek."

"Well, we'll take care of him later." He stopped talking when Alton and a Coast Guard medic climbed back into the tunnel. "Rest easy, son. We're going to put you on a backboard and lift you out of here now."

It took a few minutes to get Daniel secured onto the board and hooked up to the makeshift lift. Because he was the most awake and aware, he was the last one taken out of the tunnel. As he was being lifted out of the shaft, he heard a loud din coming from the ground above. "What's going on?"

"Cheering," Todd told him. "All y'all have kept this entire island awake. You have a lot of apologies to make when you feel better. I wouldn't want to be you when it's Marylee's turn."

Daniel grinned as church bells rang out, and boats and ferries blew their whistles. The village was celebrating the return of four children who, for a short time, thought they'd never see outside of that tunnel again. Daniel would never forget that night. He was pretty sure no one on the island would ever let him forget it either.

"Thanks for finding us, Dad."

"Thanks for staying alive."

It was past midnight when the four children were loaded into Coast Guard helicopters and flown to the hospital in Elizabeth City. Billy and Daniel had recovered enough to enjoy their first helicopter ride, but Stefanie and Mark remained unconscious.

When Daniel was settled into his hospital bed, he asked his dad to wait before joining his mother and sister at the hotel. "I need you to do something for me," he said secretively. "You have to go back down into the tunnel and bring out the treasure."

"What?!"

"No, listen," explained Daniel. "If you don't go down there and get it out, someone else will find it and steal the stuff. Mrs. McNemmish left that treasure to us for bur..."

He stopped midword. Now was not the time for confessions, and the medicine that was going into the tube in his hand was making him drowsy. "Did you see the key and the tickets that were in my pocket?" he asked, switching the topic of conversation. "Wait 'til you see the rest of the stuff we found. There's Civil War stuff, and pirate stuff, and coins, and guns. Did you know it was a pirate tunnel, *and* a Civil War tunnel, and part of the Underground Railroad?"

"Daniel, that's all very interesting and I'm sure y'all had a great adventure, but no one is going back into that tunnel for any reason. I don't care what kind of treasure you found. Do you know how lucky the four of you are to be alive? If we hadn't found you when we did, Stefanie and Mark could have died. How long do you think you and Billy could have survived without fresh air and water?" Todd took a deep, weary breath. "I'm exhausted, Daniel. We'll talk about this in the morning, but I promise you, the fire department's going to have that tunnel shored up before anyone goes back down into it. I don't think you have to worry about anyone stealing your treasure. We put the lock back on Mrs. McNemmish's treasure chest, so you don't have to worry about that entrance either."

"You don't understand," argued Daniel.

"I understand you need to get some sleep. So do I. How's your leg?"

Daniel wiggled his toes and felt the soft cast that went from the bottom of his foot all the way up his calf. "It's still pretty numb. So is my arm."

"The doctor said it's a reaction to some kind of spider bite. He wasn't sure what kind."

"Billy said it was something southern."

Todd laughed. "I suppose it was. You and Billy did okay," he told Daniel approvingly. "I'm really proud of you guys. I'm proud of all four of you. That blanket over Mark's eye saved his life. He's going to have surgery tomorrow, but the doctor thinks he'll be fine."

"What about Billy and Stefanie?"

"Billy has a few dings and dangs. Nothing too serious. But Stefanie has pneumonia and a collapsed lung. She'll be in the hospital for a while."

Daniel leaned back against his pillow and stared out the window. Even the gray sky and steady rain seemed beautiful. "We were really scared, but Stefanie did okay. At first she was pretty freaked out by the skeletons, but after a while she got used to seeing them and didn't mind them anymore. Except the last two. She had real issues about those guys." His voice was beginning to weaken as the medicine took effect and he was tiring quickly. "All she kept saying was how she wanted to see her mom again. I felt so bad for her. I think I felt worse for her than I did for myself."

"You're a good friend, Daniel. I'm sure the four of you kept each other going."

Daniel snickered. "When Stefanie's better, she's going to be really annoyed that we didn't find any diamonds. That was the one thing she wanted to find and the only thing not down there. And don't be surprised if she makes y'all put a bathroom in down there." Daniel looked at his father, his eyes drooping with fatigue. "It was like being buried alive down there. We didn't have too much time to think about it, though. Not with bats, and skeletons, and leaks, and cave-ins, and treasure chests. I just wish Stefanie would have shut up about having to pee every two minutes."

Before Todd left the hospital, he took possession of the key, tickets, collection of currency, and pocketful of Mark's white seeds. "I'll be back in the morning," he said, rising from his chair. "We both need some sleep."

"Promise you won't tell anyone about the treasure or the key or what's in the tunnel?"

"I promise."

"And promise you won't ask us about anything until we're all together at the same time."

"For heaven's sake, Daniel."

"Promise!"

"Okay! I promise. Go to sleep!"

"Dad?"

"Yes, Daniel?"

"How did you know about the tunnel underneath..." Daniel was asleep.

"Luck," whispered his father.

A few minutes after Todd left the hospital, Daniel reawakened and scooted down between the covers on his bed. He had been awakened by the presence of someone walking around his room. But when he opened his eyes expecting to see a nurse or doctor, he found the room to be both silent and empty. His half-opened eyes wandered toward the door where the warm glow of the hallway light spilled into his room. He again closed his eyes, but soon the presence returned. It was a warm and inviting presence, as welcomed as the hallway glow. It was as if someone had climbed into his bed and wrapped their long, comforting arms around his entire body, drawing him into their safety. It reminded him of sitting in front of the widow's fireplace on a cold winter afternoon, sipping hot chocolate, and listening to a ghost tale, which of course included a tale about Blackbeard the pirate. Then he understood. He sighed deeply and with a smile let go of the day. "Goodnight, Mrs. McNemmish. Thank you."

Mrs. McNemmish also smiled as she watched a shooting star sail above Blackbeard's ship. "You're very welcome, child. Sweet dreams. Sweet dreams to all of you."

Blackbeard stood proud and statuesque beside his petite shipmate. Staring out at the backdrop of black sky and ever-twinkling stars, he took a long, satisfying draw on his favorite clay pipe and blew out a cloud of sweet-smelling smoke. "Success stirs the blood and fires the soul of man, Theodora! Ezekiel Beacon was no match for me crew of dastardly scourge and ghostly apparitions. True villainy is well thought out, mate. One must have brains and cunning. Beacon is but a blight on humanity, a leech upon the sea, bloated by his own ego. Yer four courageous children beat him at his own game."

Mrs. McNemmish understood and agreed with this fine gentleman pirate. "May I?" she implored the captain. She held out her hand and received the pipe from Teach's masterful fingers and balanced it lovingly in her hand. "My Arthur loved this pipe. It was the thing I treasured most after he died. Zeek may have crushed the clay, but not the memories."

"Zeek is a fool, Madam, as was his great-grandfather times three." Teach chuckled softly as he rested his hands along the deck rail. "Shall I tell ye of the day I acquired this very pipe?"

"Please," implored the widow, always keen to hear an inviting good story.

Blackbeard's eyes crinkled with delight. He began his monologue with eagerness and expressive hand movement. "It was during a game of chance in a pub in Bath, England, in the year 1718, a few months before me unfortunate demise. I remember that it was a hot, sticky afternoon, and even though sweat ran freely down their sweet faces, the maidens who serviced us were well done up and most flirtatious. Ah, they drove me crazy, Theodora, with their captivating smell of fresh soap and lavender. I couldn't help but offer the dear maids a few pints of chilled ale, being the gentleman that I was. Later, I took one of the mistresses for me wife, governing the service meself aboard me own ship. But it was during the flow of ale that Israel Hands took advantage of me wandering eye and snuck a peek at me winning card. He called me Liar, Madam, saying I called the winning hand differently than the one I produced. So, I showed the clapperclaw all me cards, as would any gentleman enduring the same scrutiny, guzzled a few more pints, removed the precious pipe from his possession, making it my own, and shot him in his card-holding hand. I mostly sailed without the scourge after that. A few years later, after he died, he was sent down to Davy Jones, who spit him back up to me ghost ship." Blackbeard reclaimed the pipe, took a long draw of smoke, and blew out a cloud of satisfaction. "Yer Arthur was right, Madam. It has a wonderful draw."

Mrs. McNemmish peered into the horizon. Above the wavy line and cresting waves, ribbons of feathery clouds crossed the Milky Way, casting shadows in front of the Swan and Cassiopeia. Below the star-speckled sky, a handful of tall-masted ships played among the moonlit rockers. The soft wind carried age-old songs, sung by sailors who hung like monkeys from crisscrossed nautical rigging. Their voices blended with the cries of gulls, whales, dolphins, and pelicans that sat bobbing on a nearby wave.

"Zeek had no right endangering those children," fretted Mrs. McNemmish.

"Sharp spines bear sweet fruit, me lady. If the youngsters have suffered, their rewards will be sweet."

Mrs. McNemmish took in the night view once again, then turned toward the captain, ready and eager for her next orders. "When do we stir the wind again, Captain? I'm rarin' for another fight."

"All in good time, fair mistress. All in good time."

It was nearing one in the morning when Zeek Beacon and Birdie were dragged into the Coast Guard station and shoved into a holding room. "What about my boat!" Beacon yelled for the fortieth time. "You said as soon as the storm blew over, you'd get out there and look for those idiots who were shooting at us all night. I want them arrested for endangering our lives and crippling my craft!"

"Pipe down!" Pete warned him. He yawned and stretched, fighting to keep his eyes open long enough to type his report. "We'll send somebody out there later. Whoever it was, they're gone now. A few more hours won't make any difference one way or the other."

Keith Cutler hung up the phone and discreetly gave the other two officers thumbs up that the children had been found. They pretended otherwise, however, hoping to trick Zeek into a confession.

"I was thinking," Keith told Beacon candidly. "There might be a way of getting that boat of yours taken care of a little faster."

"Oh, yeah? How's that?"

Keith pressed a button on his telephone and a young Coast Guard officer entered the room. He was carrying a heavy bundle wrapped in a hand-quilted bedspread. When the bundle was opened, a treasure trove of Mrs. McNemmish's personal belongings was placed on the officer's desk.

Beacon stared at the items, expressionless.

"Ever see these things?"

Zeek shook his head. "Nope."

"That's really funny," said Rudy, joining them. "Because we found them in your stow."

"Must be a coincidence, 'cause I never saw those things."

"Is that so? Well, maybe they belong to Birdie. How about it, Birdie? Have you ever seen these things?"

Birdie took a good look at the swords, pictures, bell, and other assorted items displayed on Rudy's desk. "Sure," he announced confidently. "That's a bell. And that's a sword. And those are pictures."

Zeek made a motion to smack Birdie in the head, but his pudgy first mate was out of reach.

Rudy looked back over at Zeek and grinned. "See? Birdie says he's seen these things."

"Birdie's a moron. That's not what he meant, and you know it."

Birdie, who was always eager to serve the Coast Guard, munched on his bag of peanuts and pointed to the widow's collection. "I like the bell the best," he told Rudy.

"Me, too," Rudy told him.

Zeek Beacon groaned. "Are you going to arrest the morons who shot at me, or what?"

"We'll get around to that." Keith pulled up a chair next to Beacon and handed him a cup of coffee. "Seems your fingerprints are all over Theodora's trunk lock. I don't suppose you'd remember how they got there?"

"I bought that lock for her so no one would snoop around in her stuff. She'll tell you. Oh, yeah! She's dead! That's too bad. She was a nice old lady."

Keith pursed his lips and nodded. "That was a very thoughtful thing to do for her. And why do you suppose Stefanie and Billy have their prints all over the lock and trunk, as well?"

"How should I know? Ask them."

"I'd love to!" hollered Keith, becoming enraged at the captain's casual demeanor. "But they're missing!"

This time Zeek did react. He caught his reaction and settled down. "Oh yeah? That's too bad."

Rudy walked over to Birdie, who had started on his hot dog and milkshake, and sat down beside him. "Say, Birdie? Did Zeek say anything to you about a couple of kids who might be missing?"

Birdie scrunched his eyebrows and thought hard. He made sure not to look at Rudy in case Beacon's eye rule applied to him, as well. "No," he said quite certainly. "No kids. But he was real upset about some missing blowfish!"

"Blowfish?"

"That's what he said. Somebody was gonna be real upset when they found out about the missing blowfish." He looked over at Zeek with pity written across his face. "He was very disturbed."

"Blowfish, huh? I'll bet he was disturbed." A slow grin spread across Rudy's face, and he patted Birdie on the shoulder. "Thanks, Birdie. Good memory."

Birdie looked over at Beacon with his mouth half-stuffed and his eyes glued to the man's left shoulder. "When do I get my parrot?" he mumbled.

Beacon dropped his shaking, aching head into his hands. "Moron."

Keith was losing patience. "Come on, Zeek. Why don't you make it easy on yourself and tell us what you did with the kids."

"Hey, man! You don't have a thing on me. I didn't touch those termites, and I don't know how that stuff got onto my boat. Birdie and I were on a simple, little fishing trip and got caught up in a gale. Next thing we know, we're being hammered by cannonballs."

"Don't start with that again." Keith was thoroughly disgusted. "Lock him up," he told Pete. "Birdie, you come with me. I'm taking you over to Miss May Belle's house. You can stay there for a few days."

"Hey!" Beacon objected loudly as he was being escorted from the holding room to the cell. "What's the charge?"

Rudy kept walking. "Hunting fish without a license."

Early the next morning, Tom O'Neal's shrimping boat listed starboard. The motorized pulley heaved and moaned as it hauled up one of its larger nets.

"It's real big!" hollered Tom. "Feels like a shark!"

Tom and his men guided the net out of the water as the pulley ropes fought with the catch. Years back, a seven-hundred-pound shark got snagged in Bobby Garrish's net. They had to cut the shark free in order to right the boat, but the Smithsonian Institution in Washington, D.C., said it was a great find, considering the shark was believed to be extinct. Tom was sure he had netted the same shark.

When the payload was dropped onto the deck, Tom and Calvin Gaskins rushed forward. "Lordy! Will you look at that!" whistled Tom.

Calvin grabbed a knife and slit the net open. A large box fell out. "It's...."

"...the widow," ogled the captain. Tom examined the bottom half of the coffin that had been securely wrapped in its own fishing net and duct tape. He noted that the net was still securely tied in place, making the next discovery all the more startling.

"What do you mean it's empty?" shouted Teddy an hour later when he met Tom's crew on the dock of the Silver Lake Harbor. He helped tie off the boat and unload the coffin, then cut Daniel's fishing net and tape with a fileting knife. "Where is she?"

"Don't ask me," said Tom. "I just hauled it up."

Teddy slammed his foot into a piling. "How can she be missing if the net was still attached? There's no way she could have floated out! There isn't a shark skinny enough to get in there and pull her out. So, where in the devil is she?"

Tom shrugged. "Maybe she was never in there to begin with."

"Of course she was in there. Why else would there be netting over it?" Teddy looked up sharply. "This has gone far enough. I have got to talk with those kids."

"We can't talk to the kids," explained Todd over the phone from his room at the hotel. "The doctor says they're in shock. We're not supposed to ask them any questions until they're out of the hospital. He thinks they've been traumatized enough."

"They've been traumatized?" shouted Teddy. "What about Theodora?"

"I doubt Theodora's having psychological problems! Who else knows about the coffin?"

"Tom's crew and the Coast Guard."

"And whoever took her out," said Todd, feeling the same frustration he knew Teddy was feeling.

"Todd? What if the kids took her out of the coffin before dumping it into the ocean? We haven't got a clue what they did with her."

"Why in the world would they take her out of the coffin?" shrilled Todd. "I don't know. I don't know anything. Maybe they're not even the ones who broke into the church."

"Give it up, Todd. The four of them practically drew their initials on the carpet with the extinguisher foam. Look, Daniel and Billy are coming home the day after tomorrow. Either we get some answers from them, or I swear, I'll traumatize them myself!"

Night comes,

And the stars that are hidden by day shine

brightly through the terrifying darkness.

Evil stirs,

And goodness rushes in and chokes it with

finger-vines of deliciously smelling lavender

and sweet strawberries.

Death comes,

And the cooing and toothless grin of a

newborn or the cuddly warmth of a beagle

puppy melts away the tears and fills the

void with laughter.

Thus is the legacy of

a woman remembered.

CHAPTER XIX

Todd Garrish stood next to his wife and children on Howard Street just above Miss Dixie's rental cottage. The hurricane had taken two of the island's oldest trees and had left a watermark on the walls of the Village Craftsmen. The road itself was riddled with deep holes and wind-blown sand mounds that crept up the white picket fences that guarded the ten small cemeteries that lined both sides of the street. The once-famous canopy of branches overhead now smiled openly, allowing sunlight to touch places that had been in the shadows for four hundred years. Howard Street was changed in contour, but not in character. Today, Todd stared down at the newest gravestone rising from the McNemmish family cemetery plot. A beautifully engraved, polished cedar casket rested on the ground in front of the newest marble stone.

"I know it's not funny," Todd said in a voice low enough so only his wife could hear. "But there are four graves in this graveyard, and not one, single body! Don't you think it's just a little weird to continue sticking stones in the ground where there aren't any bodies? And now we're putting a casket into the ground that doesn't have a body. Why don't we just make a plaque, put everybody's name on it, and hang it up in the church?"

"Will you be quiet before somebody hears you," hissed Elizabeth. "You can't visit a plaque. This cemetery gave Theodora a place to come and visit Arthur and her sons."

"But they're not here!"

"So what? She still needed a place to visit."

"That's just plain nuts!"

"No one asked your opinion."

Todd looked around impatiently. The reverend was busying himself with welcoming people as they gathered onto Howard Street. Villagers and off-islanders were greeting each other with handshakes and hugs, fretting over the mysterious loss of Mrs. McNemmish's body from the coffin, and gloating over the heroic rescue of the four children. "I still say we should have had this funeral at the beach," Todd continued. "It's a beautiful day, and that's where she was the happiest. As a matter of fact, if Daniel's right, she's happier where she is now."

"We don't know where she is."

"She knows where she is!"

Elizabeth frowned at her husband. "Why are you so annoying? I told you, we're doing this for the kids. So stuff a sock in it and deal with the situation."

"May I have everyone's attention, please!" Reverend Woods stood on top of a peach crate and drew people toward him with a wave of his arms. "I believe the children are ready to begin their service!" He waited another moment for the last of the islanders to gather around the McNemmish gravesite.

"Friends, we are here today to bid a final farewell to Theodora Teach McNemmish, who died and disappeared three weeks ago. We are also here to celebrate the safe return of Billy, Daniel, Stefanie, and Mark. Before the children begin their ceremony, I would like to offer a moment of silence for the unknown persons whose remains were found in the tunnel. May their spirits be free now that several of them have a permanent home in a small cemetery behind Teeter's Campground. I only wish we could put names to their poor souls."

Billy leaned in to Daniel and giggled: "I only wish we could put glue to their poor bones."

"That's not nice," whispered Stefanie.

As the church bells rang out across the tiny village, Jeffrey Tillet stepped up to the empty, handmade coffin he had spent the past several weeks carving. The new coffin replaced Mrs. McNemmish's original coffin due to the fact that it was both waterlogged and too broken to use, even though all of its parts had been collected. Mark, his mother, and his younger sister joined Jeffrey. Each held a small wicker basket containing various items.

Mark pulled down the blue knit hat that covered the shaved part of his head and the single row of stitches that arched above his eyebrow, then adjusted the camo-colored patch stretching across his injured eye. He looked at his father and nodded.

Jeffrey spoke in the soft, southern brogue that was indigenous to the tiny island. "This leaf is from one of the widow's yaupons. This particular leaf came from the side of her shack that overlooks the cove." He reached into his son's basket and held up the thick, prickly leaf for everyone to see. He then reached across and pulled something out of little Jennifer's basket. "This branch is from one of the live oaks near Blackbeard's trading post beside Sam Jones's cemetery yonder. I carved the lighthouse and a few pelicans onto it and put her name and Arthur's, and her two sons, Nathan and Gabriel." He reached into the basket again. "This is a shaving from the Toothache Tree. Theodora was partial to that tree in particular since that tree is older than novocaine and works better."

"Remember when Beach Scarborough put too much bark in her mouth and couldn't move her tongue for the whole day?" whispered Daniel.

Billy nodded. "Pauletta told everyone she had 'numb tongue disease' and that if she kissed anyone while she had it, their tongue would fall out of their mouth."

"Will you two be quiet," the ranger admonished them.

Mr. Tillet waited while Mark put the branch, the leaf, and the shaving into the empty coffin, and then continued by reaching into his wife's basket. "This is the leather pouch Mark found in the trunk in the widow's shack. When he found it, it was full of Snow Duck seeds. Mark wanted to put all of the seeds he found in the widow's coffin, but Mr. Springer asked that he keep them. Instead of the seeds, the children filled the pouch with some of Theodora's tinier seashells." He reached over and put the pouch into the casket, then held up the final item. "This is a picture album our family put together with the help of Daniel, Stefanie, and Billy. It has photographs of Arthur, Mrs. McNemmish, the boys, most of us, and just about every place important to the widow on Ocracoke, Portsmith Island, Hatteras, and Nags Head."

Mark placed the album into the empty coffin and smiled. Every time he thought about the coffin being filled with the things she loved, but vacant of her, he'd know that she was somewhere, someplace, sometime, serving aboard the ghost ship *Queen Anne's Revenge*. "Have fun," he told her, using pirate sense. With that, he and his family returned to their place beside the reverend.

After applause, Stefanie was next to speak.

"Well, at least she can't talk too long," Daniel whispered into Billy's ear. "She'll start coughing."

"That never stopped her before."

"I heard that." Stefanie stepped onto the peach crate and coughed dramatically. Captain Austin, Marylee, and Matt stood on the ground beside her. "This is one of the Snow Ducks Mrs. McNemmish made that isn't needed anymore, because the person it belonged to is dead. And even though we didn't find any *diamonds* or anything, we found lots of silver and gold coins, so we put some inside the duck so Mrs. McNemmish will have real pirate money. Of course, she can't buy anything with it, so I don't know why we're putting it in there, but Billy and Daniel and Mark wanted to, SO WE ARE!" she announced with great exaggeration.

She reached over and took something from her father and held it up for everyone to see. "This is a piece of the cement Mrs. McNemmish made out of the seashells she collected her whole life. I'm not supposed to talk about the tunnel, but trust me, she made a whole lot of this stuff."

She reached over and received something from her mother. "This was the widow's favorite Bible. I put it in a plastic bag so it would stay nice. Inside the book on the first page, it tells who her mother was, and grandmother, and all of her great-grandmothers and great-grandfathers and her great-uncle, Edward Drummand Teach."

She bent down and received a stack of papers from Matt. "These are a bunch of letters from her husband Arthur. I wanted to read them but my mother wouldn't let me. And Clinton carved her two laughing gulls." She leaned down and told Matt to hold up the gulls.

Following that latest display, Stefanie got down off the crate and she and her brother put all of the items into the coffin. She then walked over to her mother and retrieved an emerald-green bed pillow with colorful stitching on both sides. "This is my favorite pillow," she told the coffin. "I hope you have a very comfortable life in heaven, or on Blackbeard's ghost ship. The pillow has hearts and ducks and things on it in case you need something to look at while you're dead, even though we all know you're not really in there. And listen. I'm really glad we did what we did, even if we didn't get any diamonds. And don't worry about your cats. Everybody's taking care of them." She said something too quiet for anyone else to hear, and then she and her family returned to the gathering.

Billy and Drum waited for the applause to fade, then followed the Austins. Even though most of Billy's bumps and bruises were on the mend, his left arm was still in a sling from a shoulder injury he had sustained during the cave-in. "This is the newspaper we found in the widow's trunk," he said, holding it up for everyone to view. "It tells about the capture of Blackbeard. We had it copied, so it's okay that it's going into the coffin. This other piece of parchment is the missing Howard Map we got back from Zeek. We're not sure if it's real or not, so we offered it to Philip Howard, but he said to go ahead and give it to Mrs. McNemmish's coffin." Billy grinned. "Zeek was really angry when we took the map away from him. It was worth it just to hear him scream."

Reverend Woods cleared his throat, as several members of the audience applauded at Zeek's reaction. "Anyway...since Miss Theo was always telling stories because she liked them so much, we had everyone at school write her a story. It was my idea to put a flashlight in the coffin just in case she reappeared someday and wanted to read. Anyway, we collected a bunch of knick-knacks and statues of the lighthouse, and the ponies, and some of the wildlife. And this was her favorite apron." Drum helped his son lay the items to rest in the widow's coffin. Billy bent down and spoke to the coffin personally. "Tell Blackbeard hey for us. I hope you guys kick butt." Then he and his dad tipped their hats and stepped away. "Oh, I forgot!" Billy turned back toward the coffin and whispered, "Tell my mom hey, if y'all happen to see her. Thanks."

Daniel, his parents, and his sister Lena walked to the front of Mrs. McNemmish's cedar coffin. Ranger Garrish spoke first. "Mrs. McNemmish once told a story about a cedarwood staircase with thirteen steps. Her grandmother told her that whenever she stepped onto the thirteenth step, she should pretend she was stepping onto a place where her imagination took her. Of course, Mrs.

McNemmish always made the thirteenth step Blackbeard's quarterdeck. Now, when her spirit resides in this cedar coffin, she can breathe in the memory of the thirteen steps any time she likes."

Daniel stepped forward. "Since the Historical Society wants to keep Miss Theo's walking cane and some of her more personal items, we thought of some other things she might have enjoyed having in her coffin. This is a copy of Blackbeard's flag." Daniel helped Lena onto the crate where she held open the flag for everyone to see, even though everyone on the island already knew what it looked like. Then Daniel pulled a deck of cards out of his jacket pocket. "I found this deck of cards with one of the skeletons." He was careful not to say more about the cards, or more about the tunnel, or anything about their other findings on account of Mr. Springer telling him not to. Balancing himself on his crutches, he held up the playing cards for everyone to see. "When I found the cards, the skeleton was actually holding a really good poker hand."

"Daniel!" admonished his mother.

"Sorry." Daniel shrugged at the laughter, then continued. "Anyway, this is the ruby ring no one knew about until the day before Mrs. McNemmish died." He held up the ring, but only those closest to him could see it. "Miss Theo had given it to Zeek to pay for the whelk shells she used to make her Snow Ducks, but then he was all mean to her, because he thought she had more stuff. Teddy got the ring back, seeing that Zeek broke a whole bunch of her antiques. And it really does belong to Miss Theo."

Stefanie tiptoed sideways, inching her way toward Daniel. She whispered into his ear, pretending to remind him of something. "Pleeeease don't put the ring in the casket. It's not like she's going to wear it. I'll take really good care of it, and you know we were supposed to find diamonds and didn't, and this is almost as good as a diamond, and I really think she would want me to have it."

"I don't care. We already decided to put it in the coffin. Now shut up. You had your turn."

"Dimwitter."

"Dingbatter!" Daniel stepped away from Stefanie and continued. "We got Miss Theo a new pipe from Teach's Hole that looks just like her old one. Then we fixed up the mug and lantern that Zeek broke, and we're putting them into the coffin, too. The ladies from the island quilting club donated a pile of quilting squares. May Belle said the widow never got around to finishing any of the quilts she started, so she thought that would be a good thing. We're really sorry about the widow's quilt at the church. That's it," he told the reverend. After he and Lena put everything into the coffin, Lena returned to her father, concerned. "What if Mithith McNemmish showth up and wantth to uthe her coffin? There won't be any room for her."

Todd took his daughter's hand. "That's the nice thing about spirits," he told her. "They fit anywhere."

Todd Garrish remained near the coffin as the widow's family and friends filed by. Everyone carried with them a small token gift they thought would please the widow. When it was their turn, they laid their gift inside.

"Remember," he told everyone. "No one outside this community is to find out about the tunnel until after the meeting tonight. If word gets out, we'll have more treasure-seeking tourists down here than summer mosquitoes."

"And as for you four!" said Teddy, addressing Mark, Daniel, Billy, and Stefanie. "When you're feeling better, you each have two hundred hours of community service to complete for the unlawful breaking and entering of the church, borrowing two motorboats, and stealing a coffin. You will also give up ten percent of your job earnings to fix up the church and pay for Tom's new fishing nets."

"That's not fair!" objected Stefanie.

"Trust me. All y'all are getting off easy."

Stefanie glared at the boys. "I can't believe I have to do two hundred hours of community service because you three dimwitters decided to give Miss Theo a midnight burial in the ocean, where she didn't even stay anyway! And another thing. I..." She suddenly stopped talking and dissolved into a fit of coughing so loud, and so long, it rendered her speechless.

Daniel grinned. "Quick! Somebody hide her cough medicine!"

"I heard that," croaked Stefanie.

Marylee Austin overheard the conversation and yanked her daughter back home for a rest. Billy, Daniel, and Mark laughed as they got into the sheriff's car with Mustard and rode to the Pony Island Restaurant. The day was cool and crisp and smelled of pine and cedar. Winter would soon spill onto the shores and life would return to normal. It was hard to imagine Thanksgiving, or Christmas, or Halloween without the widow, but the first sighting of the headless pirate over at Try Yard Creek would yield a story even she would hover above to hear.

Listen to the sweetest music.

Watch the graceful flight of a pelican.

Look into the horizon, which stretches

above miles of dappled greenery and

below rich, thick clouds of gray, and

pink, and ivory.

Do these things, and I will take you to a

place that exists within paisley dreams

and bountiful hope called Ocracoke.

C H A P T E R   X X

Settle down, everyone. We have a lot to talk about and I'd like to get out of here before midnight." Mr. Donald Springer of the Dare County Island Bank and Real Estate Company stood on the edge of the gymnasium stage and waited for five hundred O'cockers to take their seats. "I have here Miss Theo's Last Will and Testament. It was the widow's wish that all y'all be present to hear it. I'd like to begin by…" He stopped abruptly when the back doors swung open and Pete Scarborough, Keith Cutler, and Rudy Howard burst into the room. Zeek Beacon and Birdie were in tow.

"Hey, Billy! Hey, Stefanie!" Birdie waved eagerly to the four children as he followed Keith down the center aisle to a waiting chair. "I got my parrot!"

Billy grinned and waved back. "That's great, Birdie!"

"Sure," whispered Stefanie. "Now he and the parrot can share an I.Q."

Zeek Beacon was in a far less amiable mood. He stood in the back of the room, handcuffed to Pete Scarborough. "What are you termites staring at?" he growled at the four youngsters seated up front.

Stefanie gawked in his direction, but avoided his eyes.

"There's nothing worth looking at," Daniel assured him.

Zeek made a move toward the boy, but Pete yanked him back. "Knock it off, Zeek, before I chain you to the fire door."

"I don't know why I have to be here," griped the captain.

"Well, if you'll sit down and shut up, we'll find out." Pete thrust Beacon into a seat, then took the one beside him. Stefanie stuck her tongue out at the captain, which he answered with a clawed hand the size of her throat. Captain Austin placed his hand on his daughter's head and faced her forward. Mr. Springer called the islanders back to order.

"As I was saying, when I opened the envelope containing the widow's will, I discovered an old skeleton key and a handwritten poem."

"Not another poem," whined Stefanie.

"Maybe it's another trunk!" said Daniel.

"The only trunk I want to see has an elephant attached to it."

Mr. Springer adjusted his reading glasses and unfolded a small piece of paper. He read out loud:

> *Though this key be half the prize,*
> *It holds the future of our lives.*
> *The second key in mystery lies*

For those with brave and curious eyes.
Hold those things we value most,
The sound, the beach, the island coast,
And take to heart this sacred ground,
The purest treasure ever found.

Mr. Springer removed his glasses. "At first, I hadn't a clue what the poem meant, except that this key was one of two such keys, and that whatever they opened held great importance to the widow. Daniel, Billy, Mark, and Stefanie found the matching key when they were locked into the tunnel. As it turns out, the keys opened a lockbox the widow rented over sixty years ago. When I read the documents inside the box, I understood the magnitude of the poem."

"What's in the box?" someone laughed clear across the room. "Seashells?"

"Wisdom," Mr. Springer replied pleasantly. He waited for the giggles to subside, then continued. "About sixty-five years ago, Mrs. McNemmish stumbled onto an old well cover on the northern end of Blackbeard's Cove. Without giving away her secret, she asked around to see if anyone else had ever seen or heard of a well on that part of the island. Everyone seemed to know about the shallow well in Teach's Hole, but she was assured that no deeper well could exist on the island because Ocracoke is really only a sand bar, and the water from such a well would be undrinkable. Then one day, she found an old newspaper clipping that had a picture of the land where Blackbeard had his castle and outhouse. She recognized the land and knew that the well cover she had found was on the exact same piece of property the outhouse had been on before it was destroyed in the hurricane of 1938. After finding the article, she convinced her husband Arthur to build their home around the well cover. When the house was completed and they moved in, they cut a hole in the floor, uncovered the well cover, and opened it up. It was then they discovered the steps leading into the tunnel. At first they covered up the hole with a rug and table. Later, after finding Blackbeard's treasure chest and hauling it up into their house, they fit it with a flyaway bottom and made the tunnel their project for life."

"I knew it!" squealed Billy.

"That must be the newspaper article Mark found," said Daniel.

Mrs. McNemmish's cousin stood up to speak. "Are you saying that Theodora and Arthur built their house over the well that had once been Blackbeard's outhouse? On purpose?"

"In her journal, Miss Theo said she didn't think Blackbeard ever used it as a outhouse, but only built it to look like one to hide the entrance to the tunnel."

"Oh, yeah? Well, you should smell the place," Stefanie commented to those around her.

"This whole story smells," howled someone else.

"Are you sure this isn't one of Theodora's tall tales?" asked a villager.

"How could it be a tall tale if we were down there?" asked Daniel.

"Even if this is all true," debated one of the island schoolteachers, "we don't know for sure Blackbeard's the one who dug the tunnel. Maybe somebody else found the well and built the tunnel."

"Ah! But the detail Theodora gives in her journal is quite conclusive," said Donald. "For instance..." He referred to the widow's personal diary, "I quote, 'The walls were shored with cabin logs and ships' beams dating back to the 18th century. One such beam caught my eye when a shiny piece of brass peeked through the cement, where two skeletons were shackled to the wall. I dug and swept clear the cement until the front face of a trunk stared back at me. Carved into the brass facing were the initials E.D.T., and the words 'For the Devil's Eyes Alone' were carved on the wood beneath. Two months of digging and pulling were rewarded with the trunk that remains below. This was the second trunk found with the pirate's initials in bold print. That same dig revealed the remains of the two poor souls who were sent to guard the trunk, as their hands were still shackled to the sides of the chest and not to the wall as first suspected. Arthur and I had to carefully move the remainders of both gentlemen, and with God's understanding and guidance, reassembled them. I publicly beg their forgiveness if the wrong parts were put to the wrong man. Good intentions and wheat paste are all my sweet Arthur and I had.'"

"I told you they were put together wrong!" shouted Stefanie. "Didn't I tell you they were put together wrong? But do you ever listen to me? No. I told you they looked weird." She sat back with a smug expression on her face and wasn't even aware that the entire room had broken into hysterical laughter.

Daniel, Billy, and Mark shook their heads grievously. "Man. She's going to be crowing about this for the rest of her life."

"I heard that."

Mrs. McNemmish's niece Trudy raised her hand. She was laughing so hard, tears streamed down her face.

"Theodora and Arthur pasted skeletons back together, not knowing an elbow from a leg bone, or which bone belonged to which person?"

"I'm afraid so."

It was five minutes before poor Mr. Springer got the meeting back under control.

"Look, people. I think Theodora and Arthur deserve a lot of credit trying to do right by those gentleman. She writes, 'Upon finding the tunnel, my sweet Arthur and I and our two boys ceremoniously buried over a dozen skeletons that had already fallen into ruin. We have left the remaining skeletons in their final resting place and plan to keep it as a pirate's cemetery.' End quote."

"What do you mean, 'ceremoniously'?" Todd Garrish wanted to know.

Mr. Springer cleared his throat and took a sip of water. "The McNemmishes gave the pirates a burial at sea."

"In our sea!" screeched Marylee.

"That would be my guess."

"I'm never swimming in that water again!" huffed May Belle. The sentiment was seconded by many.

"I think this whole story is hogwash!" shouted someone near the back of the gymnasium.

"Not really," said Mr. Springer. "If you'll just be patient, I'll explain everything." He carefully unfolded a second document, which had yellowed with time. Fortunately, the jet-black ink was as clear as the day it was penned.

"Now, according to Theodora, there was an eleven-foot ladder that descended from underneath the opening of the well. However, once entering the tunnel, the ceiling lowered to six feet, sometimes hovering at a mere five-and-a-half feet. Arthur and the boys had to stoop much of the time they were down there. Blackbeard was somewhere between six feet one and six feet seven inches tall. I imagine his men did most of the digging and hiding of ammunition and treasure."

"Wait a minute. How can you have a tunnel eleven feet underneath the island if there is no eleven feet underneath the island?!" asked Lawton Howard.

"Chris and I were down there," B.J. told everyone. "Both entrances are eleven feet deep!"

"I don't care where you think you were!" protested several people at once. "You can't dig a tunnel underneath a sand bar unless you have a road crew, and I doubt Blackbeard had a road crew!"

"Where do you think we got lost?" argued Daniel.

The room erupted in argument. No one even noticed the gentleman in a blue suit and tie walking onto the stage.

"May I?" The gentleman asked Mr. Springer.

Mr. Springer stepped back gladly. "Be my guest."

The stranger walked to the front of the stage and spoke through the microphone. "May I have everyone's attention?"

One by one, people took notice of the stranger and quieted down. When the room was silent, the stranger introduced himself.

"My name is Adrian Powers and I am an underground transportation advisor and contractor." He stopped talking for a moment and turned away from the microphone to whisper to Donald Springer. "Why is everyone staring at me like I just stepped off a U.F.O.?"

Mr. Springer grinned, slightly embarrassed by the question. "You're wearing a suit and tie. People around here attend weddings and funerals in t-shirts and cut-offs."

"Oh." Mr. Powers removed his jacket and tie and the audience relaxed. "I recently had the privilege of touring this beautiful island and parts of the tunnel with Mr. Springer," he began. "And I think I have come up with a plausible explanation."

"What's *plausible*?" whispered Billy.

"Believable," said Daniel. "Shh!"

Mr. Powers held up a large topographical map of the village.

"You will notice that I have marked several places on the map with a thick, black marker. The areas marked with an "X" are places around the village that either don't perk, or perk just underneath the top layer of sand, which is good. The areas marked with an "O" are places around the village that perk anywhere from six inches below the sand or deeper, which isn't good. So, as you can see for yourselves, this would not be acceptable for a project such as the tunnel."

"Speak English!" shouted someone from the right side of the room.

Everyone laughed and Mr. Powers apologized. "Percolation is the seepage of water. If water settles quickly, it's not a good place to dig. If water stays up top, it's a good place to dig. Whoever designed the tunnel underneath this island knew that. They mapped out the areas on the island that could be dug without immediately filling with water. That gave them time to shore up the walls with logs and boat planking, and then later add cement. In time, they were able to tunnel from one of those areas to another, and so on, until they reached the length of tunnel they desired. Now, here's the really interesting part. When

Blackbeard built the tunnel beneath what is now Mrs. McNemmish's shack, it dead ended. It only had one entrance and exit."

"That's impossible," said Teddy. He stood up and spoke directly to Mr. Powers. "That tunnel has two entrances. I'll agree it jig-jags a lot, but the shaft underneath the widow's shack and the shaft underneath Bobby Garrish's tree are entrances to the same tunnel."

"That's right," agreed Drum, who was usually silent about such matters. "No matter who dug the tunnel, they wouldn't have dug it without a lady dodger."

"A lady dodger?" asked Mr. Powers.

"Sure. A second way out in case your wife saw you go in with another lady."

Mr. Powers took a sip of water. His hand was trembling and he blushed slightly. He handed the microphone back over to Donald Springer, sat down, and wiped the sweat off his forehead.

Donald Springer thanked him for his participation, then continued with the meeting. "Blackbeard may not have been the horrible monster people made him out to be, but he was no angel," he told everyone, but to no one's surprise. "When he stored two of his trunks in that tunnel and put a dozen men down there to guard them, he had no intention of having his wares snuck out of a second entrance. He guarded that one entrance himself, and if any man tried to sneak out of the tunnel with any of his goods, he was taken to a secluded island, and given a bottle of water, a pistol, and a single bullet. Blackbeard's men didn't even dare look guilty. They knew Teach was ornery enough to remove the treasure and bury them."

"See?" piped Stefanie. "I told you he left them down there."

Daniel rolled his eyes. Some things never changed, and Stefanie's mouth was one of them.

Alton, who was busy writing a history about the island, seemed more curious than most. "If Blackbeard only dug the entrance under the widow's shack, who dug the shaft under the Bobby Garrish tree?"

"In the 1850s and '60s, when the islanders found out that slaves were trying to make their way north to freedom, some of the O'cockers wanted to help. They must have known about Blackbeard's tunnel, because it was to become an integral part of the Underground Railroad. Entire families were eventually hidden in that tunnel. The problem was, it only had one entrance. If anyone on the lookout for runaway slaves saw them enter the tunnel, they would have chased after them, captured them, and taken them back to their owners to be beaten, or worse. No one on the island wanted that to happen. So the villagers got together and agreed to dig a second entrance so the runaway slaves could go in one way, hide for a while, then sneak out the other way when the coast was clear. First, they had to study Blackbeard's tunnel, then find other places on the island where they could dig just as deep. They began the second part of the tunnel below Bobby Garrish's tree because it had a natural ditch beneath it, which gave them a head start. The islanders and the runaways dug from both ends at the same time until the two sides came together. The wall connecting the two tunnels is directly below Blackbeard's Cove where Teach had his trading post. The slaves helped dig while they hid out in Blackbeard's tunnel. The islanders who worked on the second entrance kept the base of the tree boarded up so that no off-islander would suspect anything. And no one did. Not even y'all."

"How come none of us ever heard that story?" asked Norton Styron. "You'd think our kin would have been proud of what they did."

"They couldn't say anything at the time, or they would have been punished along with the runaway slaves. Even after the war was over, the southern sympathizers would have been a problem. North Carolina is a southern state. Some of the emotion of that war is still present today. That information was best left alone. Or so your ancestors thought."

"I still don't understand what any of this has to do with the key the children found," said Todd.

"I promise I will explain everything, but it's important to first understand the events prior to the children finding the tunnel."

"Then get on with it!" shouted Beacon. "I could be in my cell clipping my toenails!"

Mr. Springer mumbled a comment to himself, then continued. "According to the widow, most of the cement had fallen off the tunnel walls and ceiling by the time she and Arthur ventured down there. Water and wet sand were seeping through the walls in a lot of places, and much of the wooden shoring had rotted out. The tunnel was in danger of collapsing. The first thing they did was to move Blackbeard's second trunk, the one still down there, into the newer part of the tunnel in hopes it would be safer. They actually had to take it apart and reassemble it because it was too big to fit around the corners."

"Told you," sang Stefanie.

Daniel grunted.

Mr. Springer ignored the children and continued. "That's also where the McNemmishes reconstructed the two gentlemen guarding the trunk. They truly wanted to leave as much of the tunnel as possible in its original state. After that, she, Arthur, and their two boys secretly cared for the tunnel by making their own cement out of seashells and sand to replace the cement that had fallen away. They replaced much of the shoring material with local ship-wrecks that had washed ashore. After Arthur and the boys died, the widow took care of the tunnel by herself. She spent so much time down there, she made a pet out of one of the bats that had befriended her. She writes that he used to perch on her head while she worked."

"That was her pet!" shrieked Stefanie. She turned and smacked Daniel on his sore arm. "You killed the widow's pet!"

"You told me to!"

"How could you do that?" Billy scolded him.

"I was saving you!" Daniel defended himself. "You told me to smack him with the bottle."

"I didn't know he was her pet!"

Mark gave Daniel an evil, one-eyed glare.

"Hey! The only reason I killed that bat was because the rest of you were too chicken to do it."

"That's no excuse. You're just a cruel, heartless mur-derer," Stefanie berated him.

"Fine."

"Fine."

"Hey!" Zeek Beacon bellowed so loudly, the entire gym-nasium quieted and turned in his direction. Jumping to his feet, he dragged Pete up with him. "Are you telling me that old woman had a fix on Blackbeard's treasure the whole time we were growing up, and she never divvied it up?"

"She had her hands on it, all right, but we haven't gotten to the divvied up part yet. She spent most of her time caring for the tunnel and not caring about the treasure."

"I'm sorry," laughed Trudy. "But it's hard to picture Theodora keeping a tunnel together when she had enough trouble just gluing her Snow Ducks."

"Theodora could do anything she wanted to do," Elizabeth Garrish assured everyone in the room. "She stood four feet nothing and weighed eighty nothing pounds, but I don't know anyone who was ever brave enough to tell her what she could or couldn't do."

"Amen to that," said Teddy.

"It was Theodora who researched the tunnel and found out why it had two entrances," said Mr. Springer.

"Heck! That ain't hard to figure out," chuckled Kyle Howard. He owned the pub and was already half a keg higher than high tide. "One side to fill her up, and one side to drain her out."

The children giggled when Ellen Howard smacked her husband over the head with her plastic water bottle.

Donald Springer pulled out a yellow legal pad and showed it to the villagers. "I have here a complete inventory of the items Mrs. McNemmish found in the two trunks. I understand from the children that a few of the items, such as the bodies of two Spanish maidens, were not accounted for."

"Mrs. McNemmish went a little *overboard* with the first one," teased Billy.

Donald frowned at the pun, then referred to the list on the legal pad, which he had copied from the widow's journal. "The items found and sold by Mrs. McNemmish included several mahogany boxes filled with gold and silver doubloons."

"I knew it had doubloons," cheered Billy, quite satisfied with himself.

"There were also several sets of gold and silver dinnerware and seventy-two pieces of hand-blown glassware encrusted with priceless diamonds, emeralds, rubies, and opals."

"What?" gasped Stefanie.

Daniel grinned at the seething, beet-red girl seated to his right. "What a shame," gloated the boy.

"Shut up, Daniel."

"There were also several pieces of art and sculpture along with, as she put it, 'dazzling jewelry fit for a queen.'"

The ear-piercing scream was involuntary. Donald Springer leaped backward as if an angry bear had charged him. Every heart in the room jumped, and people jumped out of their seats as Stefanie's hysterical screeching and spastic leaping turned to hyperventilating. Daniel pulled her back into her seat and slapped a hand over her mouth, while her mother leapt to her feet and fanned her daughter.

"Is she all right?" asked Mr. Springer.

"I think she's in shock," said Billy.

Stefanie threw off Daniel's hand and wriggled away from her mother. "Did you know about this?" she screamed at the boys. Her crazed eyes nearly popped out of their sockets as she unleashed her glare onto Mr. Springer. "She sold the jewels?" she repeated slowly and clearly, enunciating each word as if she were chewing them up and spitting them out. "Mrs. McNemmish sold the jewels? She didn't keep any of them? Not one diamond?" The youngster had turned so red, she looked like she was about explode into a multicolored fireworks display.

"She owed me those jewels!" Zeek Beacon raved at the top of his lungs. "That was my ring! Those brats stole everything!"

Clinton Gaskill howled so hard, he nearly fell out of his chair. "That's my Theodora," he told May Belle. "Keep the chalk and sell the carbon."

Todd Garrish slapped a hand to his forehead and groaned audibly. "God help us."

"I knew it! I knew that old biddy cheated me out of my share of the treasure!" ranted Zeek. "If she wasn't dead, I'd kill her myself!"

"Shut up and sit down!" ordered Rudy. "Donald, are you sure about this?"

"Absolutely sure."

"Wait a minute." Hannah Wehab, who now had the honor of being the oldest pirate descendant on the island, slowly rose to her feet. "If Theodora sold the treasure, how come she stayed in that shack?"

"I told you it was a good question," croaked Stefanie.

Donald Springer took a deep, weary breath. "Look, Theodora was well aware of the value of the things she found. She kept a few of the items that had historic value for her family. She also kept a little of the money to add to her meager income. But to her, there were more important things than living well. Miss Theo was very proud and very well educated about her pirate heritage. But she also understood the difference between right and wrong." When the room finally quieted, he continued. "In her journal, she calls Blackbeard 'the Robin Hood of the Sea.' He stole from ships, then gave colonial families free food and furniture so they wouldn't have to pay English prices or pay English taxes. She liked that. However, the way he lived and the *not*-so-nice things he did in the name of piracy were, in her opinion, very wrong. Theodora's desire to be buried at sea and become a pirate on Blackbeard's ghost ship was to live out the fantasy of being a pirate without hurting anyone who wasn't basically already dead."

"But our children did get hurt," said Marylee.

"That was Zeek's fault," Billy stated emphatically. "He's the one who locked us in the tunnel."

"Yeah? Well, you're lucky I didn't shoot you."

"I swear, Zeek, if you don't shut up, I'm going to sew your lips together," barked Rudy.

Daniel Garrish stood up and motioned for his three friends to stand up with him. The room quieted. "It's nobody's fault we got hurt," he told everyone in the room. "We took Mrs. McNemmish out of the church and buried her at sea because we loved her and it's what she wanted us to do. We don't know how she got out of the coffin, but she's on Blackbeard's ship now and that's what counts." He realized he had nothing else to say and sat down. The other three followed.

"She could have left us a few diamonds," whispered Stefanie.

"Get over it."

Sheriff Jackson had a question. "If she sold all of the jewelry and the other stuff of value, what did she buy with the money?"

The audience waited breathlessly for Donald Springer's answer.

"Sand," he told them. "Lots and lots of sand."

Give me diamonds,

But I cannot feed the children.

Give me emeralds,

But I cannot buy the love

of yonder gentleman.

Give me sky and sea,

And I will write great poetry.

Give me poetry,

And I will sail the ocean wide.

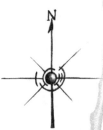

CHAPTER XXI

S and? She bought sand?" erupted the room.

"What do you mean, she bought sand?" asked Teddy.

"I told you she was nuts. Didn't I say she was nuts? Nuts and squirrels."

"Shut up, Stefanie."

"Hard arteries," chorused Marylee.

"Excuse me!" Mr. Springer rapped on the microphone. He waited for the room to quiet. "Actually," he said, pointing to the recovering adventurers, "She left the four of you the greatest treasure of all."

"Treasure. What treasure?" Stefanie leapt out of her seat and threw her hands around Mr. Springer's ankles. "What did she leave us?"

"Let him talk," Daniel told her. "What? What did she leave us?"

Donald unwrapped his ankles, then retrieved four Snow Ducks from a stand on the side of the stage. He showed them to the children. "Recognize these?"

"They're the ducks from the widow's mantle," said Daniel. "What are you doing with them?"

"We'll get to that in a moment. Do you remember what was on the bottom of the ducks?"

"Compass points," said Billy.

Mr. Springer nodded. "On the bottom of each duck was a small piece of tape that said either N.E., S.E., N.W., or S.W. Only they weren't meant to be compass points. They were meant to be areas on a land deed—a deed that was found in Mrs. McNemmish's safety deposit box."

"A deed to what?" Todd inquired, suddenly unnerved by the implication. "A little over sixty years ago, Theodora had the foresight to purchase several land deeds using the money she received from selling the dis-covered treasure. I want to show you something." Mr. Springer pulled down the large movie screen that hung from the stage rafters, then trotted to the back of the room where he cut the lights and turned on the school's slide projector.

"This first slide shows the deed area marked Northeast. It stretches from Old Hammock Creek to Molasses Creek. As per her wishes, it's now part of the Hatteras Island Preservation. This second slide shows the area marked Southwest. It stretches from the top of Teach's Hole to the tip of South Point Beach, including the entire area of Blackbeard's Cove. That, too, is now park-land and wildlife preserve. This third slide focuses on the

Southeast area. It runs east of the Jackson Tract. The revenue from that land was applied to the fourth and last area." Mr. Springer clicked onto the remaining slide. "It is this last slide that will interest everyone here tonight. This slide highlights the Northwest land deed."

"I thought that was owned by the government," said Alton.

"That's what you were meant to think," said Mr. Springer. "Theodora writes about this area, quote, 'At night, I can stand beneath the shadow of the great oaks and stare into the black ocean of sky made of satin and freckled with stars. The only interruptions in creation are the shooting stars that crisscross when passing, like wind-blown ships of yesteryear. They are the only residents of the sky I greet with such openness and love that I offer them freely and without hesitation. Touch not the trees, for they carry the legends of this island in their ever-present, welcoming arms and outstretched greetings. We have inherited them and shall pass them on to the next generations. They are as precious as the water, the sky, and the air we breathe, and we owe them that same respect. Take those that fell themselves from wind and old age and make for yourselves enduring gifts, for wood is of the earth and nowhere else. Use the land so that it may replenish itself and keep it pure. These words are your gift, the rest is for you and your conscience.' End quote."

"She gave the kids wood?" asked May Belle.

"Not exactly." Donald Springer cut off the slide projector and returned to the stage. He smiled down at the four youngsters who looked as perplexed as their parents and friends. "The Northwest land deed covers the only area in the village that is completely undeveloped. One-fourth of it now belongs to you four children to build on when you are ready to have homes of your own."

"What?!" Todd Garrish jumped to his feet, knocking his folding chair backward onto May Belle's lap. "What belongs to them? A fourth of that land belongs to them?"

"That's right," said Donald Springer.

"Billy owns part of the pirate's den?" Drum turned to Jeffrey and Margery Tillet. "The kids own part of the pirate's den!"

Marylee Austin looked like she was about to faint.

Zeek Beacon rose to his feet. His steady glare bore down on the children as he took several steps in their direction. "You little thieves," seethed the man. "She owed me!" he screamed, becoming more and more enraged. The muscles on his arms carved new slopes in his coat sleeves as he dragged Pete Scarborough halfway down the center aisle. "That was my birthright!" he yelled hysterically. "I could have sold that land!"

"Shut up and sit down!" bellowed Pete. He yanked Zeek back with such force, Beacon smacked his head on the back wall.

Daniel watched the strange goings on, and turned to Billy, Stefanie, and Mark. "I don't understand. Is he saying Mrs. McNemmish gave us the den?"

"I guess so," said Billy, slightly unnerved by everyone's reaction. "She bought it with the treasure money and now we own it."

Stefanie sat quietly thinking. She owned property! She was a twelve-year-old property owner! This was bigger than a diamond! "All right!" she told herself.

Todd Garrish had a headache. This was all too much to comprehend. "The kids own a fourth of the pirate's

den," he kept repeating to Elizabeth. "This is unbelievable! Are you sure about this?" he asked Donald. "You've
had the documents checked out?"

Mr. Springer chuckled. "It's all been taken care of,"
he told the stunned parents. "It's all quite legal. Okay,
everyone!" he shouted over the microphone. "I'd like to
continue."

"Continue?" asked Teddy. "There's more?"

"Hey! My son could have found that tunnel if he was
as nosy as those four pimples!" yelled someone standing
up in the middle of the room.

"Your son couldn't find ice in a snowball," hollered
Beacon. "If it were anybody but those four brats, they'd be
going to jail for what they did. Little monsters."

"Zeek's right! Why should they be rewarded for stealing the old lady's body?"

"Because she wanted us to!" hollered Stefanie. "And
another thing!"

"Oh, God."

"We almost died down there, and if we hadn't been
down there, y'all wouldn't even know what's left down
there, and there's plenty left down there, and we're divid-
ing it up between the four of us, but we'll probably share
some of it, unless y'all act like twits and forget about Mrs.
McNemmish." She stopped abruptly, looked at Mr.
Springer, and sat back down.

"That was short and sweet," admired Billy.

"Accidents happen."

"I heard that."

"People!" yelled Mr. Springer. He rapped on the
microphone, making it squeal. "Could you please settle
down! We're not finished!"

Teddy jumped up onto the stage and shouted into the microphone. "Sit down and be quiet! Y'all can jabber about this later." He turned to Mr. Springer when the room had settled down. "They're all yours."

"Thank you." Donald took a long drink of water and ran his fingers through his damp, sweaty hair. "I want to explain something that was made quite clear in Theodora's will. Miss Theo knew that when she died and the house was cleared out, the trunk and the tunnel would be discovered. But in her journal, she was concerned that her wishes for a burial at sea would have been overlooked. It is for that reason alone, she left the land grant to the four children who knew about and would grant her final wish. Mark, Daniel, Billy, and Stefanie provided her with a burial at sea. But she never for a moment forgot her love and devotion to the other members of her community. You were her family.

"You four are being given one-fourth of the area to share as your inheritance because you *did* see to her wishes. The other three-quarters of the area will be shared by the village's other children—the ninth and tenth generations of pirate descendants, along with future generations."

For a second time that night, the gymnasium exploded into chaos. This time it consisted mostly of cheers, laughter, and a whole lot of handshaking and friendly backslapping.

Zeek Beacon's gruff laughter rose above the din, stunning the room into silence. "She left you a hunk of sand!" chortled the man. "This ain't the Riviera. It's a stupid, little nothing of a shrimping hole infested with mosquitoes and no-see-ems, and you can't sell it 'cause she divvied it up. Don't you get it? She's condemning your kids to stay here. Personally, I would have kept the jewels and sold the island."

"What's the Riviera?" Stefanie asked her father.

"It's a place where people vacation when they can't live here."

Daniel raised his hand. "The poem said the keys were just half the prize," he reminded Mr. Springer. "What's the other half?"

"We'll get to that in a few minutes. First, I'd like to talk about these." Mr. Springer held up two strips of ancient paper with black script written across both sides.

"Our tickets!" said Billy.

"Exactly," said the banker. "But finding out what kind of tickets they were sent my workforce on a three-week-long scavenger hunt. First, we had to locate the paper company that made this brand of paper, but they went out of business in 1790. Then I had to research the writing, the date, the origin, and the meaning of the tickets. It seems," he told the children, "these tickets were part of a land pirate's registry. These particular tickets originated in Ireland and were distributed to a relative of Theodora's who lived near Jockey's Ridge on Nags Head Island. They came into Mrs. McNemmish's possession on her sixteenth birthday. She received them from her grandfather, who had received them from his grandfather, who had received them from his grandfather, and so on, all the way back to a gentleman who received them from his mother, Miss Melanie Smyth, who was the daughter of Blackbeard's sister who resided in Bath, North Carolina, on the occasion of his marriage. Both tickets were dated June 25, 1718. One ticket was given to Miss Smyth as a receipt for a pair of sticks. I'm guessing the ticket once read 'candlesticks.' The other was a receipt for an item made of sterling silver beginning with the letter 't.' Unfortunately, Miss Smyth was relieved of her prizes when Governor Spotswood confiscated everything that was on board the grounded ship.

"Because no one knew who the rightful owners were, the items were taken to the seat of government in Williamsburg, Virginia, where they have been stored in a warehouse to this day. Young Miss Smyth pocketed her tickets as a souvenir, then passed them on as gifts."

"As it turned out, the items Miss Smyth selected as her prize the night of June 25, 1718, were just a smidgen of the ill-gained goods on board. No one knows, at least not yet, how many times the cache on that grounded ship had changed hands before reaching Nags Head, as pirates were almost always looting other pirate ships." Mr. Springer grinned. "It is the express desire of Theodora Teach McNemmish that an attempt be made for these items to be returned to the descendants of the original and rightful owners who were separated from them at no fault of their own. It will take diligent research and steadfast perseverance to track these families down, especially since they are likely to live in or around Great Britain."

Stefanie knit her eyebrows. "Why is he looking at us?"

"He's not looking at us," said Daniel.

Mark glanced at Stefanie, Daniel, and Billy and faintly nodded.

"Yikes. Mark says he's looking at us."

"Why are you looking at us?" Stefanie asked him.

"I'm glad you asked," teased the banker. "Because it is the four of you who will be tracking down the rightful owners."

"Say what?!"

"Theodora loved a good mystery. She figured whoever solved the mystery of the tunnel would be the best person, or persons, to solve this one, too."

Stefanie's jaw dropped. "I can't solve a mystery! I can't even find my own socks. Besides, I'm finished helping Mrs. McNemmish. I'm still sick! See? Cough. Cough. Cough. Do I look well to you?"

"How are we supposed to find families who have been dead for three hundred years? If anyone could have done that, they would have done it already," figured Daniel.

"I guess you'll just have to go to Williamsburg and start where everyone else left off."

"Williamsburg? When?" asked Billy.

"As soon as your injuries and school schedules permit."

Billy objected. "What about our jobs? I work at the Pony and the Community Store."

Mark took in a deep breath and chuckled.

"Says you," snapped Daniel. "But I need the money."

"Well, I'm not doing it," Stefanie said obstinately. "I am so done with dead people."

Billy sat back and grumbled. "We never even saw the stuff, and we already have to return it."

Mr. Springer, once again, called the villagers to order. "If I can have everyone's attention, I'd like to get to the last piece of business."

"It's about time!" growled Zeek.

"You'll be most interested in this, Captain Beacon." Donald Springer asked the four children to join him on stage. He asked Mark to bring his collection of white seeds and the handful of assorted nuts he brought with him out of the tunnel. He then looked out into the audience and asked for a raise of hands. "How many of you still have your Snow Ducks?"

Many of the older islanders looked at each other with embarrassment, then one by one, slowly raised their hands. Even some hearty sixty- and seventy-year-old men blushed their way into honesty. Mr. Springer grinned. "Do you recall Mrs. McNemmish always put a white seed in the belly of the duck? Well, there was a reason for that." He turned to the four children beside him. "Mark has a fine collection of white seeds. Some of them, Captain Beacon passed up."

"So what?" yelled Beacon. "Finish up, already!"

Birdie stood up and waved his arms excitedly. "I have my Snow Duck. And I have the other white seeds the widow gave me."

"Well, hang onto them," Mr. Springer told him.

Birdie smiled and sat back down. "Okay, Donald."

"Now normally, white seeds and assorted nuts don't have much of a market value. That is, unless you're an aged widow who happens to like them a lot. And I should tell you, there are several cans filled with these seeds and nuts still waiting to be recovered down in the tunnel. Daniel told me that when they found the nuts and seeds, they were wise enough not to try and eat them. If they had, they would have broken a few teeth."

Mr. Springer looked out at the hundreds of curious faces. "I'm going to share a secret with you now. Probably the biggest secret the widow ever kept. But before I do, I see that we have many off-islanders standing in the hallway, listening in. And even though Mrs. McNemmish thought of many of you as family, she did make the distinction between original families and those families that came to the island later. So if you don't mind," he told Teddy, "I'd like you to close the school doors. The remainder of what I have to say is for O'cockers only."

Donald Springer turned off the microphone. A hush fell over the room except for the scraping of chairs being moved closer to the stage. Outside, people pressed their ears to the walls and doors of the gymnasium, but no sounds or voices flowed through the wooden barrier separating descendant from island friend. Minutes passed, and the only noise came from a flock of gulls laughing down at the visitors. Then...

"What? No way! That's impossible! This is not happening!" screamed a thoroughly irate Zeek Beacon. "She tricked me. Those seeds are mine. They all belong to me! I earned those seeds!"

Inside the room, a wrathful Zeek Beacon dragged Pete Scarborough across the floor as he lunged in the direction of the four children. Bruce and Rudy tackled him to the ground then escorted him out of the building, yelling and kicking, to a standing ovation.

"I knew it," sighed Stefanie. She jumped to her feet and spun around in circles. "I knew it, I knew it, I knew it," she sang as she hugged a handful of seeds and nuts.

"You did not," said Daniel.

Stefanie leaned over and kissed Daniel on the cheek. "Who cares? I don't even mind that I had to pee in a can. I don't even mind about the ring. Well, I do, sort of, but not too much."

"Zeek will have plenty to think about while he's in jail," Drum told Teddy.

"Miss Theo was a pretty smart lady, wasn't she?" Daniel asked his dad.

"She trusted the right kids. You know, Daniel, what y'all did was wrong. But you did it for the right reasons.

I'm proud of you. We all are. We're just glad it turned out as well as it did. It could have turned out a lot worse." Ranger Garrish grinned. "I bet an awful lot of people go home and rummage through their attics for missing Snow Ducks."

Mark held his jar of seeds close to his chest.

"Are you going to share the seeds with your sister?" Stefanie asked him.

Mark looked at Stefanie, his one good eye twinkling.

"All your chores?" laughed Stefanie.

Mark grinned and nodded.

"Hmmm." She looked around for her brother. "Matt, come here a minute."

Mr. Springer rapped on the microphone. "One last thing, people. I am holding a third key. It is the key to the trunk in the widow's shack. It is for anyone who wants to help preserve and take care of the tunnel. Sign-up sheets and the key will be in Teddy Jackson's office. Meeting adjourned."

Daniel walked along a stretch of beach just as the afternoon sun peeked through a puff of gray-purple cloud. "I bet you don't think she was nuts and squirrels now," he said to Stefanie the following day.

"Not entirely."

"Not at all."

"I bet Zeek is going pretty nuts," chuckled Billy. "Rudy said he screamed all the way back to the detention center about the tall ship that attacked the *Lucky Beacon* and how Mrs. McNemmish gypped him out of his rightful inheritance by selling all the treasure and giving us the den."

"Zeek Beacon got what he deserved," said Stefanie.

"Yeah, but think about this," said Billy. "If he hadn't taken the ring and messed up the widow's place, we wouldn't have known about the treasure and buried her in time to get the rest of the stuff."

"Yes, we would have," said Stefanie. "Miss Theo would have told us about all that stuff so we'd bury her at sea."

"But then, she'd have to know she was going to die."

"Of course she knew she was going to die. She was ancient, for heaven's sake."

"You know what the best part is," said Daniel. "While Zeek's rotting away in prison, Birdie's living with May Belle, working in the Creek Side kitchen, and has a piggy bank full of white seeds."

"Don't forget his parrot," said Stefanie.

"Lordy," said Billy. "You don't think he'll get confused and feed the seeds to the parrot, do you?"

Stefanie freaked. "Do you think he'd do that?"

"Doesn't matter," laughed Daniel. "He'll get them back the next day."

"Oooo, yuck. Don't be gross." Stefanie jogged over to a large shell as she and her friends walked along the dunes that neatly hemmed the Ocracoke coastline. The golden sea oats were luminescent against the rich pinks and purples of the setting sun and the wind-blown sand swirled and curved in patterns that mimicked the bark on ancient live oaks. Every so often a stray dog or interested bird would come close enough for a word of greeting, then disappear behind a dune or wash etched out by years of erosion. In the distance, a school of dolphins wove in and out of the crisp, winter water, and the kids shielded their eyes in hopes of catching a glimpse of a whale.

As they walked toward North Beach, they followed the line of snow fencing that assured the safety of next season's turtles and birds. Mrs. McNemmish always thought it was funny calling it snow fencing since Ocracoke only got snow once every hundred years. She named her whelk ducks Snow Ducks in honor of the ducks and birds that perched on it.

Stefanie walked along quietly for a while when the sound of a distant bell caught her attention.

"What was that?" she asked, glancing out to sea.

"What was what?" asked Daniel.

"That bell."

"What bell?" asked Billy.

Stefanie listened. "That bell."

"There's no bell, Stefanie. You're hearing things again."

"I am not!"

Mark pointed.

"What?" Daniel asked him.

"He wants you to look at the lights," said Stefanie.

Billy squinted into the distance. "I don't see any lights."

"They're right there," said Stefanie, getting exasperated with the two older boys.

"I don't know," teased Daniel. "But I think you and Mark definitely have issues."

"We do not have issues," huffed the girl. "I heard a bell, and we both see those lights."

"Can we forget about bells and the lights for a moment? We have bigger problems," said Billy. "I can't believe we have to find people we don't know in order to return items we've never seen, three hundred years after the stuff was stolen. Not to mention, even if we find the original ship that took the stuff and the name of the ship that ran aground, there might be ships in between."

"I'm just tired of doing stuff for dead people," said Stefanie.

"The descendants aren't dead. Anyway, I don't mind doing any of it now that Zeek's in jail having nightmares about those seeds," said Daniel. "Serves him right for being so mean to the widow."

Stefanie and Mark weren't listening. They were intrigued by the cloudy mixture of mist and sparkling lights coming from just beyond the horizon. "Can you see the lights now?" Stefanie asked the boys.

Billy shook his head. "No. But if that's the *Queen Anne's Revenge* and I see Blackbeard's headless body swimming ashore, I'm out of here."

"Not me," said Stefanie, her eyes twinkling with possibility. She grabbed the small diamond pendant that hung around her neck and swung it back and forth on the delicate chain. The memory of breaking open the large white belly-button seed on her Snow Duck would forever be at her fingertips. "If Blackbeard does appear," she said invitingly, "he might have more nuts and seeds." She turned to Billy with wide, greedy eyes and burst out laughing. "Well, he might!"

As the children walked on, the day continued as most days did. Mark was quiet. Stefanie was chatty. Daniel wanted to strangle Stefanie, and Billy was the keeper of peace.

"I always thought it was Mark who would take me place," said Ensign First-Class Pirate McNemmish. "But Stefanie will make a great pirate, I think. She's a lot like I was. I like that."

Edward Teach looked at his favorite lady and chuckled. "And I suppose you are pleased with yerself?"

"Aye, that I am," boasted the woman.

Blackbeard took flint to his mug and brought it to his mouth. His coal-black eyes reflected the firelight turning softness to devil. "Don't be too proud," he said with laughter like rolling thunder. "You never did find me third trunk."

GLOSSARY

Dingbatter: a tourist, a foreigner.

Meehonkey: a call to come out, as when playing hide-and-seek.

Mommuck: to knock about, to pick on someone.

O'cocker: a native from Ocracoke Island.

Quamish: an upset stomach.

Water fired: to be phosphorescent in water.

AUTHOR'S NOTE

If you are interested in more information about the Ocracoke Brogue, I recommend "The Ocracoke Brogue, A Portrait of Hoi Toider Speech" (1997), a video produced by the Language and Life Project, Humanities Extension/Publications, at the North Carolina State University. It is available through the Ocracoke Island Preservation Society and through the North Carolina State University Press. —A.P.

ACKNOWLEDGMENTS

This humble author could never have completed this project without the years of storytelling provided by Clinton Gaskill, Elizabeth Wahab, Lawton Howard, and Edna Miller. They were not only gracious in their sharing of stories, but equally as gracious in their willingness to listen on end to the progress of my manuscript. I would also like to thank Pierre Dery, who I trapped into the job of story consultant and who found every gap, hole, and incomplete thought I had. Finally, I would like to thank George and Mickey Roberson of Teach's Hole, Mark E. Mitchell of Original Historic Newspapers, Philip Howard of The Village Craftsmen, and my friends at the Island Inn, Pony Island Restaurant and Hotel, and Ocracoke Preservation Society.

—Audrey Penn

ABOUT THE AUTHOR

 *Mystery at Blackbeard's Cove* is Audrey Penn's tenth children's book. Best known for the *New York Times* best-selling children's title *The Kissing Hand*, she is also the author of *Sassafras, Feathers and Fur, A.D.D. not B.A.D., The Whistling Tree*, and *Pocket Full of Kisses*, among others. Ms. Penn takes her educational program, the Writing Penn, into schools, libraries, and children's hospitals, where she often shapes and refines her story ideas in partnership with kids. She is a sought-after conference speaker for groups of teachers and other professionals who work with children.

Mystery at Blackbeard's Cove is the culmination of a twenty-year project. Intending to write a novel about Blackbeard and the pirates who sailed with him and frequented the Outer Banks of North Carolina, Ms. Penn spent the better part of that time getting to know the pirate descendants who still reside on Ocracoke Island, NC, and researching the letters, journals, and diaries passed down through family and friends. She also spent many years with children from the island, who helped her bring to life the many adventures facing the story's characters.

Ms. Penn lives with her husband in Olney, Maryland, near Washington, DC. She has three children, all of whom excel at writing.

ABOUT THE ILLUSTRATORS

Joshua Miller graduated from Ohio University with a Bachelor of Fine Arts degree in Graphic Design and Illustration. He has worked for 9 years as a computer animator and lives in McLean, Virginia.

Philip Howard is the great-great-great-great-great-grandson of William Howard, Blackbeard's quarter-master. He lives on Ocracoke Island, where Blackbeard was killed on November 22, 1718. Luckily for Philip, the young William was not serving with Blackbeard at the time of the famous pirate's final battle. Philip owns and operates a quality craft shop on Ocracoke. In his spare time he collects island stories and tales.